SNARES OF THE ENEMY

Ambelhurst is a large monastic school, seemingly the last place to harbour violent death. When Dom Martin comes across the school matron's body at a quarter to six on a fine May morning, every aspect of this vast institution—monks, boys, lay masters, household staff, even visiting parents—falls under the scrutiny of Inspector Evan Morgan. Morgan, a devout Wesleyan Methodist, finds he has much to learn about many matters other than criminal investigation in a society where regard for law and order cannot obscure the fact that its values are not of this world.

SNARES OF THE ENEMY

Pauline King

Visit this house, we pray you, Lord,
drive far away from it all the snares of the
enemy.
May your holy angels stay here and guard
us in peace,
and let your blessing be always upon us.

Office of Compline

ATLANTIC LARGE PRINT
Chivers Press, Bath, England.
John Curley & Associates Inc.,
South Yarmouth, Mass., USA.

Library of Congress Cataloging in Publication Data

King, Pauline
  Snares of the enemy.

  (Atlantic large print)
  1. Large type books.   I. Title.
  [PR6061.I.467S5   1987]   823′.914   86–29268
  ISBN 1–55504–314–3 (Curley: soft: lg. print)

British Library Cataloguing in Publication Data

King, Pauline
  Snares of the enemy.—(Atlantic large
  print)
  I. Title
  823′.914[F]   PR6061.I46/

  ISBN 0–7451–9239–4

This Large Print edition is published by Chivers Press, England, and
John Curley & Associates, Inc, U.S.A. 1987

Published in the British Commonwealth by arrangement with
William Collins Sons & Co Ltd and in the U.S.A. with
The Scribner Book Companies, Inc

U.K. Hardback ISBN 0 7451 9239 4
U.S.A. Softback ISBN 1 55504 314 3

TO
The Family—with love

7130660

CHAPTER ONE

MURDER IN THE MONASTERY

Dom Martin came across the school matron's body at a quarter to six on a fine May morning. She lay in the shadows behind a heavy oak door that gave access from the north cloister to the monastery. Father Martin had known Mary O'Connell since his schooldays at Ambelhurst and, quite apart from her dishevelled and bloodstained appearance, the very fact that she lay within the Enclosure was proof enough that she had been murdered—for she would never, voluntarily, have invaded the monks' privacy: still less would she have broken the strict rule that denies all women—other than the reigning Monarch, Consort or Queen Mother—entrance to a monastery of the Order of St John the Less.

Blood had splashed over Matron's face and down her neat lace-edged collar. Dark patches stained the pin-tucked bodice of her navy uniform. But, below the hem of her dress, her stout legs encased in grey nylon looked surprisingly normal and ended in highly polished 'sensible' shoes. It was, however,

1

shockingly abnormal for Matron's starched white cap to be askew on her head.

'My God!' whispered the novice-master, crossing himself; and then—making a similar sign of the cross over the dead woman—he pronounced the words of absolution. An avid reader of detective stories, he knew better than to touch the corpse. His immediate priestly duty fulfilled, he turned on his heel and hurried back down the cloister, bent on informing the appropriate members of the community and on summoning the police. He had reached the high arched entrance to the inner hall when he almost collided with a young novice.

'Brother Charles!' he said, his voice strained and harsh. 'Matron appears to have been murdered.' He waved a hand to indicate the bundle lying a hundred and fifty yards from where they stood. 'Stay by the body, don't touch her—and let no one near until the police arrive. And, Brother! Pray! Say the *De Profundis*—or anything you like.'

The young monk neither spoke nor raised an eyebrow. He bowed his head in acknowledgement and proceeded on his way, gliding smoothly over the terrazzo flooring, his hands buried in his sleeves and hidden beneath his scapular. A model of unquestioning obedience.

Dom Martin strode towards the prior's cell, pausing only to look back down the vista of arches to where Brother Charles was kneeling beside the corpse. Undoubtedly he would be praying for Matron, the monastery and the murderer. *Omnia Amor Est!* The training given by the Order of St John the Less is equal to any emergency and the satisfied novice-master reflected that outside the cloister few people, other than members of the nursing profession, the police and most of the armed forces, would have responded so instantly to a command. Monasteries are, as yet, untroubled by Unions and negotiations.

The procurator was sent to tell the headmaster that, after thirty-five years of faithful service to Ambelhurst School, Matron had gone to her reward; and the prior, having considerable experience of boys, remembered when he reported the incident to impress upon the police the absolute necessity of bringing their vehicles to the Monastery entrance—avoiding the School at all costs. Too many pairs of sharp young eyes and ears were capable of fastening upon the least suspicion of a drama and would have set about discovering in what way the world of horror comics had impinged upon their drab lives.

Meanwhile, those monks not required to deal with the scandal in their midst proceeded

3

silently to the abbey church for Matins. Their normal route did not include the north cloister, so they saw nothing untoward, though several of the brethren noted, with surprise, the absence of Brother Charles— who had never been known to oversleep, or to neglect the *Opus Dei*. He, poor embryo monk, was on his knees, increasingly weighed down under a burden of tragedy and guilt. Being very nearly perfect, he identified himself with sinners and was, in consequence, crushed by compassion for both victim and murderer. He was, indeed, an exemplary religious and, as such, a trial to his brother novices: for it has justly been said that the martyrs are those who have to live with the saints.

★   ★   ★

Discreetly, the drama of detection began to unfold and the police, under Detective-Inspector Evan Morgan, CID, made good use of the short time available before the school came alive. The precise spot in the north cloister where Matron had been attacked was identified by a small pool of blood on the flagstones and by extensive bloodstains on the vaulted ceiling.

'Chance in a hundred!' said the police surgeon. 'Must have hit the left carotid artery direct—though it's possible the murderer aimed elsewhere and she dodged back and deflected the blow upwards. There's a penetrating stab wound in the neck caused by a slim sharp instrument. The blood would have spurted up, and—there it is.' He indicated the fan vaulting. 'Then she was dragged by the legs—she was short and slight so it would be easy for any man, woman or strong young boy—across the flagstones and she'd slide quite smoothly when they reached the marble floor beyond that door with the label. What does it mean, by the way, *Clausura*?'

'It means Enclosure and laymen are expected to keep out unless invited in. Women— religious or lay—are not so invited. Of course,' the prior added hastily, 'the police will go wherever they please.'

'Remarkable, isn't it,' said the inspector, 'that her nurse's cap should have—'

'She called it her "army square",' interrupted the monk irrelevantly—but he felt that he owed it to Matron's liking for precision that the headgear should be correctly named.

'Remarkable that her *army square* should have stayed on her head at all. She must have been a dab hand at securing it.'

'She was. Winds and boys tried to whip it off—and failed.'

'H'mm. Well I think she'd been dead for six to eight hours before the body was found, which means that she was murdered between eleven and one o'clock.'

The prior consulted his watch. 'Would it be possible to screen off this part of the cloister, or put up some barricade and lock the Enclosure door before the catering and cleaning staff arrive? Boys will soon be coming this way to the church. It *would* be a feast day—which means a full attendance at the early Mass. They can be horribly observant if there is anything to hide!'

'Yes, of course,' said the inspector. 'I think we've done all we can for the moment—now that the forensic team has finished. Apart from clearing up the bloodstains. There must have been a great deal more of a mess than that tiny pool and the ceiling stains would suggest. Someone used a mop and bucket, or cloths, to clean up last night. I've set my men on a discreet search.'

'In that case—may I offer you some coffee? It'll only be instant at this hour but I'm sure you need it. We can talk in my office,' said the prior, 'and discuss where you would like to set up working quarters here.'

*   *   *

Inspector Morgan laid down his cup and asked, 'May I take it that the whole place—school and monastery—is locked up at night?'

'Yes. The night watchman checks on all gates and doors and windows. But as most schoolboys and staff are capable of discovering ways in and out when they set their minds to it, presumably others could do the same.'

'Do you get tramps or similar invaders here? I don't recall hearing that you've asked for our help.'

'We have had tramps—and Old Boys—breaking in at night: occasionally they are synonymous. Ardent young junior monks feel that we ought to welcome tramps. Usually they will doss down in the cricket pavilion or an outhouse, but we have woken up to find someone sleeping it off in the cloisters—or in a vacant cell.'

'Cell?'

'Not your kind—a monk's! And an empty one, of course. We get our share of drop-outs and weirdos, as one would expect. Religious houses are fair game.'

'Whoever killed your matron must have had a good deal of inside knowledge. I suspect it was premeditated. No fingerprints—no blood trails leading from the area. It suggests that somebody came prepared with weapon and gloves—and even a mop and bucket: or knew

7

where to find them.'

'Are you excluding outside intervention?'

'Not entirely—yet. But somehow I doubt it.' Inspector Morgan looked genuinely sorry. He was a devout Wesleyan Methodist with ecumenical tendencies—and he did not enjoy suggesting that someone within a Roman Catholic establishment had been indulging in murder.

CHAPTER TWO

THE HEADMASTER

Dom Erkenwald Ward, headmaster of Ambelhurst School for the past eight years, was asleep in the bedroom above his study on the east side of the main gate. Unless school business had kept him up until after midnight he was accustomed to wake—alert and clear-brained—on the stroke of five-forty-five, but on the previous evening he had been wrestling with a peculiarly difficult adolescent and, at a later hour than he had intended, with an even more difficult member of his staff. In consequence the procurator, Dom Paulinus Hovingham, found him at rather less than his best.

'Matron? Dead?' he repeated. 'Dead?' he inquired, as if unable to grasp the news.

'I'm afraid, Dom, it looks like murder.' The procurator saw no point in disguising the full scale of the disaster; it had to be faced, and the headmaster would have to organize the school to meet the unexpected situation. 'Martin found her body in the Petit Cloister. He'd gone round that way because he had a note to leave in my office. Thank God he did! Otherwise she'd have been found by cleaners or the boys. There's blood on her face and uniform. The police are coming and the prior will cope. It could be a case of armed robbery. She may have intercepted someone.' The headmaster's face turned white and Paulinus said quickly, 'It's all right. We've sent Robert and Martin to rouse the housemasters and get them to check studies and dormitories. I knew you wouldn't want any delay.'

'Quite right. What are our chances of keeping it from the school until the police have investigated?'

'Not a lot. Edward's asked them to use the monastery entrance and avoid prying eyes. I imagine they'll screen off the body and luckily it's in the Enclosure. I mean *she's* in the Enclosure. Incongruous, isn't it? The only time in her life. Let's hope we get things cleared up before the domestic staff come on

9

duty. The cooks will be down at any moment and we don't want any reports going off to the Press.'

The headmaster groaned. He had memories of a fire at the school five years earlier when an enterprising boy, with distinct commercial potential, had earned ten pounds for the outlay of ten pence in a call-box. The thought that some parents might have another scare set his adrenalin flowing fast as he made contingency plans. 'The infirmary staff! They must be told before Matron is missed. I'll see the laymasters before the first period and the school at first Break. Has Dr Patterson been informed?'

'The prior or Martin will surely have sent for him—I'll check: but Matron looks very dead so it's really only a matter for the police surgeon, forensic, and the Coroner.'

'*And* the Press—and endless speculation—when we should be working up steadily towards the A and O levels *and* the Academies! What a feast day!'

'Feast day? Oh, good Lord! I'd forgotten! Augustine of Canterbury. The housekeeper's laid on one of her banquets and she won't appreciate any distraction from her culinary marvels—least of all if her staff waste time gossiping. They're going to *love* this! I'd better go and see her now before she gets wind of the disaster from one of her minions. There'll be hell to pay if she's not in the picture before them!' He started for the door, then paused. 'I'll be in touch with our solicitor. He has a soothing way with the Press. D'you remember when the Spanish chef cut his throat and he persuaded a reporter to put in a meagre paragraph? He said: "I'm sure you wouldn't want to blow up anything so *banal*!"—and the fellow agreed with him! Incidentally, I believe he made a Will for Matron and you'll want to know about her funeral wishes—if any.'

'Yes. Thanks. Send me word when you get feed-back from the Houses. I'll go straight to the infirmary. Can't telephone because it will be switched through to Matron's flat at this hour.'

The headmaster had dressed rapidly as they talked: shaving could wait. He went down the turret staircase to his ante-room and crossed the courtyard to the west side of the main gate. His crêpe-soled sandals made scarcely a sound. No one was about. The horrible thought occurred to him that violence could have spread to this area of the school and he paused before ringing the bell of Sister Wilbraham's flat.

'Yes? Who is it?'

'The headmaster, Sister. May I have a word

11

with you?'

'Certainly, Father.' He heard the automatic lock click and pushed the door open, calling out, 'I'll wait in your sitting-room.'

At the threshold he felt that he'd entered another—distinctly feminine—world, with books, flowers, paintings and sewing, immaculate but lived-in. He sat in a winged armchair facing the door and approved the entrance she made after a brief interval. Her blonde hair was swept up into its usual French pleat and her frilled nurse's cap sat becomingly atop. From her white drill overall, fastened by a silver-buckled navy petersham belt, to her black court shoes, she looked a paragon of cool professional competence: certainly not the type to faint. Nevertheless, he thought it prudent to invite her to sit down. He was already on his feet and motioned her to the chair he had vacated.

'Sister, there has been an unfortunate accident during the night—involving Matron.'

'Matron, Father?'

'Yes. I'm afraid she's dead. In fact, Father Paulinus seems certain that she has been murdered.'

'Murdered?' Her eyes opened wide and for an instant he felt foolish. What if he had had a nightmare and imagined all this? But the procurator's visit had been real enough.

'I'm sorry. It's a shock, I know. I haven't seen her. It appears that she was attacked in the north cloister and dragged into the Enclosure.'

The knuckles of Sister Wilbraham's clasped hands whitened. She stared at the headmaster, her face tense and eyes strained.

'A terrible shock,' he said. 'We're checking the whole school—but there's no reason to imagine that anyone else has been attacked. The important thing is to keep it quiet until the police have finished their work and the body has been removed. There will have to be a post mortem and an inquest, of course, and no doubt the Press will descend in force. We can't do much about warning the parents but I do *not* want the boys, or the domestic staff, giving lurid interviews to the gutter press.'

'Of course, Father. You may safely leave the infirmary servants to me. I cannot answer for the housekeeper's—' She permitted herself a wan smile.

He was aware of the traditional antagonism that existed between the departments and interrupted smoothly, 'Thank you, Sister.'

'I'll take the morning surgery, as usual. I'll tell Sister Hanlon that Matron's having a day off and I'll put a "Don't Disturb" notice on her door. Sister Hanlon gets a little excited so

13

it might be better to delay telling her.'

'Whatever you think best. I have confidence in your judgement.'

The headmaster left as quickly as he had come and Sister Wilbraham went to the deep-embrasured window and threw wide the casement. The early sun had not yet reached the walled garden that lay between the infirmary and the monastery: a ground mist swirled and drifted in pale wisps over the lawn and herbaceous border. She breathed deeply, inhaling the scent of hawthorn and lilacs. Beneath the window deep crimson peonies and a few late wallflowers contributed their velvet smell. The birds sang. Murder and maytime—they just did not mix.

*   *   *

The headmaster went straight from the infirmary to his study where he found a note from Father Robert. 'All well, D.G. All boys accounted for and asleep in their beds. R.A.'

'Thank God, indeed.' he echoed aloud, and climbed the turret stairs to his bathroom where he prayed as he shaved.

He was due to say Mass at seven-fifteen and he just had time to type out two notices and pin them to the appropriate boards on his way up to the abbey church. One requested the members of the teaching staff to meet him in their staff room at 09.00 hours and the other summoned the whole school to the academy room at 11.00 hours.

To his relief, there were no indications of the night's work in the north cloister, which preserved its customary aura of serenity and scrubbed woodwork, and the door to the Enclosure was locked. In the sacristy after Mass, Dom Erkenwald advised his head boy that morning classes might start late; he would be addressing the staff at nine o'clock and would speak to the boys at the end of Break. He ignored Bryant's inquiring look and approved the impassive expression which instantly took its place: a dignified head of the school whose discretion he would reward by breaking the news to him immediately before he spoke to the Assembly.

On the way down to breakfast in the school refectory he fell into step with three of the housemasters and, surrounded as they were by boys, they did not refer to the tragedy until, having collected what they needed at the hot-plate, they sat down at the Top Table.

'Revolting!' commented Dom Placid Knowles, housemaster of St Boniface, pulling a disapproving face.

'A messy death, I agree,' replied the headmaster.

'No—I mean this brew purporting to be coffee. The housekeeper's economies have reduced us to instant *ersatz* this term. One used to be able to count on a respectable Continental roast in the old days, but now—!' He cradled his handleless monastic bowl and gazed with distaste at the grey-brown liquid within. 'Until this summer one could have guaranteed that the coffee, at least, would put one in a good mood.'

'The early morning Office—or Mass—is supposed to do that, Dom.' The headmaster's reproving tone was belied by a sly grin. 'But I agree that it would have been particularly acceptable this morning. Not that—in the days when real coffee was served—you were invariably the Sunny Jim of the Top Table at breakfast-time. The toast was soggy ... someone had stolen your *Times* ... the scrambled eggs had achieved the distinction of being both hard and watery—'

'Oh, all right! I'm a night owl—not a bloody lark greeting the morning with song! However, today I shall *enjoy* my *Times* while drinking this witches' brew. Tomorrow it will be parading banner headlines proclaiming: MURDER AT WELL-KNOWN PUBLIC SCHOOL. WOMAN STABBED IN MONASTERY!'

'I doubt it! That treatment savours of the *Sun, Mirror* and *Mail. The Times* will be more

16

dignified: TRAGEDY AT AMBELHURST. UNKNOWN ASSAILANT IN CLOISTER!'

'Not so! You are thinking of the Rees-Mogg era. The style has been somewhat debased since he resigned to govern the BBC, chair the Arts Council, run his classical eighteenth-century bookshop—and advise Big Business! There are also more printing errors. However, Frank Johnson, Philip Howard, and some superb cricket reports, cheer me enormously. Also, I must admit that being able to find the radio and TV programmes on the inside back page for six days of the week—instead of having a ridiculous chase through Saturday's paper—is a great bonus.'

'I believe they did tell you where to look for the programmes—if you had troubled to consult the front page.'

'Maybe. Nevertheless, I do deplore the increase in women's features—and the fact that printers' ink is more lavishly distributed over my fingers than ever before. That does make me sour!'

'But—how unusual!' the headmaster murmured softly. For once, Dom Placid, whose name in religion had been chosen for him by an abbot and novice-master with a sense of humour, elected not to hear.

CHAPTER THREE

THE GUEST-MASTER

Inspector Morgan stood in the shadow of a doorway and scanned the uniformed tide of boys flooding up the north cloister. Their feet clattered on the stone-flagged floor and then struck hollow echoes out of a flight of shallow wooden steps leading up to the church. They were a typical mixture: some scrubbed, some scruffy; some scholarly, some athletic; a few were already wearing an air of maturity and, occasionally, of latent distinction. The shambling, uncoordinated gait of some adolescents contrasted with casual grace and confidence in others. There were boys with dreamy, uncomprehending faces who could not have said just how they had washed, dressed and joined the herd.

For most of its length the cloister was dim and shadowy—except where the early morning sun streamed through stained glass windows bearing the coats of arms of founder families, or of individual Old Boys killed in various parts of the British Empire: no doubt their deaths had been as violent as Matron's. Few of the present inhabitants of Ambelhurst

18

noticed Morgan and those who did were incurious; they were accustomed to seeing the abbey's guests in this part of the house. When the last of the hurrying or sauntering figures had disappeared through the studded leather doors at the top of the staircase, Morgan followed and found that the right-hand door was still swinging; a touch pushed it open and he passed into relative darkness in which a strange, spicy smell—as of woodsmoke and rosemary with eastern overtones—assailed his Welsh Methodist nostrils.

Incense! he thought, and the word hinted at popish practices: he was more accustomed to such smells being used as a cover for pot-smoking than for liturgical worship. Scarcely a cough or shuffle marred the deep silence within the abbey church: it was as though the boys had been swallowed up among the granite pillars and soaring arches of a great stone forest. Beneath his feet, soft brown coconut matting reminded the inspector of dead beech leaves in a winter wood. His eyes gradually adapted to the gloom and he saw that people were kneeling at rush-seated chairs in the body of the nave, but he made his way to a side chapel and found an unoccupied seat close to a large tomb, over which the impressive red hat of a cardinal hung in the gathering dust. A service was about to begin, lights were turned on to counter the fitful sunlight, and Morgan decided to stay and 'get the feel of the place'—a tenet impressed upon him at the police college. It was warm and it was peaceful and he had, after all, been hauled out of bed at five minutes to six . . .

He awoke with a start, to find a black-robed figure bending over him and murmuring, 'Inspector! May I offer you some breakfast?' He glanced at his watch—it was ten to eight—and with an embarrassed smile he apologized for falling asleep. The monk smiled.

'You've had a disturbed night, I'm afraid, and this short rest will have done you good.'

They paced slowly down the side aisle and passed through a wooden double door into the monastery, while the monk explained that he was Father Henry, the guest-master, and suggested that they would probably be seeing a lot of each other.

'Would you like breakfast in the monks' refectory—or would you prefer to eat alone?'

'Thank you, the—er—refectory would be splendid.' The inspector stumbled slightly as he tried to adjust to the Catholic way of pronouncing the word with the accent on the first syllable.

They entered a long room with tables ranged along three sides and Dom Henry led his guest to a hot-plate where he poured coffee

20

into thick white bowls and indicated fruit juice, cereals, scrambled egg and the means of making toast. The refectory was quiet but for the gentle scrape of knives and forks.

A disturbance at the far end caused the inspector to look up as a remarkable old man entered the room. His dog-collar proclaimed him a clergyman but the gown he wore was of a narrow, severe cut; more like that of a poor student at Oxford as portrayed in a series of prints that Morgan had seen on the walls of the Randolph, than the gracefully flowing robes worn by monks of the Order of St John the Less. The priest looked like a turtle as he advanced on the serving table with hands clasped waist high, and his head waving from side to side at the end of a long neck arising from a collar possibly two sizes too large for him. He wore his thick silver hair cut in a cap fashion with a fringe; it would not have disgraced a pop singer and contrasted with the clipped hair of many of the monks.

The policeman observed, with surprise, a look of benign malevolence on the turtle's face and he noted also that several of the monks had stopped eating and were watching his progress with expressions varying from frank amusement to bored tolerance. There's a character in every Mess! Morgan reflected, and was not displeased when the elderly

21

gentleman seated himself on his right and broke the silence to ask:

'Am I right in deducing that you are the police officer in charge of the—ah—ahem—investigations?'

'I'm Detective-Inspector Morgan.' A broad grin on the priest's face surprised and somehow nettled the inspector. It seemed inappropriate even in one who dealt professionally in Life after Death. Morgan was disinclined towards conversation at breakfast and surmised that talking in a monastic refectory was not encouraged, so he frowned slightly when the high thin voice continued:

'I predict some unfortunate publicity. Would you not agree on the inevitability of this, Inspector?'

'Unfortunately, yes. It's a bad business for you people with a school to run. The media is bound to blow it up out of all proportion.'

'For Ambelhurst—yes! But not for *us*! Quite to the contrary, I would say. You see, I am a Christite father and we also run schools.' His laugh was like the croak of a raven and the inspector's shocked amazement at such a callous retort led him to glance round the refectory for confirmation of his own embarrassed reaction. To his surprise, amusement rippled the faces of all within earshot.

'Hmmm.' The turtle prepared to speak again and this time the precise enunciation was more devastatingly clear. 'I am told, Dom Henry, that your—ah—Mother Abbess—was—ah—murdered during the night.'

'Matron,' corrected the guest-master, unmoved by the casually inquisitive tone.

'What's that, young man?' The priest cupped a deaf ear. 'Precisely! Ma-ter. Latin for mother. That is exactly what I said. Half you young men don't know your Latin since the Council saw fit to introduce the vernacular liturgy—and those who do mispronounce it! I understand that your Mother Abbess was—ah—e-lim-in-ated within the monastic precincts last night.'

'The school matron, Father,' said the guest-master, calmly continuing with his breakfast. Morgan marvelled at his control in face of such unsuitable levity.

'Shocking bad taste!' he whispered, with a nod towards the Christite, who was now attacking his breakfast with the zest of an elderly schoolmaster who has shown that he is still capable of handling Lower 4c.

'Father John Knox-Wesley is a law unto himself,' Father Henry whispered. 'He probably feels we need distracting and helping over the shock. It is his way of cheering us up.'

'Knox-Wesley? He's surely not a Roman Catholic with a name like *that*?'

'Oh yes, he is. His name gives him immense pleasure.' Breakfast was completed in silence, after which the guest-master suggested that the inspector might like to meet the procurator.

'The procurator?'

'Father Paulinus. He does the work of a bursar and is responsible for business management and financial affairs. He is assisted by an economus who takes charge of domestic and maintenance staff and their deployment. Paulinus is an old friend of Matron and he could tell you of her relationship with others.'

'That seems a useful suggestion. Lead on!'

CHAPTER FOUR

THE PROCURATOR

The procurator's office was furnished with practical elegance and might have been the estate room of any country landowner. The large flat-topped desk and the chairs were Chippendale and the inspector found himself wondering whether they were gifts from a benefactor, the dowry of a novice, or acquired in settlement of a bad debt.

'Father Paulinus—Detective-Inspector Morgan. If you will excuse me, Inspector, I will go and make sure that all your men have breakfasted.' The guest-master smiled and withdrew.

'Please sit down, Inspector. This is a sorry business.'

'It is, indeed.'

'We've sent for our legal adviser—but if there is anything I can do to help you in your investigations, I shall be most happy.' The procurator sat back, cool, suave and shrewd, and Morgan deduced that he would be in command of any situation. Someone here knew how to pick the right person for each job. This man was in his proper sphere—just as Father Henry, interested in people and quick in the uptake, was an ideal guest-master.

'Would you explain, sir, how it was possible for the murdered woman to have remained undiscovered until 05.45 hours? I had rather thought that monks get up to pray, on and off, throughout the night.'

'Not in all monasteries. We have Compline at eight-thirty-five—or 20.35—after which monks who have no duties in the school may have some recreation for a while; but many

25

retire to their cells. It's the Greater Silence and lights are put out in the monastery at 23.00 hours. From then until 05.45, when the monks rise and go down to choir for Matins, or morning prayers, there would be no one about in the cloister apart from—apart from a very occasional member of staff on school business. Kitchen and refectory staff are off duty soon after 20.15 at latest: the housekeeper has an internal staircase to her flat; the offices in my department are locked up. Matron may well have been on her way up here when she was attacked. She used to come up in the late evening, after her television programme ended, with requisition slips.'

'Perhaps you know that there was a note clutched in her hand?'

'Yes. We saw it, but of course didn't touch.'

'It's been taken away with other items required as evidence—but I've had a copy made for you. It's a request for attention to the electric sterilizer in the dispensary. I expect you'll want to get the job put in hand. Have you other nursing staff to cover her work?'

'Fortunately, yes, but Matron had been with us for over thirty-five years and we're going to miss her. She was part of the place and knew her job backwards. She was near retiring age, but she had the stamina of a

Connemara pony; she could have gone on for a while yet. She was utterly reliable—and loyal.'

'Excellent testimonial, Procurator. Or do I say father?'

'As you please, Inspector.'

Morgan decided that he would listen and catch on to the prevailing form of address. He made entries in a notebook before asking,

'Was she popular?'

'Well—that depends. The headmaster, school doctor and myself approved of her wholeheartedly. Many Old Boys loved her: but no doubt some of the present boys and domestic staff would have reservations. Not, I hasten to add, that they would resort to murder, but anyone in authority exerting firm discipline is bound to be unpopular with someone.'

'She had enemies, then?'

'That's putting it somewhat strongly, Inspector.'

'I see. Of course you will appreciate that this murder looks like an inside job. There were no fingerprints; no weapon has been discovered and, more importantly, the murderer managed to move away from the scene without leaving a trail. Either he came prepared—or he knew where to find mops and cloths.'

'Yes, I see. We would have preferred to

think that she had intercepted a burglar, but I have had everything of value checked and there is nothing missing from the museum, libraries, sacristy, armoury, stores or school shop. No one appears to have broken in: nothing seems to have been taken.'

'That's most helpful.' Morgan approved the speed and efficiency with which the check had been made. 'The armoury—what is that?'

'The weapons store for the Combined Cadet Force. Sergeant-Major Cookson and the Corps Commander have the keys. There are several locks on the door and all windows are barred. The CSM reports that there is nothing missing and no sign of tampering with locks.'

'Have you any ideas? Anyone you can think of who might have borne a grudge against her?'

'No. I'm afraid I can't help you at all. It's a relief to be able to say so with a clear conscience.'

'I take it that doesn't mean that you would have given the same answer despite an *un*clear conscience?' The inspector's voice was steely, but his look was only mildly malicious.

'Not really. I would have replied more— circumspectly—had I entertained vague suspicions of anyone. If I actually *knew* anything it would probably be my duty to come clean.'

'Only probably? Why not certainly? Or are you claiming a priest's privilege?'

'I would have to if someone had confessed to me as a priest. Fortunately, they haven't.'

'H'mm.' Inspector Morgan snapped the band on his notebook. 'Not a very popular doctrine with my profession. I mean, the privilege claim—not confession. As far as that goes, I reckon it's as valuable as any consultation with the headshrinkers.'

'We have a rather brilliant psychologist in the Community if you should need help, Inspector.' The procurator's voice was silk smooth but the corners of his mouth twitched. 'Father Leonard Witzenstein fled from Hitler's Germany—a fascinating character. However, I expect you like to follow your own hunches as far as possible. I wonder if you would like to meet the headmaster next? Or have you other plans?'

'No, that would be splendid. I should have to go through him, I assume, if I need to interview any of the boys or teaching staff?'

'That's right. Domestic staff come under the housekeeper or myself. Matron did have charge of certain domestic cleaners with specific jobs but now she is dead we shall centralize. The five outlying Houses and the Junior House have separate arrangements but we can deal with those as need arises.'

'Outlying Houses?'

'Common room, dormitory, study-bedroom and similar accommodation for fifty boys apiece. We outgrew the original buildings long ago but there are still five Houses under what one might call one roof—or a series of roofs. We came here from Flanders at the outbreak of the French Revolution. Schools and colleges had been established in the Low Countries for the use of Catholics during the penal times and, when we came home, one of our Old Boys offered us his Ambelhurst property. Apart from the original quadrangle there's nothing much left of the mediæval buildings. I believe that you arrived this morning at the monastery entrance—' He stood up and indicated the position on a wall map. 'But if you had driven up the avenue, between these two duck ponds, you would have come through the main gate into a courtyard. The headmaster's offices and the school library are on the right of the gateway and the opposite side of the gate leads—beyond the porter's lodge—to parlours and accommodation for visitors; and then, beyond those, to the infirmary wing running in a southerly direction. Had you turned right—that is *away* from the infirmary—you would have passed the matron's and sisters' accommodation and headed north into a gallery and then into the north cloister where Matron met her end; that is, where you found bloodstains on the vaulted ceiling.'

'Sisters? Those are nuns, I take it?'

'No, they're two trained nurses—lay women. Sister Wilbraham—coolly efficient—who, I suppose, is almost nun-like in her attendance at several of our monastic offices in the abbey church; and Sister Hanlon, a pretty, fluffy blonde whom I would describe as bird-like—though I have heard boys express appreciation in terms more modern and explicit. They are a bit starved of female companionship here and the attributes of nurses, maids and cleaners don't go unremarked.'

'You don't select women for the plainness of their appearance, then?'

'No! For good references! A few are so attractive you may find this hard to believe—but, for all that, the generic term for a woman in this school is hag and that goes for nurses too. I believe that Sister Wilbraham, who is rather beautiful, was dismayed when Matron—not without malice—told her that she was classed as a hag. She found it unchristian.'

'Understandably.' The inspector looked out of the office windows upon green lawns from which the silver grey stone of the abbey church swept up and was outlined against a sky of nursery blue. 'One would think it had been there for centuries!' he said.

'Almost fifty years. There was an earlier ch—' The procurator was interrupted by a deep-toned bell that evidently rang from the belfry and had all history in its tongue. 'The conventual Mass,' he explained. 'Which reminds me to tell you that the abbot is away from home. He's been in Peru where we have five monks working and is taking in a conference of major religious superiors on his way back. If you should want to interview any of the monks it would probably be easiest to arrange it either through the prior or myself. Unless of course they are on the school staff and come under the headmaster.'

'Thank you.' Morgan made a note and asked, 'Can I be sure of finding you here for most of the day?'

'You can. I'm rather desk-bound at the moment but if I should be out of the office I'll leave a message with Father Aidan, our accountant, or one of the clerks. I had arranged to see our farm manager at two-fifteen but I could postpone it if you would rather.'

'No, please don't do that. How do I find the headmaster?'

'I'll call his secretary.' Father Paulinus

pressed a button on the intercom panel and spoke to a Mrs Macdonald. A pleasant Scottish voice replied that the school doctor was due to visit the headmaster, but that he would not be staying long as she knew that he had an appointment with the infirmarian, and would nine-forty be convenient.

'Who is the infirmarian? Is that your assistant matron?'

'No, he's the monk detailed to look after the sick brethren. If they need highly skilled nursing then they may be removed to a hospital, or if the school infirmary is not over-busy, Matron and the sisters nurse sick monks down there. Michael, our present infirmarian, had embarked on a medical training before he entered the monastery and, though not a qualified doctor, he's pretty useful; he also teaches biology in the school and is a lay instructor for the local Red Cross. The monastic rule insists that care must be taken of the sick before all else.'

'I see.' The inspector consulted his notebook. 'Were there people who disliked Matron?'

'Inevitably, in her position. One of the maids, I am told, swore vengeance upon her only yesterday. But this is nothing out of the way. We employ a strong and heady mixture of bog Irish, Spanish and Italian maids and

33

menservants, plus a few Maltese and one Hungarian. Several of the girls settle down and marry local men—often those on the estate. It brings a dash of volatile new blood into the stolid yeoman stock we breed in these parts. The Irish, Italians and Spanish are inclined to indulge in histrionics but if ugly threats are uttered they do not, as a rule, amount to anything. In Mary Burke's case I am sure it was just an outburst of frustration and bad temper. It appears that Matron had condemned her in strong terms for associating with some man.'

'Do you know the name of the man?'

'No. I only heard the story this morning from Susan, the senior housemaid in the school infirmary. Sister Wilbraham had told her, in confidence, of Matron's death and Susan felt it her duty to advise me of this trouble; although she emphasized her belief that Mary is incapable of murder and is "just a silly young girl out for attention".' The procurator mimicked a gentle female voice with a touch of the brogue. 'Susan is a splendid person,' he continued, 'calm, well-balanced, and entirely discreet; we're lucky to have her in the infirmary. She told me of this episode only in order that I should learn the true story before the rest of the staff discover what's happened and start casting around for suspects.'

'Had anyone else threatened Matron?'

'Not that I know of. Possibly some boys will be found to have uttered dire threats—that wouldn't surprise me in the least. But on the whole I would think that Matron was popular. The nursing staff in a monastic boarding-school provide some female interest and, unless they are women completely lacking in personality, they are bound to make an impression of some kind. Perhaps matrons are only fully appreciated in retrospect—like several of the masters!' He smiled sardonically. 'At all events, a good many of our Old Boys find their way down to the infirmary when they come back here and, since calling on Matron is a voluntary affair, one must conclude that they liked her. She never forgot a face, or a name.

'She could scent epidemics and lead-swingers a mile away and there wasn't much she didn't know about boys of all ages—including, one often thought, the community. Of course she'd known several of the monks when they were boys here. The headmaster will be able to tell you more and would, no doubt, agree that she had her critics among the idlers who strive to get off Corps or to land in the infirmary with some trivial, and possibly self-induced, malaise just as the exams loom up. There *are* ways of achieving a few days of desirable rest—as any old soldier knows; but Matron knew them too.'

'Is the Combined Cadet Force compulsory here?'

'For the lower school, yes. Partly, I think, because we have a rather good record. We can't compete with Stonyhurst which, though small until after the Second World War, has produced seven VCs, but we have a strong Service tradition. It's a matter of pride that the corps should get good reports, notwithstanding the malingerers, and Matron felt it was up to her to discourage any slacking. She also had a distaste for low comedians and every school has a few of that breed; sometimes amusing, but not to a busy matron.'

'Comedians?'

'Practical jokers. Fake wounds, soap slides in the infirmary—that sort of thing, don't you know? Childish, often funny, sometimes dangerous. Sisters may smile—but matrons never! At least, not in public.'

'So—in general, she was popular?'

'I would think so. In the way that characters in schools and other institutions do become popular. The older they get the more eccentric they become; legends grow around them and they become part of school history.

"O'Courtesy O'Connell" the boys called her, because she insisted on good manners. "Let's have a little courtesy" became a catchphrase—especially outside the dispensary when young thugs, queueing for medicine or whatever, are apt to push and shove and make a general nuisance of themselves. At busy times she demanded the presence of a monitor who, inevitably, was labelled "the courtesy cop", but she rarely reported boys to their housemasters or to the headmaster. No, I can't think that anyone would actively dislike her—certainly not enough to murder her.'

'What about the use of the north cloister in the late evening? Who would know that Matron was in the habit of bringing chits to your office?'

'Almost anyone. Monks, boys, masters, domestic staff. Over the years she must have been seen by hundreds of people and anyone interested could have worked out her movements pretty exactly. However, although anyone *could* have been in the cloister late in the evening, in fact very few people do come this way after dark. At nine-thirty the church is locked for the night and most of the monks retire to their cells. I am referring to those living in the monastery—not to those who have rooms in the school. Lay masters mostly live out in the village. Any of them could use

37

the north cloister, but they are much more likely to enter and leave by the main gate—until it is locked, in the summer at ten-thirty.

'The kitchens would be closed soon after eight. The men servants all live out and the maids who do live in are mostly young, silly and frightened of the dark. They have a recreation hut, as I think I told you, in the grounds and there is always some form of entertainment going on there. They return to their rooms here after voluntary night prayers at ten. The older cleaners, whom you will see around, are local, married women and would not be here in the evenings unless they were working in the kitchens. Most of them go off duty in the afternoons. As far as the boys are concerned, this is not part of the house they would have any reason to visit after nine o'clock. At the time Matron was murdered they should all have been in their rooms and dormitories at some distance from the north cloister.'

'What about the lay masters who live in? Some of them must be out late at times and want to get back into the school; or supposing a lay master, who lives out, has to come back to collect books or papers—what then?'

'A good question, if I may say so. The Kestrel gate and north hall door are locked at ten-thirty by the night watchman and, after that, the only official entrance is through the side door in the infirmary wing which is left unlocked until around midnight, simply to allow any of the staff who have been out late to get back in. Matron, or one of the infirmary staff, sees that it is locked and anyone arriving after that has to ring the bell and brave Matron's wrath. Just inside the infirmary door is a staircase leading down to the basement and from there it's possible to travel underground and come up by another staircase opening into the gallery near the kitchens and refectories. It's called the Tunnel, is out of bounds to boys, and used only by domestics or, as I have said, by lay masters returning late. In their case the idea would be to avoid any noise in the infirmary passage where they would have to pass by Matron's office and flat and she is, or rather *was*, a light sleeper. The nursing staff's dining-room and bedrooms are on the first floor.' Father Paulinus looked at his watch, 'I think, Inspector, that it is time we made our way across to the headmaster.'

CHAPTER FIVE

THE STAFF COMMON ROOM

By nine o'clock, sixteen of Ambelhurst's lay masters, one lay mistress and several of the monks who taught in the school were waiting in the staff common room. There was little speculation as to what might have prompted the headmaster to call a meeting that must inevitably delay the start of the first teaching period of the day; some were content to talk, others marked books or attempted *The Times* crossword. There was little sense of frustration and a minimum of impatience; Dom Erkenwald had long enjoyed the confidence of his staff and not even a confirmed grouser, such as Claude le Mesurier, the senior history specialist, could suppose that he would interfere with the timetable for the sake of an idle whim. Claude was a superb teacher fuelled by nervous energy who had had the sense to marry a slow, placid wife. Sheila complemented his tautly strung personality and reacted as calmly as a good children's nanny whenever he gave her the benefit of his overstrained and overeducated nerves. In her presence he shed exhaustion as a snake sheds its skin. At one minute past nine on the morning of May the twenty-seventh, Claude could be described as tuning up his orchestra of irritation, a process which presaged a lively period for Upper Va when he was free to join them.

'Mercifully,' he announced to anyone who cared to listen, 'the Erk—when he *does* come—will put a jerk in it, make his points, and depart. He has a—' But at that moment the headmaster walked in and, as Claude had predicted, he wasted no time.

'Good morning, Miss Mynor, Gentlemen.' He paused, looking grave and allowing them to catch his mood. 'I regret having to tell you that the school matron has been murdered. She was found dead early this morning, having been attacked in the north cloister and dragged into the Enclosure. The police are, of course, in charge of the case and for the moment I do not want any rumours to reach the ears of the boys. You may recall that when we had a fire here, some years ago, one of our more enterprising scholars lost no time in briefing the Press and consequently alarming the parents unnecessarily. I shall give the school the bare facts—as I know them— during this morning's First Break, and no doubt certain of the more imaginative will entertain us all with their improved versions

41

later in the day. This is neither the time nor the place to refer to Miss O'Connell's work among us but may I ask you to remember her in your prayers.'

Dom Erkenwald, as usual, disappeared as quickly as he had come and there was a stunned silence which le Mesurier broke.

'An assassination—or an assignation—or both?' he inquired.

★   ★   ★

The procurator and the inspector emerged from the former's office into a narrow passage on the west side of which were offices labelled Sub-Procurator and Economus. Along the south side, the passage was half-glazed to below shoulder height and they could see into a general office where clerks and typists were at work.

'This looks like a well-run business house,' Morgan commented. 'Have you a big property to administer?'

'Three thousand acres of farmland, mechanized and modernized. There is good shooting, lakes are stocked with trout and we run a pack of beagles. The kennelman is famous and our hounds are in demand for breeding purposes. Our estate carpenter's son is both an artist and a craftsman and we have been able to provide the capital for a flourishing small business, which employs local men and turns out sturdy cottage-style furniture to Seed's designs. He has evolved his own signature-gimmick; not as charming as Thompson's famous mouse—Seed signs his pieces with a wheat-ear—but it is attractively done. We also have a guesthouse in the village—run for the benefit of parents and relations of the monks and boys. We own houses and cottages around Ambelhurst: we have to, otherwise we shouldn't be able to accommodate the staff we need for teaching and maintenance. Of course there is much reassessment going on nowadays. Some of the younger monks deplore the fact that we are landowners and business men. They regard it as unchristian. It's a point of view. Because of our ancient history they can scarcely label it unmonastic. We work and pray—that's traditional.'

Leaving the procurator's department, they turned right and descended the flight of wooden steps up which Morgan had earlier followed the boys into the church. A barrel-vaulted roof curving overhead and the stone arch above the lowest step prevented them from seeing down the full length of the north cloister. The inspector judged that only a quarter, or less, of its total length was visible

43

from this viewpoint.

'This,' Father Paulinus explained, 'is part of a temporary building linking the school with the church. Visitors are surprised by the sudden transition from dignified cloister to clattering staircase and assume that we miscalculated the distance and filled in the gap as cheaply as possible. It will probably last another fifty years—'

A scream of piercing quality, followed by a series of louder screams, interrupted him and both men turned and leapt back up the stairs, following the direction of cries and imprecations that could only have emanated from a feminine and Latin throat. Turning towards the stores, they burst upon a scene reminiscent of operatic tragedy.

'*Aie, aie, Madre de Dios!*' shrieked a Spanish voice and, from kitchens, refectories and stores, a flood of young men and women, with a sprinkling of more mature cleaners and cooks, flowed into the narrow passage.

'Pray God, it's just hysteria!' muttered Dom Paulinus, pausing to let the police officer pass him. A slim dark girl with a mop of curly hair was cowering against the wall, shuddering dramatically, with her forearms crossed and her hands clutching at her shoulders.

'Issa baby!' she moaned. '*Si, bambino, si, si,*

si . . .'

Another girl was poking about in a plastic bucket with the end of a mop and, as the inspector drew level, she retrieved a once white cloth and held it up, dripping with heavily bloodstained water, as she crooned reassuringly:

'No-a, no-a! Issa not-a baby. Issa dirty water. Issa floor-cloth—floating. See! You believ-a Regina—not so? Regina tell-a you the truth!' Then—with a dramatic change of tone from reassurance to fierce anger—she shouted, 'Carmelita! You stupid! You silly cow!' Carmelita's sobs were lessening and she was able to look about her as well as at the dripping cloth. The insult had wounded her pride but she was loath to see the quickly gathering audience disappear. Throwing the front panel of a floral pinafore over her head, she uttered a succession of shrieks that pierced the eardrums of all.

Dom Paulinus did not hesitate. Two quick strides and he seized hold of the colourful pinafore, pulled it down and administered a ringing smack to the girl's right cheek. There was a stunned silence—then Carmelita gasped in surprise and relapsed into muffled moans.

'Someone see if the doctor has arrived and get him!' the procurator commanded. 'Regina—you have shown common sense!

45

Take her to the maids' day room. Rosalita and the rest of you—get back to your work.' Chastened, they shuffled obediently away though with many a backward glance and disgruntled sigh. The subdued Carmelita allowed herself to be led off stage muttering under her breath as she massaged her smarting face.

'Tell the doctor what's happened. I expect he will provide some arnica—and tranquillizers!' the monk said. 'Sorry about that, Inspector. We don't indulge hysterics here in our multi-racial society!'

'You acted very swiftly, sir,' said the policeman approvingly. 'I don't expect it's the first time.'

'No, it isn't. But don't imagine that we go in for muscular Christianity here—or for striking women like gongs.'

'I'm sure you don't,' said the inspector, though he marvelled how he had reached such a conclusion in so short a time at Ambelhurst. 'Don't let anyone empty that pail, I shall need that for investigation of the blood group— and, with any luck, fingerprints.'

From the direction of the north hall a tall, broad man lumbered into sight and Morgan hailed him with relief. 'Archie! Something for you here, the usual processing—sharpish— please. Got your gloves?'

'Yessir!'

'I served in Italy at the end of the war,' explained Dom Paulinus as he and Morgan walked back down the wooden staircase into the north cloister. 'Lovely people, the Italians, but a bit apt to indulge in histrionics. I learnt that the occasional slap could quieten down a riot—even if it was strictly against the Geneva Convention. By the time the Red Cross could have arrived the whole thing would have been out of hand; but nursery tactics, allied to supreme courtesy on other occasions, kept things under reasonable control.'

'You don't have to apologize to me. We are no longer allowed to slap naughty boys caught stealing apples, of course, but—' Morgan smiled mischievously—'I'm interested to see the Church Militant.'

The deep-toned abbey bell once again interrupted the conversation. One, two, three, it tolled: then a pause, and again one, two, three.

'The Elevation,' said Dom Paulinus by way of explanation: and seeing a cloud of mystification come over the inspector's face, he added, 'of the Mass.'

Morgan frowned. In pre-ecumenical days he had heard his Baptist grandfather dilate upon the subject of the 'blasphemous Mass'

... he had slept through one such earlier in the day and had now twice heard church bells tolling to indicate the beginning and progress of the mysterious liturgy. He had also been to investigate the murder of a woman in a monastery. His grandfather's warning of the 'whore of Babylon' stirred in his memory.

They had reached the spot where Matron had been murdered, and the inspector noted again how easy it would have been to hide in the deeply embrasured doorways on either side of the cloister and be swallowed up in the shadows.

'Is it lit at night?'

'Dimly—until eleven o'clock. Matron used to carry a torch because, although she knew the place like the back of her hand, she had once tripped up over a black cat. The flagstones are worn—which explains the pool of blood left behind after the killer's cleaning-up operation.'

'Whoever lay in wait could mark her progress by the torch—which, incidentally, we found. It had rolled into a corner.'

They did not talk again until Dom Paulinus stopped at a heavy oak door and, holding it open, said, 'After you, Inspector.'

Morgan stepped out into the sunlit courtyard and drew a deep breath. Around him, superbly indifferent to time or fashion, lay the core of sixteenth-century Ambelhurst. The style was as forthrightly severe as the Lancashire masons who had hewn each stone. There was no concession to popular appeal; none of the unmistakable charm which the golden stone of Oxford and the Cotswold country exerted so easily. The men who had designed and built the old Ambelhurst would have been unconcerned with easy acclaim. They built solidly, magnificently and to the purpose, with a certainty that bordered on arrogance. Morgan was silent.

'I can see that she's got under your skin,' said the procurator. Morgan noted the pronoun and thought it appropriate. The quadrangle lay like a stage-set—expectant, attentive, utterly still—yet very much alive. It was as though players waited in the wings and would shortly come through one or more of the six doorways, engaged in quiet or animated conversation: or perhaps, Morgan thought, a man on horseback would ride up the shallow steps of the great gateway and clatter across the cobbles and flagstones, shouting for servants to hold his mount. Whatever might happen here would probably have happened before. For five hundred years people had stood at the casements of the mullioned windows and looked through the leaded panes at aspects of life repeated again and again as one generation succeeded the last. He looked down at the dark grey setts at his feet, noting that no weed or blade of grass, scarcely a suggestion of moss, softened the outline of the ancient stones. He thought the starkness was symbolic: there was a take-me-or-leave-me air about this historic core of Ambelhurst that was not precisely disdainful but somehow expressed unconcern as to whether strangers liked or rejected all that it had been and what it now stood for.

'People visiting Ambelhurst for the first time,' said Dom Paulinus, 'are seldom indifferent; they can be overawed or nonplussed. Superficial people who will never understand her start talking fast—compulsively—gushing about her splendour or complaining about the cold. The ones who can take it—who will eventually make a positive response to the place—are temporarily silent. Ambelhurst makes no attempt to conciliate: she just is—take her or leave her. Those who have fallen under her spell love her for ever and when they come back—it's home.' He paused, then added, 'Why don't we go and stand in that patch of sunlight over there—part of the courtyard is always in shadow however high the sun may be.'

'Do you believe—as I do,' asked Morgan,

'that people become like the places they live in and vice versa?'

'Oh, most certainly; unless they are completely unreceptive and insensitive to atmosphere. It depends, not so much upon the length of time spent in any given place, as on what people give—and what they take.'

'Exactly! I should expect Ambelhurst to imprint a firm character on staff and pupils—particularly the young.' He smiled. 'Are your average Old Boys sound in belief, honest and uncompromising?'

'We have our rogues. I hope you are not already finding us inflexible and so rooted in tradition that we are also narrow and ruthless?'

'No, indeed! Quite the reverse. But with your feet planted firmly on the earth and your gaze on the heavens.' He pointed upwards as, for the first time, he noticed the twin towers soaring on either side of the main gateway and silhouetted against a cloudless blue sky. Each was capped with a silvery-green dome that glittered in the sun. Morgan's eyes watered and he looked away. The buildings surrounding the quadrangle were four floors high and the symmetrical perfection of each window, door, stringcourse and carving was repeated, until the east and west wings ended at the base of their respective towers to be united by an ornate central building over the entrance porch. The archway was at least thirty feet deep and stone benches ran along the walls, with racks for fishing rods above them; it was closed by a wrought-iron screen and a pair of beautiful gates which, at this hour, stood open at the top of a flight of shallow stone steps.

'You can see from the ornamental ironwork why this is called the Kestrel gate,' said the procurator. 'The hawk is the crest of the Keshawke family who built Ambelhurst and whose descendants gave it to our Order. If you go down the avenue and look back you can see the bird theme repeated, in stone, at the top of the towers. The school coat-of-arms over the gateway and the Keshawke crests have just been repainted, so you are seeing them at their best. On your right is the porter's lodge and the parlours—used for receiving parents and other guests—and on the left of the gateway are the headmaster's offices and his bedroom overhead. Ah! I see Dr Patterson getting into his car—so we have timed our arrival well. Let's be quick before Sam Brown catches us! He's the porter standing by the doctor's car.'

CHAPTER SIX

AN INSIDE JOB?

It was nearly half past nine when the school doctor, having examined Carmelita, confirmed the procurator's diagnosis, and approved his swift action, arrived at the headmaster's office.

'Dreadful news, Dom!' said James Patterson, accustomed to coming straight to the point.

'Yes. Have you seen Matron?'

'No, but the police surgeon tells me that death was practically instantaneous. An artery in the neck pierced by a sharp instrument. She would have lost a great deal of blood very quickly. They'd removed her body before I arrived. I knew you were busy so I went home for breakfast and to collect her case history for the police. Since I got back there have been old Dom Oliver and Brother Hilary to see; and I got called to a maid with hysteria. But— here I am. Mind if I smoke? I'm really upset about the old girl—having worked with her so long. And I bet you are too: you always got on. I had my moments of disagreement with her but—dammit—she was always right! I've tried to knock these cancer sticks,' he said, lighting one and inhaling deeply, 'but at a time like this—'

'You could always try prayer—much less harmful to your health!' Dom Erkenwald's voice was quietly ironic but he smiled sympathetically. 'I hope you're not going to become a heavy smoker again now that you don't have to prove your superiority to Matron in your ability to kick the habit?'

'I must admit that I enjoyed scoring off her. She just couldn't give it up and now I won't be able to prove that she has contracted some dire disease as a result. She's got the last laugh—as usual!' He sighed and continued, 'She'd have been upset to land us in this sort of scandal. The Press will love it! I saw the police sergeant on my way up to you. He's a man I know—discreet, reliable chap—a patient, actually—and he told me that it looks like an inside job.'

'An *inside* job? Surely not?'

'Apparently there's no sign of a weapon, no fingerprints and no bloodstained footsteps or trail leading away from where the body was found. The first two points suggest merely that the murderer wore gloves and took the weapon with him, but the third rather indicates special precautions; because it was a messy sort of death and one would have expected to find blood trails had it been an

54

unpremeditated job thrust on a burglar in a moment of panic. The murderer seems to have dragged the body into the Enclosure and then used a mop and bucket to clean up the mess in the north cloister.'

'It sounds fantastic!'

'I agree. But a squeegee mop and a bucket of bloodstained water were found in a housemaid's cupboard in the north passage. I was called to the Spanish girl who discovered it. Hysterical. She swore there was a baby in the pail but it turned out to be a white cloth—floating.'

'Oh Lord! This means the housekeeper's staff already know what's happened. I broke the news to Sister Wilbraham and she is telling her staff as she thinks fit.' The intercom buzzed.

'Yes?'

'The procurator would like to bring Detective-Inspector Morgan down—as soon as it is convenient for you to see him. I suggested that nine-forty would suit you, Father.'

'Very well. Dr Patterson and I have almost finished—I think?' He raised an inquiring eyebrow and the doctor nodded. 'Yes, that's all right, Mrs Macdonald.' He turned to the doctor. 'Anything new for this morning's surgery?'

'The list suggests nothing urgent. One sprained wrist, one pre-patellar bursitis—Wright and O'Gorman respectively. That means Wright won't be playing in the Eleven for the next three matches. Butcher has hay fever and Montague and McCleery-O'Prentiss both have mild athlete's foot. If anything else turns up I'll let you know. In the circumstances it seemed best to come and see you first thing, this morning. It's a shocking business. I still can't believe that Matron's dead. By the way, Hayden—as you know—cut his elbow and forearm badly yesterday. I looked in on him before coming here and he's in good shape and rather enjoying being the only patient in the infirmary. We may have to ward Butcher if he doesn't respond to treatment for his asthma—but Sister Wilbraham knows his case.'

'Good thing we have her to fall back on. She's the obvious successor to Matron; but I didn't expect there would be a vacancy quite so soon.'

'No, indeed. Matron had two or three years to run before retirement. Actually—I wondered whether Sister would stay on beyond this year. She's exceptionally well qualified and ought to be running an acute ward, or a big department—or even a hospital. They appoint hospital officers young

56

these days and she has the right qualifications and is good administrative material.'

'Tch! It hadn't crossed my mind that she might want to leave in order to better herself. I've taken it for granted that school nursing is her métier and I know she appreciates the religious background. She was an agnostic until five years ago; did you know?'

'I didn't. I've seen rows of religious books in her sitting-room. But she reads widely—art, poetry, biography, philosophy, medicine—the lot! We've never discussed religion. I'd have guessed her to be a cradle Catholic—possibly a spoilt nun.'

'Well, you'd be wrong about the former, certainly—and possibly with the latter. I'm tolerably certain she's not tried her vocation in a convent. Reverting to your assessment of her chances of a career in hospital, perhaps I'd better sound her out and discover what she feels about succeeding Matron. It's rather soon to be discussing the matter—scarcely decent—but if she's looking elsewhere we'd better know. It's not much of a promotion that we can offer—but if she enjoys the work and the religious atmosphere she could do worse. What are your views? You'd have to work with her. Apart from her professional suitability, does the prospect please you?'

'If you can secure her as matron of

Ambelhurst I'd say you were fortunate. Since she came I've been able to do all kinds of minor surgery impossible before. It saves the boys missing classes attending outpatients departments; not to mention travelling expenses. She's an excellent surgical nurse with theatre experience; and she's done intensive care. I'd say you'd be lucky beyond our deserts—because the infirmary wing is pretty grotty, you know. It has atmosphere all right—but it's inconvenient. To quote Sister Wilbraham: it "reeks of mice, leaking gas, dry rot and woodworm". She forgot to mention the deathwatch beetle and the bats!'

'Good Lord! I suppose I'm used to it. It's thirty years since I arrived as a new boy and went down with bronchitis on my second day. It seemed a homely place compared to the dormitory where I'd spent the first night, feeling ill and homesick. I confess to an affection for the place.'

'Enjoy your nostalgia while you may. I'd like to bring in the sanitary authorities and see it razed to the ground. However, I'd better not launch out on the subject today!' Dr Patterson rose and stood by the desk, looking grave. 'I've worked with Hag O'Connell for twenty-three years and she was here twelve years before me. It's a sad day for us all. She was absolutely reliable and utterly loyal. Out

58

of date, perhaps, in some ways—but she could spot an infectious disease a mile away and she had a sixth sense for disaster of any kind.'

'Yet not, apparently,' the headmaster countered drily, 'for disaster involving herself!'

★　　★　　★

The headmaster rose to his feet as Morgan and Dom Paulinus entered his study and the policeman was conscious of being in the presence of a man of considerable distinction. The inspector's reading matter did not include the deliberations of the Headmasters' Conference but he had occasionally seen on television, or read of, interviews with the Headmaster of Ambelhurst, from whom the mass media was accustomed to seek enlightenment and a discreetly presented point of view worth matching against the militant opposers of the public school system. Dom Erkenwald looked even taller and more impressive in his black monk's habit than he did on the TV screen, but his quiet and gentle manner was disarming. Morgan enjoyed making snap judgements at a first meeting and he was careful to revalue his assessments on closer acquaintance: but he was not often wrong. Humility, sense of humour, love of people were the qualities he discerned in this man.

'Inspector!' Father Paulinus's incisive voice cut across Morgan's reverie almost as though he had guessed that the Welshman was lost in intuitive appreciation. 'This is Father Erkenwald Ward, the headmaster—Detective-Inspector Morgan.'

'How do you do, Inspector? I'm sorry that your first visit to Ambelhurst should be occasioned by this tragedy. Do sit down. Will you stay, Paulinus?'

'I think I must return to my office—unless you need me?'

'No, that's all right.'

'Then I'll see you later, Inspector. Would you care to join me for a glass of sherry at about twelve-forty-five? You know where to find me.'

'Thank you. I'll fit it in somehow, you may be sure.' The inspector drew out his notebook as the door closed, and said, 'I'm afraid I can't spell your name, Headmaster. Latin was never my strong subject.'

'It's an old English name—an Anglo-Saxon saint,' he replied and spelt it out.

'Hmmm, I keep expecting to find things a bit foreign here but Ambelhurst seems much like any other boys' school—apart from your monastic uniforms!'

'They're really rather practical and comfortable to wear. They may look like mediæval fancy dress but they're economical—provided one doesn't use the scapular—that's the loose garment hanging free from the shoulders—as blackboard duster or oven cloth! Habits are blessed before we're allowed to wear them and we are supposed to treat them with respect. Like the King's or Queen's uniform!'

'I'm Welsh Methodist, myself,' the inspector ventured—drawing out his vowels, 'so one or two things in a Roman Catholic school are bound to look, sound and smell a bit strange.'

'Smell?' inquired the monk in surprise.

'In the church. The incense, you know. I don't suppose you notice it.' Reassured by the headmaster's courteous smile, he relaxed completely and looked about him with approval. It was a beautiful old room—a comfortable working study facing south. The windows, framed by the glossy leaves of a *Magnolia grandiflora*, were wide open on this sunny morning, and from his chair Morgan could see a long straight avenue running for almost a mile in a southerly direction. Nearest the school buildings the roadway was flanked by oblong ponds, broad lawns and shrubberies until a white railing marked a boundary separating the garden from the meadows beyond. A belt of trees and a statue surmounting a tall pedestal closed the vista at the far end where the road swung left towards Ambelhurst village.

'It all looks so normal,' the inspector mused aloud, 'considering the circumstances.'

'The news of matron's death is known only to a few, as yet.'

'I really meant—' He hesitated, then continued with slow Welsh humour: 'Well! Being called up in the early morning and told there'd been a Murder in a Monastery—and of a woman too!'

Dom Erkenwald's eyes glinted with amusement. 'Distinctly mediæval—Maria Monk and all that!' he suggested.

'Well—yes.' Morgan suddenly felt he had been a little tactless but there had been no resentful reaction—quite the reverse. Encouraged by the sympathetic atmosphere, he went on: 'On the way here, my sergeant informed me that I'd be entering a nest of papists. He's a Catholic himself, and I rather think he wants me to feel a complete outsider and is just hoping I'll put my foot in it and—er—burn my Welsh Methodist fingers.'

The headmaster grinned delightedly. 'We'll have to preserve you from your subordinate's scorn. Just ask me anything you want to know

62

and he won't have a chance to mystify you. Incidentally, I'm afraid that the Press will write it up as luridly as possible: one could hardly expect them to bypass such a glorious opportunity. Maria Monk will be left standing.'

'I'm afraid you're right but it will blow over.'

'I understand that you have decided this was an inside job?'

'Regrettably, yes. I wish it could be otherwise but all the signs point that way. Have you any idea why anyone should hate Matron enough to murder her? Had she many enemies?'

Dom Erkenwald thrust out his chin in a characteristic gesture and looked at Morgan steadily. 'Hate. That's rather a strong term; but then, murder itself is pretty drastic. The idea that someone in this house disliked Matron enough to plan her death seems incredible—at the moment. One hardly knows where to begin in considering such a possibility.'

'Had she *no* enemies?'

There was a pause, but Morgan felt confident that none of the monks he had so far met would seek to evade or obstruct police inquiries: they would take their time and weigh their words but they would cooperate fully and their opinion—when given—would be worth having. He wished that, in similar situations, there could be more lay people who talked less and uttered only what was of value.

The headmaster seemed disinclined to make a hurried statement: he sat with head bent, reflecting, and Morgan approved his unflurried calm. Behind Dom Erkenwald's desk a carved wooden crucifix was flanked on one side by a well-hung group of prints of Oxford and, on the other, by an exquisite mediæval alabaster carving of the Madonna and Child. Morgan turned and examined the long wall where, above crammed bookshelves, a selection of modern paintings appeared to be representative of the school's artistic talent. An abstract that could have been inspired by a nuclear holocaust or a mental breakdown was hung near a long panel depicting the evolution of man. Morgan was studying the latter when the headmaster spoke.

'You ask if Matron had enemies. I can think of three people who had reason to dislike her. You understand, of course, that I don't suspect any of the persons I shall mention; I only hope that by bringing their trouble with Matron into the open, they may be cleared of any suspicion. The grievances are known to several besides myself, so it would be quite useless for me to attempt to conceal the facts.

'First, an Irish maid, Mary Burke, who—as Father Paulinus will confirm—had publicly threatened to "murther" Miss O'Connell. I believe the Welsh to be less volatile than their cousins across the Irish sea but it seems to be a characteristic of the Celts that they experience black feelings which, when expressed with violence and venom, can evaporate. I think this to be the case with Mary Burke. She is a good-hearted girl, somewhat simple and liable to flare into a passionate rage but, if ignored, her anger blows over and dies away into sullen mutterings. I would think that her religious beliefs would prevent her from translating hot words into evil deed. She sees black and white too clearly and it would not be at all in character to plan a cold-blooded murder.

'Secondly, Juan-Pedro Ortiz y Gonzalez McCreaghane-O'Riordan. A mouthful of name—I will write it out for you.' The headmaster's face looked more strained than Morgan had yet seen it, as he printed the name in elegant italic script. 'This boy comes from Peru and has had an extremely unsettled childhood which, now that he's fifteen, is not making adolescence easy. His father, a ne'er-do-well of Mexican-Irish origin, was killed two years ago by guerrillas. His widow is still grieving: he was an attractive rogue—brave, inconsequent, charming, spoilt, and every bit

65

as rich as she is herself. The Marquesa is over here on a visit and staying in our guesthouse. She seems to enjoy its unaccustomed simplicity and, of course, likes to be near her son.

'Juan-Pedro developed tonsillitis shortly before she arrived—ran a temperature and was warded. The infection cleared too quickly, from his point of view, and he was passed fit for a CCF exercise on Friday last. That meant that he couldn't join his mother for lunch on the day after her arrival. Had he malingered Matron would have kept him in the infirmary—having admitted recovery he was passed fit for the Field Day. In view of the rarity of his mother's visits I would have let him lunch with her but, since the decision had been made and in fury Juan-Pedro had treated Matron to a scene worthy of all his more irascible Irish, Peruvian, Mexican and Spanish ancestors rolled into one; and had also sworn vengeance in highly dramatic terms—I had to support Matron when she put in a complaint. She had offered to telephone his mother at the guesthouse to explain and she pointed out that he would have the weekend free to spend with her: but he was beside himself with rage. Matron said that he "looked as though he could have killed her" and shrieked, "I'll have your blood for this, you vicious old hag!"''

'What action did you take?'

'I left the young man to cool off. It is important not to give hot-blooded South Americans any chance to start a vendetta or to feel themselves victims of persecution. Healthy neglect and the opportunity to cool off and feel foolish are required. When O'Riordan was once more capable of listening to reason I intended to send for him and extract an apology. We are quite good friends and I meant to ignore him pointedly and coldly, until he could appreciate that his behaviour was beneath contempt. Of course, this treatment would be ineffective with most English boys—who would probably interpret it as weakness; but O'Riordan is a civilized savage. From his Castilian ancestors he has inherited an innate courtesy and he would not, in cold blood, insult a woman in Matron's position. I think he is already feeling a fool and regretting his undignified loss of temper; I would be surprised indeed to learn that he fulfilled his threat.'

'Boys of fifteen have committed murder.'

'But rarely in cold blood—I would think. Also, I doubt if O'Riordan would have been able to resist a grand gesture of defiance— such as a note pinned to Matron's dress.'

'Nevertheless, the murder weapon was

67

evidently a thin stiletto-type knife and that would be in character, I imagine? Had he got such a toy?'

'You've found the knife, then?'

'No. But my men are searching every likely place.' The inspector consulted his notes. 'Burke and McCreaghane-O'Riordan. I'll skip the Spanish bits. Who is your third "enemy", Headmaster?'

'Regrettably, an Old Boy of Ambelhurst—Charles Bolton. He is an assistant games master; no degree—he was sent down—but he was a double Blue: apart from his coaching and the organizing of games generally, he does little beyond invigilating the Big Study. An effective invigilator as he has a fine physique. He is also second-in-command of the CCF and helps with the Duke of Edinburgh's Award adventure training and similar activities. Towards the end of last term, Matron complained that Mr Bolton was paying marked attention to her maids. He used his not inconsiderable charm to distract them from their work.'

'I surmise that they would not be averse to Mr Bolton's attentions. Did he know that he had been reported to you?'

'He did. I left him in no doubt before Easter that such behaviour could not be tolerated, in view of its probable effect on the boys. Charles is, as one would expect, admired and imitated. He promised to take a pull at himself and I insisted that if there was one more complaint he would have to go. He loves the place and all its traditions and runs the Wanderers—that's the Old Boys' sports club—and I had hoped that the threat would be effective. But unfortunately, Matron had further serious grounds for complaint and a fortnight ago I gave Mr Bolton notice. In view of his special position in the school and the fact—' the headmaster gave a wintry smile—'that we badly need his help with our cricket teams—especially with the Wanderers' and Emeriti weekends coming up—I felt that we should allow him to finish out the term; but I had—and have—misgivings. His charm is his undoing and he has a compelling attraction for almost all women.'

'The other complaint to which you referred?'

'Matron had engaged two new and very sophisticated girls from Ireland, Tessie O'Regan and Cissie Sheridan: she found Mr Bolton paying court to each alternately, thus setting them at odds and causing them to neglect their work. I happen to know both girls as they cleaned this part of the house together—until they fell out and had to be separated.'

'The other girls to whom Mr Bolton paid attention?'

'Principally, Rosie Beale—who is expecting his child and is quite contented with her lot. She would have no grudge against Matron, who has been most kind to her. Mary Burke, Tessie O'Regan and Cissie Sheridan may possibly have groused about Matron and called her "a murtherin' ould cow" and so forth, but not one of them, I am convinced, would go so far as to murder her. I dare say they will all weep copiously at her funeral.'

'They wouldn't be clever enough to dispose of the weapon and eliminate trails of blood?'

'I doubt it. Their code of sin would preclude it. They were brought up to fear hell and damnation and to have a healthy respect for monks. When Cissie first came here she was sent up to our slaughter-house to collect offal for Matron's cat. Two men dressed in overalls were at work: the taller happened to be the Abbot. He told Cissie that they were too busy to attend to her that morning.

'"Is dat so?" she returned. "An' I'm too busy to be talkin' with the likes of you!" Picking up a knife, she hacked off some meat, and with a contemptuous smirk flounced to the door, saying, "'Tis a disobligin' creature y'are—an' I'll be tellin' the matron—so I will!"

'The next time she went up to the butcher's for offal the shorter man, who was the professional butcher, asked her if she had realized that the man she had castigated was the "Lord Abbot of Ambelhurst himself". The poor girl was distraught! "Holy Mother of God!" she whispered, crossing herself, and she ran back to the infirmary in floods of tears, convinced that she was damned or at least in a state of mortal sin. Matron had a hopeless time trying to calm her, and she eventually sent for me to reassure the girl. I really don't think, Inspector, that Cissie or her compatriots would brave the wrath of the entire Church by committing murder! However, I mustn't waste your valuable time. What you want are the names of people who just conceivably might have felt angry enough to kill Matron. Again, I can't think that any of them would do so in cold blood. But, since you ask, Miss Melsdon—the housekeeper— was a sworn enemy; in fact they conducted a ding-dong battle of complaints and counter-blasts. Matron believed that the housekeeper deliberately sent down too little, dried-up or otherwise unpalatable food and she reacted with displays of pent-up frustration and bad temper. When the battle became too rowdy either the procurator or myself would take it in turns to counsel our respective protagonists

71

and there'd be peace for a while. I don't know if Father Paulinus mentioned Miss Melsdon?'

'He didn't. Of course she is well situated geographically for an attack in the north cloister, and kitchen skewers would provide a handy weapon. I'll have to go and see her.' He made more notes and, without looking up, asked: 'When would it be convenient for me to see the boy O'Riordan? And what about the nursing staff? Did they get on with Matron?'

'As far as I know. Matron sometimes complained that Sister Wilbraham spent too much time in church, but I couldn't agree that going to Mass and Compline amounted to a neglect of her duties—provided that she arranged for Sister Hanlon or Matron herself to cover her absence. I found by discreet inquiry that Sister Wilbraham never went up to the abbey except by prior arrangement. It was just that anything more than Mass on Sundays and holy days spelt religious mania for Matron. She could be unreasonable.'

'And Sister Hanlon?'

'No religious mania there! Attractive and feather-brained. There were grumbles about her work from time to time, but nothing serious; and she is competent in a subordinate position.'

'Anyone else who had crossed swords with Matron?'

'Not that I know of.'

'So that's the lot!' The inspector examined his list. 'Mary Burke, mentioned by the procurator and yourself; Juan-Pedro McCreaghane-O'Riordan, Charles Bolton and Miss Melsdon—those are the only persons known to have quarrelled with Matron. I take it that Mary Burke sleeps above the kitchen quarters? And that she could have followed Matron up the cloister and lain in wait? The boy, Juan-Pedro, where does he sleep?'

'He is in St Augustine's House attached to the main building, and could have reached the cloister by a number of different routes.'

'What about Mr Bolton?'

'He has a room in St Aldhelm's—one of the separate houses—and he also could have taken any route at all: locked doors present no problem to an athlete. Actually the infirmary door would have remained open until Matron returned from the procurator's office and locked up for the night—which means, I suppose, that it might not have been locked at all, last night.'

'When could I interview Mr Bolton?'

'It will have to be some time tomorrow. He's up in London today—at Lord's—and will be returning overnight. But let me repeat, Inspector, that I don't believe that any of these "suspects" has the temperament, or is sufficiently unbalanced, to have murdered Matron.'

'So we are left with Miss Melsdon who, I take it, you *could* just envisage as a murderer?'

'If you are determined on one of these four—then, yes, she would be the only one I could envisage in that role. She is good at her job, but—well! no doubt Dom Paulinus, or our economus, Dom Anthony, would be able to tell you more about her temperament and character. Have you met Father Anthony? He is speaking to the domestic staff at ten-thirty, so, if we go up now, we might catch him in the staff dining hall and he could arrange for you to interview Mary Burke and Miss Melsdon. I will engage to have O'Riordan here at any time after eleven o'clock assembly. Shall we say eleven-fifteen? I would, of course, wish to be present when you see him and, although his mother is in the village, I think that my presence will steady him more than hers would. About Charles Bolton: I will ask him to be available at nine-fifteen tomorrow morning—if that suits you?'

'Perfectly, Headmaster.'

'I wonder, Inspector, whether you and your staff would care to use one of the guest rooms opposite for your interviews? We have a dining-room and kitchen on this side of the gate and you could lunch either here or, if you prefer, in the van Dyck parlour—if that is more convenient. We should be delighted to see you in the monks' refectory but I wonder if you would appreciate being read to throughout your meal?'

'Personally, I should find it restful, but I doubt if my sergeant would, and in any case we must work as fast as possible on this case. I don't suppose that you are anxious to have us here any longer than is necessary?'

The headmaster smiled absently and a trifle wearily. The whole thing seemed to have taken on the inevitability of a nightmare. Here he was, calmly, arranging for interviews which might result in a charge of murder being brought against a boy, an Old Boy, or a member of the staff.

'Shall we go, Inspector—in pursuit of Dom Anthony?'

CHAPTER SEVEN

THE ECONOMUS

Dom Anthony was concluding his announcement to the domestic staff and enjoining them to give their full cooperation to the police. A girl screamed hysterically and was brusquely ordered to 'Stop that row!' which she accordingly did, subsiding into a muffled sobbing. This was clearly annoying to Father Anthony who wagged an admonishing finger in her direction, but her distress excited the sympathy of her neighbour. Morgan thought that the two young girls—the one with dark curly hair who had screamed, and her Titian-haired friend whose compassion had been evoked—looked irresistibly appealing as they clung together, extracting every ounce of drama from the occasion: but the monk was unaffected by the sight. No doubt one had to be firm with a staff of men and women of whom over half were drawn from various underprivileged European and South American countries. The inspector conjectured that an admixture of solid local stock must provide a very necessary antidote to so volatile a mixture.

'I am sure,' said Father Anthony with heavy emphasis, 'that you will remember Matron in your prayers. Arrangements for her funeral will be announced later and there will be a requiem Mass in the abbey church. I know that as many of you as possible will wish to be present, but I must ask you to remember that some will have to remain on duty.'

The inspector wondered how many would willingly forgo the morbid pleasure of assisting at Matron's obsequies.

'That is all. You may go.' Father Anthony wound up the proceedings with impressive deliberation and sat watching his staff as, in chatty excited groups, they flooded out of the hall: on his face was an expression of world-weary cynicism and Morgan judged that nothing in human nature would ever surprise him. The economus rose to his feet as the headmaster moved forward and introduced the inspector.

'My dear sir, this is indeed a pleasure!' said Dom Anthony, somewhat to the policeman's surprise, 'I have already heard of you from my friend Father Knox-Wesley who fears he has scandalized you. He is quite obsessively eccentric at breakfast-time and he has begged me to offer you his apologies, and to explain that, at his age, the temptation to shock people, though reprehensible, is well-nigh irresistible. I surmise that someone must have taken him to task as he tends to be unaware of the remarkable effect he has on strangers.'

Morgan attempted repudiation but his words were confused and he was acutely aware that the economus was enjoying his discomfiture. He suspected that Dom Anthony could find entertainment in many situations. They repaired to a cubbyhole next door to Father Paulinus's more spacious office and here Father Anthony motioned his guests to two upright chairs, seated himself at his large untidy desk and, in what was probably a characteristic pose, planted his elbows and approximated the tips of his fingers. His massive head seemed to rise out of his folded hood on a tide of double chins.

'And how may I be permitted to help you?' he inquired. His manner and voice were so precisely like those of a distinguished judge before whom Morgan had once, when an extremely raw constable, had the misfortune to give evidence, that the experienced detective became all fingers and thumbs and dropped his notebook. The headmaster had known others to be disconcerted by Dom Anthony's intimidating manner and he kindly came to the rescue.

'The inspector would like your opinion on possible suspects, Anthony, and wondered if he might interview Mary Burke and Miss Melsdon. He has an appointment with Paulinus at twelve-forty-five. If you could lay on lunch for two in the van Dyck parlour, Mr Morgan and his sergeant would prefer that to the monks' refectory. I must go now as I have to speak to the school at eleven. I leave you in good hands, Inspector. Dom Anthony knows his staff backwards. Give him the chance and he'll cross-examine for you; he had a

78

distinguished career at the Bar before he decided to join us.' With a smiling salute, he disappeared.

'So, Inspector—' the richly rumbling voice held a faintly sinister note of inquiry—'you have suspicions, I perceive?'

'Vague ones, Father. I understand that Matron crossed swords with a few people and I must, of course, interview anyone known to have quarrelled with her.'

'Just so, Inspector—just so. And may one inquire if these two are your only suspects? Are your investigations to be concentrated solely upon my staff?' He rose, as though in awful warning, but Morgan realized that the slightly theatrical manner was bluff and that, alone of the community, the economus was extracting a measure of enjoyment from the Ambelhurst murder; in the most harmless and Christian way, of course; priests could scarcely be suspected of rejoicing in murder but, the deed having been done, it would have been difficult for this particular man not to have derived some pleasure from a situation that might just as well be faced cheerfully.

'Not on your staff alone, Father. I shall be seeing a boy called O'Riordan, and a master, Charles Bolton.' He saw the monk's eyes kindle with interest. 'Perhaps, as the headmaster suggested, you will have other

79

names to put forward?'

'I think not, Inspector, I think not.' Evidently he had given some thought to the matter and was not disposed to waste time in considering the improbable. 'I would think that you could exclude Mary Burke—an unlikely murderess indeed! But Miss Melsdon! Or *Ms* Melsdon as she prefers to be called! Now there we have a woman who might well plan and execute a murder in cold blood. Though mark you—' he raised a minatory finger—'I bring no accusation, no proof, not a ghost of a suspicion. I would simply say that, given the motive and opportunity, given sufficient resentment and frustration, she might *conceivably* commit murder.'

'Dear me! Arsenic in the soup, perhaps? She doesn't sound the ideal housekeeper.' Morgan had recovered his equilibrium and was beginning to enjoy this conversation.

'She isn't! But her predecessor was taken ill, retiring unexpectedly at the beginning of the school year, and our choice was limited to two. Both were at a difficult age; this one had the better qualifications.'

'So she had known Matron only since last autumn. Had Matron many friends?'

'Not close friends, I would say; or rather, not many who lived locally. She kept herself to herself and avoided the village because, not unnaturally, people would try and pump her for information about the school. The village gossips would never get anything out of Matron—she was a model of loyalty and discretion.'

'And the housekeeper? I understand that she and the dead woman were always at loggerheads.'

'Well, Miss Melsdon is a frequenter of the Black Swan, known locally as Fenny's, the name of a long-dead publican, and her conversation is not limited by the professional discretion expected of nurses. Many of the lay masters, clerical staff and so on, are also regular customers and the school, being the largest local employer, is of abiding interest to just about everyone. For some people it is essential to be in the know, and what one cannot *know*, it is tempting to invent: Miss Melsdon is of this breed. Knowledge of the housekeeper's weakness in this respect inspired dislike and distrust on Matron's part and she was not a person who could or would hide her feelings. There was also trouble about the quality and quantity of food supplied to the infirmary. Unfortunately we are saddled with our housekeeper until the end of this year. I have to give her a measure of support, and in any case Matron could be pretty vitriolic at times. The headmaster and myself endeavour to preserve a balance of power. I must confess to being of the school that deplores the necessity of employing women in any capacity. I find them clever at deception and they rarely behave—when settled in—as one would have expected from their convent school behaviour at interview prior to appointment. This Miss Melsdon is a case in point.' Here Dom Anthony hitched up his scapular and buried his hands underneath—a sure sign, as Morgan learnt on closer acquaintance, that he intended to make a long speech. 'She was a demure version of the hockey-playing female when I engaged her. Masculine in appearance—cropped hair, shirt and tie, that sort of thing. But very pat with her "Yes, Father, No, Father, Three bags full, Father"—so I hoped that she combined a healthy disregard for feminine wiles with a reverence for the cloth. But no! From the moment that she took up residence she has made a favourite of the chefs and male staff generally (apart from the butler, who loathes her), behaved like a cat with the women, and—latterly—she's started banging her fist on *my* desk when she disagrees with *me*! She refers to the monks as "a community of country gentlemen" and is altogether the most offensive product of a Catholic Convent school that I have encountered in years of experience.

'She'll have to go, of course. I can give her a term's notice at any time after the expiration of her twelve months' contract. But—' he sighed—'how I hate working with people under notice, especially women! You will think me a complete misogynist! Be assured that I have a great liking for reasonable and intelligent women. However, I digress . . . we were discussing Miss Melsdon, and Miss Melsdon's flaws, like my own, are all too apparent; she has a temper like the fiends of hell and a vocabulary to match—while I, I lack patience and tolerance. Your impression of the lady may be a very different one but, for myself, I cannot overlook the possibility that—in ungovernable rage—Miss Melsdon might commit murder. I only hope that I am not a potential victim. Perhaps you'd like to meet her now?'

'Not particularly, after that masterly survey; but I suppose I must. Or would it be advisable to go and visit her on her home ground?'

'Less provocative than summoning her, certainly. I will send for Mary Burke, who is on my staff—as opposed to Matron's—and when you have interviewed her, we will go down to the kitchens and observe the virago in action.'

'Would it be possible to contact Sergeant Arrowsmith, Father? I shall need him for note-taking.'

'Certainly. He was in the general office just before you arrived. I'll find him for you.' The big man rose with surprising agility and, as he reached the door, turned with a broad grin on his face.

'I have said that I deplore the necessity of employing women, Inspector. When you see the—er—Rose of Tralee, whom I shall shortly bring in, you will think me a misogynist indeed.'

CHAPTER EIGHT

WOMEN

If Mary Burke was a fair sample of what Sergeant Arrowsmith would describe as 'the local bird talent', then the inspector felt that one could have a certain sympathy with Charles Bolton's promiscuous behaviour, for black curling hair, thickly lashed eyes of a compelling blue, a milk and roses complexion and an entirely enchanting smile were allied to a shapeliness that not even a nylon overall could effectively disguise. He sensed the sergeant's unspoken 'Cor!' hovering in the air. One hoped that Miss Burke had not been exposed to temptation beyond her powers of resistance, but even if she had succumbed there was little danger that she would fail to attract an honourable proposal and conclude a favourable alliance with one of the local farmers or college servants: men are not blind and beauty earns forgiveness for fallen virtue. Such were the inspector's first reactions, but he banished these amoral and quite uncharacteristic sentiments and determined to give Arrowsmith an example of impersonal and impartial professionalism that would be worthy of the CID.

'Come along and sit down,' he said, with a carefully controlled version of a reassuring smile. 'I am Inspector Morgan, Miss Burke, and this is Sergeant Arrowsmith. I expect that Father Anthony has told you that I would like to ask you one or two questions in connection with Matron's death?'

'He has, sor! And ah, God rest her, the poor creature, and may she rest in peace!' She accompanied the pious utterance with a sketchy sign of the cross, and added, ''Tis terrible news, sor, so 'tis.'

'Indeed it is,' the inspector replied and was amazed to hear his voice assume an Irish lilt

85

entirely foreign to it and still more surprised at the hibernian flavour of his next question. 'Did you ever wish harm to her, Miss Burke? Before you answer this I must caution you that whatever you say will be taken down in writing. You will have an opportunity to read and sign it before it is submitted as evidence.'

Mary looked bewildered so the inspector rephrased his question.

'Did you ever threaten Matron O'Connell?'

'I did, sor, and may de Lord forgive me! But sure, she was a dreadful hard woman—so she was.'

'What did you say to her? Did you ever threaten to harm her?'

'Ah, God now! I did, sor! Sure, I said I'd kill 'er.' Mary crossed herself again.

'And did you?'

'Indeed I did not! What for would I be killing an innocent body?'

'But—if matron had annoyed you? Perhaps—?'

'Ah, she did. Sure she was forever interferin' and tellin' me to keep away from *her* part of the house an' not to be a-standin' an' a-talkin' wid wun of the lay masthers.'

'And who might that be?'

'Sure 'twas Misther Bolton. An' a nicer gentleman there wouldn't be—unless 'twas the abbot himself.'

'Did you go out with Mr Bolton last night?'

'I did not—though I had a word wid him in the tunnel. "Mary," says he, "I've me work to do arrangin' dem at'letic teams. I'll be seein' you annudder night," says he, "but for now I've to be away."'

'Were you out yourself last night?'

'I was not, sor. Why so?'

'I would be glad if you could tell me what you did after you left Mr Bolton.'

'Ah, sure, I'll tell you, sor. 'Tis simple enough. I went to me room, that I share wid Bridie O'Keefe, an' wept till me eyes were red an' sore. An' that's the truth of it.'

'Dear me!' The inspector was genuinely concerned at the thought of this poor little thing realizing she had been stood up and breaking her heart over a worthless young man. 'I am sorry that you were upset. You did not go out again?'

'I did not.'

'Did you go straight to bed, then?'

'Ah, I did—when Bridie cum up!'

'And when would that be? Would you know what time it was?'

'Sure—'twas just afther a quarter past ten, sor.'

'How can you be so certain, Miss Burke?'

'Well, sor, y'see, Bridie 'ud been up at the recreation hut—an' the Father says night prayers at a quarter to ten—an' afther that the hut is closed—unless 'tis a dance night. An' when Bridie comes up I axes her de toime an' she says 'tis twenty past ten o'clock—but Patsy O'Leary, her wid de tongue of de serpent, says 'tis afther half past ten. An' Bridie went down wid her to see de clock on the stairs—an' sure, 'twas twenty-five past ten exactly.'

'Thank you, Miss Burke. That is most helpful.' Morgan beamed at her in a fatherly way and she dimpled engagingly—but, alas, her eyes were on Sergeant Arrowsmith. The inspector coughed to withdraw her attention to himself and asked, 'Would you know where I could find your friend Bridie?'

'I would, sor. She's in the kitchen now preparin' de vegetables. Will I find her for you, sor?'

'That would be most kind. I will ask Constable Gray to go with you and bring her back here. Sergeant! explain to Gray, will you? He should be in the general office.'

Bridie O'Keefe was perhaps less ravishing than her compatriot but she had a certain charm and her copper curls presaged a lively temperament.

'Good morning, Miss O'Keefe,' the inspector greeted her as she marched boldly in and, with a somewhat brazen and defiant glance at both policemen, settled herself on a chair. 'You know, I think, that the school matron died last night?'

'Sure, father was tellin' us th'ould cow—' She broke off and had the grace to look ashamed.

'Ummm,' said the inspector and looked at her searchingly. 'I see. I take it that you did not care for her?'

'Ah, she's dead, sor!' The pious ejaculation was omitted by this witness. 'She was all right—but always mitherin' an'—' Again she stopped in mid-sentence and this time she blushed. Morgan waited but she did not continue and he asked:

'Could you tell me how you spent last evening after you came off duty?'

'I can, sor. Afther our supper I axed Mary Burke to come down to the hut wid me; but she was delayin' around, so I went by meself.'

'And Mary never joined you?'

'She did not.'

'What time did you leave the hut?'

' 'Twas around ten to ten when the father had finished the prayers, an' Jim Malone— him that works in the Shtores—says to me: " 'Tis a fine night for a walk!" "Ah, 'tis," sayd I—an' he axes me to go up wid him to the shtile. An' that's what I did.'

'And how long did you stay there?'

'Well, sor, we went up by the byre—an' back by the road: an' then an' owl hooted an' wasn't I scared out of me wits entirely? An' I runs in by the infirmary door an' back to me room.'

The voice of conscience thought Morgan perceptively and, as it happened, correctly.

'Was Mary Burke there?'

'She was, sor. An' her eyes on fire wid weeping.'

'Did you go straight to bed?'

'I did, sor—after I'd settled Patsy O'Leary—the disbelievin' creature!'

'Disbelieving?'

'Sure she swore 'twas afther half past ten whin I came in, an' she axed me what I'd been up to wid Jim Malone. An' I proved to her—'twas twenty-five past ten o'clock exactly.'

'How did you do that?'

'Didn't I make her look at the clock on the shtairs? Sure that one 'ud disbelieve the blessed saints themselves, so she would!'

'Did you see anyone about when you came in through the infirmary door?'

'No, sor. I came up by the tunnel an' there was no one at all—until I saw Mary and Patsy in our bedroom.'

'Thank you, Miss O'Keefe. You've been most helpful. And now, could you find Father Anthony for me?'

The housekeeper was busy supervising the preparation of the midday dinners when the inspector was ushered into the kitchens and, although she noticed the intrusion, she did nothing to acknowledge the existence of the three men. Miss Melsdon darted around issuing orders in a stentorian voice that rose to a siren shriek when a cook set some fat on fire. Morgan assessed her as a highly strung, nervy woman in imperfect control of herself.

'We'd better retire defeated,' murmured the economus. 'There is no prospect of interviewing her until all the dinners are served. I suggest that we withdraw to the van Dyck parlour where I will introduce you to our excellent madeira.'

'That sounds splendid. Thank you.'

They left the kitchens by a door leading into the north cloister and were accosted by Father Knox-Wesley who hailed them with delight and inquired whether the abbot had yet arrived home and whether he or the prior would be busying themselves with Bell, Book and Candle to exorcize the evil in their midst. 'Or,' he added with relish, 'perhaps, Father Minister, you are awaiting the ministrations of our Grey Eminence or one of his Visitors?'

'You think that would be more effective?' queried Dom Anthony.

'Yes, I think so. This scandal may, in any case, put you out of business altogether—in which case we should be prepared to take over.'

'You shall dance at our funeral, John.'

'I'll be there,' said the Christite and croaked with laughter as Father Anthony and the inspector moved away.

Being a sincere Christian, the policeman was scandalized by so offensive a suggestion made at such an unhappy time. 'He's a lunatic and ought to be locked up!' said Morgan emphatically. 'Who is the Grey Eminence he was muttering about? Is it another name for the devil?'

'Oh no. Just a nickname for the Christite Father General in Rome.'

'Father Knox-Wesley is not a *Jesuit*, then?' Generations of Welsh suspicion went into the word, suggesting that the inspector was not descended from those Welsh farmers who had loved and hidden Jesuit priests throughout the long years of recusancy.

'No. The Christites are like us—they take a vow of stability to a particular monastery and they run schools. The Jesuits also run schools—but they are mostly men of no fixed abode: they are liable to be sent anywhere at short notice, wherever they are needed: Third World mission fields, British slums, universities, colleges. You could say that they live with a suitcase at hand—ready to leave at a moment's notice.'

'Sounds like Commandos—or S.A.S.!'

'Not a bad analogy! They adapt to the situation of a country, a province, or the world—and go where they are most needed. I would find it a very difficult vocation: I like to put down roots. But then—' he smiled slyly at Morgan—'my bulk is a handicap! The Christites are a relatively small congregation—the Jesuits being by far the largest in our church. The J's are great preachers and spiritual directors. Their philosophers, theologians, historians, and scientists are world famous. Oddly enough, they don't seem to produce—or should I say attract—many artists and, so far as I know, only one major British poet—Gerard Manley Hopkins. But I digress!'

'Why did Knox-Wesley call you "Father Minister"?'

'That's the title given to the man who does my job in a Christite house. He knows I'm called the "economus"—he's just teasing. He's a harmless eccentric; brilliantly clever and probably the oddest character in the Company of Christ. They're not all like that!'

'I'm relieved to hear it. "Odd" is hardly an adequate description! Judging by the way he is gloating, it wouldn't surprise me to find that he's murdered your matron himself—merely to annoy you all.'

'Ah! but you'd be wrong. Actually he's a very holy man and he loves us like a brother— in fact, he's one of our Old Boys. He's here for a few days' holiday.'

'Well—really!' exclaimed the inspector.

CHAPTER NINE

SCHOOL ASSEMBLY

Meanwhile, Dom Erkenwald had been greeted by his head boy outside the academy room and they retired into a window embrasure while the monk gave Bryant advance information, and also asked him to collect McCreaghane-O'Riordan and bring him down to the headmaster's study immediately after Assembly.

'Don't let him slip away. Would you mind waiting in Mrs Macdonald's office while he's being interviewed—I may need you to take care of him if he's upset.'

'Right, sir.' They entered the big room

crowded with boys and the talking died abruptly. Dom Erkenwald mounted the steps and stood on the apron stage looking about him; he had everyone's full attention.

'You will be shocked to hear that Matron died last night. The police have reason to believe that she may have been murdered.' There was a ripple as heads were raised and the whole school appeared to give him a closer look, their eyes opening wide as though in disbelief; the brows of some shot up; the mouths of several dropped open in a singularly unattractive manner; the faces of a few sharpened as they evinced an awareness of the main chance and what might be in it for them. These last were the boys for whom any experienced headmaster could comfortably predict material success. 'All there—and half way back' was how Dom Erkenwald was prepared to describe them and he issued his warning. 'Before anyone thinks he sees in this tragedy an opportunity for financial gain, I should perhaps advise you that the Press has already been briefed—in a *discreet* fashion; and that any boy found guilty of giving interviews, or of communicating with the Press *in any way whatever* will be expelled. I trust I make myself clear?

'If any of you recollects having seen Matron between nine and eleven last night, or considers that he has seen or heard anything at all unusual or significant, then I expect that boy to come straight to me and to avoid discussing the matter with anyone other than myself. Gossip can only harm the school. I can harm the gossipers. You have been warned.'

Dom Erkenwald paused impressively and, with his chin thrust out, gazed steadily round the room. 'Ambelhurst is great enough to survive a shock of this nature but I would remind you that murder, if it was murder, is a grave sin and, while praying for the repose of Matron's soul and remembering the long years of service she so generously gave to this school, I would ask you, please, to pray also for the person who caused this tragedy and who—if of sound mind—is probably guilty of mortal sin.'

The headmaster stepped down from his dais and it was a tribute to his authority that not a boy stirred or whispered to his neighbour until he had swept out of the room. He had observed Bryant moving purposefully towards O'Riordan and knew that the head boy and his charge would soon follow. In the gallery he was met by the inspector, Sergeant Arrowsmith and Dom Anthony and, as he fell into step with the policemen, he asked if they would be good enough to wait in Mrs Macdonald's office while he prepared

O'Riordan for questioning.

'I've known this boy since he was seven and think it important not to antagonize him. He's bound to be a bit frightened. If you will let me handle him, I think I can promise his cooperation.'

'That's perfectly all right, Headmaster. We'll wait until you call us in.' They were out of sight when Bryant arrived with his charge in tow and ushered him into Dom Erkenwald's study.

'Come in, Juan-Pedro.' The headmaster felt it advisable to use the boy's Christian name and reduce the incident to the safe level of a nursery escapade. 'Sit down. You've been rather silly and uttered threats and, now that the police suspect that Matron may have been murdered, I expect you realize that you will have to answer some questions?'

The boy nodded dumbly and his olive skin took on a greenish tinge.

'You've nothing to fear. Just speak the truth and no one can hurt you.' Dom Erkenwald fixed him with a penetrating gaze and added slowly, 'I must ask you this. *Did* you kill Matron?'

Juan-Pedro shook all over but he clasped his hands tightly together and, staring back, his eyes widening with terror, he stammered: 'No! No! How could you think it?'

'I didn't and I don't. You give me your word?'

'Yes, of course. I didn't do it.' The boy burst into tears.

'All right, Juan-Pedro. Steady now. I believe you and the police will believe you. Just be sensible and get a grip on yourself. I'm here to help you and as soon as you are ready we'll get the inspector in and have this business over and done with.' He went on talking quietly, murmuring reassuring information about the sergeant who would be taking notes and the inspector who was a Wesleyan Methodist and found a Catholic school rather strange and must therefore be treated with special respect. In a few minutes he had made it sound quite an ordinary situation and Juan-Pedro's confidence was visibly returning.

'All right now? Then we'll call them in. Stand up when the inspector comes in, and remember—I'm here to help you.'

*   *   *

'Come and sit down, Inspector. Sergeant, will you be all right in that corner? This is Juan-Pedro who, I think, had better sit here beside me.'

The inspector saw an undersized fifteen-year-old with a sallow, oval face and brilliant dark eyes; strong, wiry and extremely tense. He judged that his control would not be long-lasting and decided to complete the interrogation as quickly as possible.

'I believe that you were angry with Matron because she would not let you lunch with your mother but passed you fit for duty with the Corps?'

'Yes.'

'And you threatened her?'

'Yes.' The boy was shaking violently.

'Did you plan to hurt her?'

'No! No!'

'Did you go up to the north cloister last night?'

'No—I didn't!'

'Where were you after Lights Out?'

'In my dormitory.'

'Did you leave it at any time?'

'Only to get a drink of water.'

'What time was that?'

'I think it was eleven, because I heard a clock striking, and I looked at my watch when I got back to my cubicle and—it—it was t-ten past el-eleven.' The boy's control was fast evaporating and Morgan asked quickly:

'Did you go to sleep soon after—or were you lying awake?'

'I w-went to sleep. At l-least, I think so.'

'What woke you?'

'*Nothing* woke me.' His voice rose hysterically and Dom Erkenwald put out a restraining hand. 'Oh! I see! I-I thought—I mean—I slept until the bell rang and it was time to get up.'

'Very well, That's all, then.' The inspector cocked an eyebrow at the headmaster, who decided that unusual measures were called for.

'Juan-Pedro, do you think that your mother would offer you lunch if I sent you down to the guesthouse?'

'Oh yes, sir.'

'And will you go straight down and be back for your class at ten past two?'

'Yes, sir.'

'Good. You can tell your mother about Matron and about this interview—but don't alarm her.'

The boy slipped quickly out of the room, his face expressing relief. Dom Erkenwald buzzed his secretary and told her that Bryant would no longer be needed, that O'Riordan had permission to lunch with his mother, and that he would be grateful if Bryant would kindly inform Father Robert.

'Well, Inspector?'

'What do you think, Headmaster? Is he speaking the truth?'

'I think so. He's scared, of course—but I am sure of it. He is a truthful boy.'

'This guesthouse he has gone to—is it in the school grounds?'

'Not precisely—it's in the village, just on the school boundary; you will have passed it on your way here. It's owned by the monastery and used as a private hotel and retreat house by parents and visitors to Ambelhurst. Juan-Pedro won't run away, Inspector, and if he did you would soon pick him up.'

'Oh, that's all right. I'm not worried—just interested. Idle curiosity and finding out about the place, you know. Could we check his statement about the dormitory?'

'Certainly. Would you like me to ask his dormitory monitor and the boys sleeping in cubicles on either side of him—or would you prefer to interview them yourself?'

'No, I'm happy to accept your findings. If you should be doubtful then I will recheck.'

'Good. Now about your luncheon. It is being served for you and your staff in the van Dyck parlour and the room next door has been assigned to you for an office. Your bedrooms are directly above on the first floor. Please do let the guest-master or myself know if there is anything you want. Would you like me to take you across there now?'

'No, indeed. I'm beginning to know my way around. We won't interrupt your morning any further, Headmaster. Thank you for your assistance.'

CHAPTER TEN

SISTER WILBRAHAM

Sister Wilbraham had been locking up the dispensary after the doctor's morning surgery when the school porter brought her a note.

Sister Wilbraham
The Headmaster presents his compliments and would be grateful if you would call at his study at twelve noon.

May 27th

It was eleven o'clock—which meant that she would have time to give the doctor his mid-morning coffee.

Understandably, Dr James Patterson could not resist telling the tale of the Spanish maid and the bucket of blood. Sister Wilbraham shuddered but she said crisply, 'Stupid girl!'

'The whole thing's macabre!' he continued, 'and the sooner the identity of the murderer is discovered, the better. Prolonged inquiries can only harm the school. I doubt if you'll have trouble with nightmares, Sister, the little beasts will thoroughly enjoy the murder but, if a few over-stimulated neurotics should be brought to the infirmary, I recommend tranquillizers and occupational therapy. Plenty of school work and games until they fall asleep tired out. I didn't venture to prescribe "study and exercise for all" to the headmaster—he knows his job better than anyone. Let's hope we don't discover that one of his boys is the murderer. I think it would kill him. Anyone else, but *not* a boy.'

'Do you think it might be a boy, then?'

'Could be. Someone with a grudge and a sharp weapon. The opportunity was there and an excited adolescent might think that he had a motive. But, for my money, it's young Bolton.' He hesitated and then continued, 'I'm speaking in confidence, of course, but—did Matron tell you that one of the maids is pregnant?'

'No. She regarded me as a newcomer. I have only been here two years and I think Matron had an idea that no one could be loyal to Ambelhurst until they had been here at least ten. Which girl is it? And do you want me to take her to ante-natal clinics?'

'Rosie Beale. Her parents have been told

and are, fortunately, warm-hearted and forgiving and will welcome her home with open arms. I've advised her to return to Devon in a month's time. She's sturdy and healthy enough to continue working up to full term, but we don't want her condition to become apparent to one and all; some eagle-eyed mother might recognize that the girl is pregnant and draw the wrong conclusions— we don't want the boys' reputations damaged! I've examined her and she is as strong as a Suffolk Punch. No prize for guessing who the father is: Charles Bolton, of course. He admits paternity and is prepared to support the child; she doesn't expect him to marry her and has so many younger brothers and sisters at home that one more will be lost in the crowd.'

'But I thought Mr Bolton was—I mean—' Sister Wilbraham looked slightly confused— 'he seems to have someone else in tow.'

'Oh, surely! Several, in fact. The fellow's impossible. Pity the head ever let him come back here; but he's devoted to his "boys"— whatever their ages and faults—and I suppose he hoped for the best. I happen to know that he's "sacked" Bolton as from the end of this term, but is allowing him to stay on until then—provided that there are no other incidents, of course—because, frankly, they need him to cope with the cricket.'

'Then that explains the row I overheard between Matron and Mr Bolton. He was shouting at her.'

'I'm not surprised. He loves Ambelhurst, for all his irresponsibility, and although he's brought dismissal on himself, I can well imagine that he's pretty sore about it all. Also, he must know that it was Matron, and not Rosie, who reported him to the headmaster. Rosie knows the rules and abides by them. She knew what she was doing all right and has absolutely no regrets. A child of the soil—half animal, I always think. To give Bolton his due, I don't think he'd take advantage of an innocent—he plays it fair.'

'Fair to everyone except the headmaster who trusted him to behave. Which reminds me—' she looked at her fob watch—'I should be going across to his study.'

'Mmm. Better not keep him waiting on a day like this when everyone must be chasing him. I saw the procurator and the detective fellow going over there as I was leaving, and there'll be reporters and parents and the business of keeping the school down to normal routine.' He watched Sister Wilbraham as she adjusted the cap on her swept-up golden hair and thought, not for the first time, that she was a fine-looking young woman.

Father Erkenwald stood up as the sister came in and offered her a chair opposite his desk. He approved the poise and grace with which she sat down and clasped her hands loosely on her lap. Controlled, strong-willed, utterly sure of herself, he thought. She was almost too much of a good thing. He had rather enjoyed the quirks and eccentricities of the dead matron, who had been nothing if not human. The girl might be more up to date, possibly more efficient even, but her very professionalism was a trifle austere; faults can be endearing and perfection somewhat daunting. He liked warm people, himself. The headmaster realized that there had been at least thirty seconds' complete silence while these and other thoughts passed through his head, but Sister Wilbraham was apparently undismayed. She neither shuffled nor looked embarrassed but sat quietly awaiting his opening gambit: such serenity was rare, and was especially admirable in the exciting and unusual circumstances of the day. Many women would have been restless and bursting with questions and the desire to gossip.

'I want to ask you, Sister, if you are willing to take on Matron's responsibilities as from today and—if all goes well for the rest of the term—if you would be prepared to fill the post permanently? You need not answer or commit yourself now. Think it over. You don't need me to tell you that there are many careers in the nursing profession open to you, and I would not want you to stay on at Ambelhurst if you felt that you should be working elsewhere.'

'There is nowhere I would rather be.' She spoke emphatically and met his penetrating gaze. 'I shall not chànge.'

'In that case I will ask the procurator to prepare a contract and we'll engage a temporary sister through the Nurses' Agency. We can appoint a permanent assistant matron as from next September; I doubt if we should find anyone suitable this term.' He paused, then asked abruptly, 'How do you feel about occupying Matron's flat? There would be no need to move in until next term and we can have the whole place redecorated first. Would it worry you to occupy a murdered woman's rooms?'

'I don't think so, Father, thank you. She didn't die there, after all.'

'Good. Have you told Sister Hanlon?'

'Yes. She was extremely agitated and says she will only go up to the procurator's office through the garden in future, and will never go to the abbey church other than by the outside route.'

'Silly girl! Tell her the cloister will be specially blessed; it has probably been done already. I'll see her myself, later on, and talk some sense into her. This kind of nonsense is catching and she should be setting an example to the maids, not adopting an attitude that is excusable only in the uneducated. However, I suppose she can't help her temperament. She's not irreplaceable, but it will be a nuisance if we have to make another change.' He stood up, 'Well, Sister, I think that's all. Except that—I think we'd better wait until next term before addressing you as "matron". Thank you for coming.'

She rose. They exchanged smiles of mutual satisfaction and he silently applauded the cool dignity with which she withdrew.

CHAPTER ELEVEN

THE VAN DYCK PARLOUR

The van Dyck parlour, a well-preserved relic of former glory, was in the oldest part of Ambelhurst and its oak-panelled walls were hung with one of the finest collections of van Dyck portraits to be found outside the

National Gallery. The curtains were of crimson damask and the furniture, silver and china were collectors' pieces.

'Matron had a gift for arranging flowers,' said Dom Anthony, indicating an alcove in which white peonies were silhouetted against deep red flock wallpaper. He picked up a silver salver and carried it over to a side table that stood below the alcove. Fumbling for a key with his right hand, he touched the classical urn in which the flowers were displayed and sniffed appreciatively, 'What a glorious scent this variety has!' He unlocked a cupboard and produced a decanter and three exquisite glasses.

'No seed cake, I'm afraid,' he said as he poured the wine. 'When I visited my grandmother she always offered it with a glass of madeira. I loathe caraway seeds—but the smell is nostalgic. Perhaps it's as well we have none to offer you—I've inherited a family tendency to put on weight!' He sat down heavily, on a Hepplewhite chair designed for one of his build, and indicated that the police officers should join him at the fireplace end of the long, mahogany dining-table.

They sipped their wine in contented silence for a few minutes, then the monk sighed. 'What peace!' he commented. 'Women tend to destroy one's full appreciation of good wine by continual chit-chat. We bring VIPs and reluctant mums in here for the "madeira treatment".' He smiled sardonically. 'I refer to the mothers of small boys—or rather, male infants—whose husbands are staunch Old Boys but whose wives have affiliations elsewhere.'

'Affiliations?'

'Yes. Women are curious creatures. They are not always insistent upon sending their daughters to be educated at their *own* former convent schools, however much they may cherish happy girlhood memories! But they tend to believe, implicitly, in everything their fathers and brothers have told them about their own and rival public schools. In consequence, we—sometimes—have prejudice to overcome and men bring their wives up here—forewarning us, of course— and soliciting our help in swinging the balance in favour of Ambelhurst. It's amazing how an urbane interlude—spent in enjoying an excellent madeira, in discovering mutual friends, discussing the old Catholic families, boasting gently of the school's academic, artistic or athletic successes, or—if interest lies that way—talking of the Ambelhurst farm, of fishing or shooting prospects—it's *intriguing* to see how this can erase an unfavourable view. Dilating upon other people's sons and their progress through the school, reminiscing about the good old days when we were all young and delightfully devilish, that sort of thing ... works wonders! Remarkable, really, how such a simple episode can break down barriers and rout opposition. The "madeira treatment" is a softening-up process—an eirenicon.' He held up his glass to the sunlight and gazed at it thoughtfully. 'Not at all sinister ... just—common sense! The reluctant wives, or rather mums, get to know us, the Old Boy husbands are grateful, an atmosphere of mutual respect and tolerance is evoked, and as often as not, no more is heard of the claims of the rival establishments. The wives are enchanted by their own unselfish submission to their husbands' wishes—and, in the course of time, forget that they had ever wanted their sons to go elsewhere.'

'Fiendish cunning, it seems to me,' said Morgan. 'The sort of thing attributed to Jesuits!'

'No. Just diplomacy. We appreciate that the dissenting wives have a valid objection. But we also know that men tend to be strongly prejudiced in favour of their own Alma Mater—even, it sometimes happens, when their school careers have been singularly unsuccessful. We therefore make it possible for the wives to accept us—and we welcome them into the Ambelhurst family. Thus, we promote marital harmony—and that's practical charity, as I'm sure you'll agree.'

He leant forward to refill their glasses and murmured, 'As a matter of fact, in marriage—as in life generally—the person who sacrifices his or her will in order to give legitimate pleasure to the other, frequently experiences great sweetness and joy as a result: a reward that is as delightful as it is unexpected. Love and unselfishness never fail to bring happiness.'

Inspector Morgan gave him a shrewd glance but was uncertain whether the monk's face expressed innocent pleasure or machiavellian satisfaction. Perhaps it was both. He considered awhile—and thought he had detected a practical snag.

'Your reasoning seems sound, Father, but what if the wife dislikes madeira, or is teetotal?'

'Why then—we offer alternatives. Tonic water, Perrier, tomato juice—or even tea or coffee. The latter poured, of course from good silver into delicate china cups—all given by past benefactors. Just—simple—hospitality!'

'Very disarming,' murmured the inspector, and considered his second glass of wine. 'Dear me!' he said. 'I arranged to be with the procurator at twelve forty-five—and a glass of sherry on top of this madeira will send me to sleep all afternoon. Do you think that we could cancel the appointment and take a brief walk instead?'

*   *   *

Inspector Morgan liked to get away on his own for some period of each day—especially when his cases brought him to a countryside as beautiful as that around Ambelhurst. Solitary exercise helped him to sort out his impressions and, quite often, flashes of intuition—which he attributed to his Celtic sixth sense—occurred when he was relaxed and, as he expressed it, 'hypnotized' by his long, rhythmic stride. So, after lunching with his juniors in the van Dyck parlour, followed by coffee taken with the monks in a room known as 'the calefactory', he explained to an understanding guest-master his need for solitude and slipped away.

He walked through the monks' woods where the beech trees were at their best and the silky, translucent green leaves, still fringed with soft brown hairs, stirred lightly overhead. The air smelt good and flowed like silk against his skin. A delicious sensation of peace and happiness washed over him. This was the state of euphoria that most commonly heralded his flashes of intuition: but he was in no hurry to solve the mystery and depart. Ambelhurst was a novelty and it suited him very well. He was vastly entertained by everything he saw and heard, and the warm hospitality and absence of tension were like balm to the spirit. They provided a refreshing contrast to the squalid scenes which had surrounded most of the murders he had been sent to investigate.

Morgan drew out his cigarette case—and found it empty. A nuisance, but it did not shatter his mood. He had already turned in the direction of Amberry village and he might as well call in at the newsagent's: a brief visit was hardly likely to disrupt his sense of anticipation.

From the village he continued down the road that led to the river, where he spent a long time in the shadow of the bridge, watching the trout rise. When the fickle May sunshine finally disappeared, he set off briskly to return to the school—noticing as he turned down the avenue that a cold wind was driving scurrying clouds across the sky. The buildings looked dark and sinister now and he marvelled at a change in his mood which had become one of unexpected depression. The wind gusted fiercely as he walked through the Kestrel gateway and he was glad to escape into the shelter of the headmaster's ante-room where Mrs Macdonald hailed him with relief.

'I've been trying to contact you, Inspector!'

'Sorry. I was out for a walk. Anything urgent?'

'Juan-Pedro's mother has telephoned. She's coming up from the guesthouse any minute now to see the headmaster. He wondered if you would like to be present at the interview?'

'Thank you—I would.'

'Will you go straight in, please.'

*   *   *

'Inspector! Well timed! The Marquesa is upset. I was engaged when she rang but I gather she was dramatically voluble on the subject of persecution by the British police. Mrs Macdonald tells me that she made it sound like the Spanish Inquisition.'

'Oh dear!'

'She's over-protective where her son is concerned. The only boy among five daughters—'

The door was opened by Mrs Macdonald and a beautiful little creature, superbly dressed and expensively coiffed and scented, exploded into the room. From the top of her shining dark head to the tips of her very high-heeled court shoes she was the quintessence of elegance, and she appeared to be in the grip of an overpowering emotion.

'Fa-ather! *What* are you *do*ing to my *son?*' Her enormous black eyes were bright with tragedy and, as yet, unshed tears. The arms which she flung out in an extravagant gesture of despair seemed too fragile to bear the weight of the solid gold bracelets and the diamond and emerald rings on her fingers. She wore a tangerine linen sheath dress of an expensive simplicity that proclaimed its couture origin, and on it was pinned a brooch that was undoubtedly worth a film star's alimony. Inspector Morgan drew back into the shadows, grateful for the opportunity of witnessing a vivid episode in the life of the school.

'I *trust*-ed him to you. And you! You have be-*tray*ed my trust and denounced him to the Policia!' Her voice soared and throbbed like an organ under the hands of a maestro and drew from Morgan emotions of which he had not thought himself capable. The poor mother, like a broken butterfly, sank with consummate grace into a chair opposite the headmaster, dropped her head on to her outstretched arms and sobbed as though her heart would break. The inspector had seen hysterical women and loathed and detested

116

them, but this was not hysteria; this was the high peak of tragedy, the apotheosis and perfection of distressed motherhood. He swallowed hard and looked fiercely at the headmaster, who had subsided into the chair from which he had started to rise on the Marquesa's entrance. To Morgan's incredulous and indignant astonishment, he was looking weary, worldly and slightly bored.

'Nonsense!' said Father Erkenwald loudly and crisply. 'Pull yourself together, Marquesa, and listen to what I have to say. Indulging in these histrionics does credit neither to your common sense nor to your maternal instinct. You are an intelligent woman—so try and behave like one. That is the best way to help your son.'

The beauty snapped back into animated and angry life again, like a ballerina moving on to the next pas-de-dance. She threw back her head, showing a shapely throat to its best advantage, and with furious intensity hissed:

'Oh! you are so pr-roud! And so cr-ruel and ar-r-rogant! You have no feelings! Well, I—I too am pr-roud and arr-r-rogant. But I care for my son and—I will listen.' Then, with a transformation so complete that Morgan was astounded, she sat in absolute silence, with stillness and dignity, and listened intently

117

while the headmaster quietly explained all that she, as Juan-Pedro's mother, had a right to know.

This type of woman was outside Morgan's experience and he was glad to have an opportunity of seeing how she could be managed. It would, he reflected, have been unfortunate if the headmaster had entrusted her handling to the police. Heaven alone knew what drama might have been enacted.

'So, you see,' Dom Erkenwald concluded calmly, 'you have no reason whatsoever for withdrawing your trust from the school and you can best help Juan-Pedro by your sensible cooperation.'

'You ar-re r-r-right! Always I know that you will help me.' The voice, now, was musically low and the head bent in childlike submission. She held the pose for perhaps half a minute— and then, as though at the snap of invisible fingers, or the crash of a chord striking into the silence following a pianissimo passage, the Marquesa sat bolt upright, gave a graceful flick of her head in the direction of the policeman, and demanded imperiously:

'Who is that man? Introduce him, if you please.'

Morgan, bewildered by the protean intensity of this tiny creature's passions, rose to his feet as the introduction was effected.

The Marquesa was disposed to be gracious and, with languid elegance, extended a hand which the inspector felt it would be more proper to kiss than to shake. He hesitated—and the opportunity vanished as the buzzer on the headmaster's desk indicated that his secretary was about to intervene.

'Yes, Mrs Macdonald?'

'Murphy and Petre are here, Father, with information that they feel you should have.'

'Does it concern Matron's death?'

'Yes, Father.'

'Very well. One moment, please—' He looked without speaking at the Marquesa, who inclined her head, rose to her feet in one swift and graceful movement, and with the intelligence and accomplished ease of an experienced hostess, made her escape before either of the men could open the door.

'Send them in, please,' said the headmaster.

The boys who entered were, the inspector guessed, about seventeen years old and they looked responsible types.

'Well, Petre?' queried Dom Erkenwald in mildly encouraging tones.

'Sir, you asked us to tell you if we'd overheard anything "unusual or significant" and we think we may have. But we don't want to—er—get Mr le Mesurier into trouble. It's just that—' Petre looked for help towards

119

Murphy but that young gentleman was studiously examining the nails on his left hand. There was silence.

'Well, Murphy?' prompted the headmaster.

'Matron and Mr le Mesurier were always having rows, sir.'

'And—?'

'We—er—heard them at it last evening, sir.'

'That—I take it—was nothing *unusual*?'

'Probably not, sir.'

'Anything *significant*, then?'

'Not really, sir—except that Mr le Mesurier called Matron a "bloody bitch".'

'To her face?'

'Not exactly. He'd left the dispensary and slammed the door behind him.'

'And of course you have never been tempted to describe Matron in similar terms?' The sarcasm was thinly veiled. Again there was silence. Evidently the headmaster was satisfied that his visitors were acting 'solely in the public interest' and were not motivated by spite, for after a brief pause he spoke more gently.

'You know as well as I do that Mr le Mesurier is a brilliantly clever man who functions almost entirely on nervous energy. Because he is a genius, somewhat eccentric behaviour that would be unpardonable in

120

me—or, indeed, in you two—is excusable in him. You were quite right to report this, but I do not think that it indicates any murderous intent.' He turned to the policeman. 'Inspector—?'

'Not unless there were other grounds for suspicion. Was he seen in or near the north cloister late last night? When you say "evening", I presume that you mean some time between five and eight o'clock?' Murphy nodded. 'Does Mr le Mesurier sleep in the school, Headmaster, or live out?'

'He is a married man and has a house in the village but he could be here in the late evening. He helps a great deal with extra-curricular activities—debating, the archæological society and so forth. I could not say whether he was here last night. Does either of you know?'

'No, sir.'

'It would be quite easy for me to check, if you wish, Inspector. If Murphy and Petre have no real evidence to give, perhaps we need not detain them?'

'No. Thank you.' He smiled benignly at both boys.

'Very well,' said the headmaster. 'You were absolutely right to come and see me about this—but you must not, of course, mention the matter in the school. To do so might harm

121

an innocent man.' He nodded in dismissal and when the boys had gone, said:

'I hope that when you have had a chance to meet le Mesurier, you will agree with me that he is just not the murdering type. But then—who is? *Is* there such a thing—or do the circumstances produce both murderer and victim?' He raised a quizzical eyebrow.

'Both, in my opinion. I've had experience of the born crook, and of the man moulded by circumstances and apparently driven to crime.'

'I take it then you don't absolve either from responsibility for his actions?'

'Oh no. But I do find cause for pity—and very great sympathy, sometimes.'

'Even policemen can hate the sin and love the sinner, I perceive,' said the monk drily. 'Shall I tell you about Claude le Mesurier?'

'If you would be so kind.'

'He crossed swords with Matron because he frequently sent boys to the dispensary with instructions to "ask Matron for a couple of Veganin". Quite rightly, she had very strong views about what she called "reliance on or addiction to drugs" and I agreed with her that simple remedies and a measure of self-control should be encouraged—rather than recourse to drugs for every slight headache.'

'Remedies such as—?'

'A cup of tea; checking the position in which a boy works or sits at his desk; the siting of the desk itself (some of them change round the furniture in their studies without any reference to the available light—daylight or artificial); opening windows—stale air can give one a headache; possibly a bit of neck massage to relieve tension, or a boy might need to have his eyes tested. I was well satisfied with Matron's judgement and experience—she had a flair for diagnosing schoolboy ills—and our school doctor had enormous confidence in her.'

'But not, it would seem, Mr le Mesurier.'

'No. He would get very cross when she sent a boy back without so much as an aspirin and he was liable to be just as angry if she kept another in the infirmary for rest and treatment. His idea was to keep his pupils at work at all costs. Instead of accepting her judgement, he created a tense atmosphere, declared that Matron was (I quote) "a contentious creature wielding despotic power over her chemist's shop armoury of synthetic drugs", and that "Florence Nightingale might have been tolerable at Scutari but her subsequent history provided a singularly unfortunate example of a determinedly power-hungry sadist, who had imbued all nurses with a propensity for waving the Dangerous

Drugs Act in the face of suffering humanity!"
He can produce a flow of invective quite
easily, and I had to ask him to stop
persecuting Matron. Not that she really
required my defence. She never wasted words
and had a habit—infuriating to some earnest
housemasters as well as to Claude le
Mesurier—of concluding any argument or
disagreement simply by walking away.
Somehow the sight of the starched triangle of
her Army square bobbing behind her head
was so very final and it exasperated her routed
opponents. Most men, I find, hate to be
worsted by a woman who doesn't even trouble
to utter the last word.'

'She sounds formidable!'

'I suppose she was. If Matron had views on
any subject, it was as though the entire
General Nursing Council backed by the Royal
College of Nursing marched breast forward,
shoulder to shoulder; "a monstrous regiment
of women". Even I hesitated to question her
handling of certain matters!'

'I rather wish I had known her. I haven't
yet examined her rooms. I suppose they could
tell me a lot?'

'They might. Would you like to go over to
her flat now? I had it locked up, of course, as
soon as her death was reported. We gave one
key to your sergeant—the other is here.'

'Don't let me trouble you, Headmaster,' the inspector protested as Dom Erkenwald rose, 'I can find my own way there.'

★　　★　　★

Matron's flat accorded perfectly with the impression that Morgan had so far received of a sturdy, independent, utterly loyal, somewhat inflexible, yet very human and shrewd woman. Her sitting-room, with a double row of pelargonium and geranium plants crowding the deep windowsill, had the cosy appearance of a country cottage; the walls were painted white and the low ceiling was supported by heavy oak beams.

He moved around slowly, getting the feel of the place and absorbing the personality and interests of the dead woman. The attachment of the Irish to their country and to racing is so general that it was no surprise to discover prints and photographs of Connemara, 'the Liberator', 'Dev' and Garret Fitzgerald on the walls; and copies of the *Turf Guide and Racing Times* at her bedside. He learnt that she was an expert needlewoman; but, over and above all, her abiding interest had been Ambelhurst itself. It was obvious that the headmaster had both affection and respect for her and, judging by her souvenir photographs of monks and

125

boys, it seemed that many others held her in the same high regard. Somehow the picture that formed in the inspector's mind of a neat little person seated at her desk or in her small, upright armchair, was much warmer than he had expected.

He wondered again who could have found it possible to dislike her so much as to be driven to plan and encompass her death. Many people, it was true, had quarrelled with her and she had been capable of inspiring intense irritation: the stories of strife and dissension caused by the way in which she had interpreted her duties illustrated this. But it was a far cry from mere dislike to murderous hatred.

Morgan took a last look round the pleasant little sitting-room before locking the door to the flat. She must have been quite a Character—and he wished that he had known her. But that she did have enemies was undeniable.

CHAPTER TWELVE

THE HOUSEKEEPER

It was five-thirty that evening before the inspector had the doubtful pleasure of meeting Miss Melsdon. The economus had somehow prevailed upon her to visit the police in their parlour-office, under the pretext that Morgan had called at her kitchen department earlier in the day in order to pay his respects, but had found her preoccupied with the feeding arrangements for over seven hundred people and thus unable to give the inspector any of her valuable time. The housekeeper was supremely conscious of her exalted position and consquently happy that the police should have been subdued by the sight of her responsibilities. Full of importance, she sailed into the parlour, making, as she did so, a double check of her wristwatch against the clock on the chimney piece.

'I can allow you just forty minutes,' she said impressively, 'and must then leave you to superintend the Suppers.' She swept a firm hand over the seat of a chair, swung it round so that the back faced the inspector, and straddled it as if it were a horse. Morgan wondered faintly whether he could survive forty minutes of this amazon's time and attention, but, with his customary courtesy, he acknowledged her goodness in permitting him to trespass on some part of her overcrowded day.

'Overcrowded? Nonsense! No orderly administrator—such as myself—permits his day to be overcrowded.' Morgan noted the pronoun employed and, despite the skirt at present tucked up to reveal a pair of massive knees, he felt it appropriate. The cropped hair, the deep voice and the firm gestures were scarcely feminine.

'Miss Melsdon, you know of course that we suspect foul play. Do you know of anyone who might have harmed Matron?'

'Miss O'Connell,' said Miss Melsdon authoritatively, 'was a vicious, vindictive woman who seemed to think that she had a prescriptive right to the attention, obedience and admiration of every member of the Ambelhurst staff, school and community.' She crossed her arms and glared at the inspector as if daring him to contradict one word of her statement. There was a pause. Morgan was considerably taken aback by the venom in her voice and thought it remarkable that Matron had survived so long.

'I expect you think that I'm either mad or

jealous? I'm probably both—but I didn't murder your Flo Nightingale. I see no point in canonizing her now she is dead, though doubtless several of her former enemies will see fit to do so. Ask me where I was last night,' she commanded. 'Go on!' The inspector felt that the control of the interview had passed right out of his hands—if, indeed, it had ever lain there.

'Er—where were you?' he asked feebly.

'Last night? I was, as usual, in the Black Swan bar until nine forty-five, and then I came back to my flat in order to listen to a radio programme. You can check the first part of my statement with the publican; the second part you must take on trust. I saw no one.'

'Not even Matron?'

'Was she alive then?'

'We think so.'

'No. I came in by the infirmary door, then by way of the tunnel to my own staircase.'

'You saw no one?'

'I have said so, haven't I?'

'Oh, certainly. I am sorry—I was just recapping.'

'Then don't. I am not likely to have made a mistake—nor shall I deviate by one iota from my statement. "What I have said, I have said!" I am not one of your shaky witnesses.'

The inspector was outclassed and he knew

it. He would willingly have brought the interview to a close but doubted that the initiative was his. This vixen would go when she wanted and not before. The economus's description of her had scarcely prepared him sufficiently and he found it difficult to accept the story that, at the initial interview, she had behaved 'as demurely as any convent schoolgirl'. He could imagine her saying 'No, Father!' but never 'Yes, Father!'—other than in a purely contradictory sense.

'Does your man want me to sign the statement?' She nodded towards Sergeant Arrowsmith, who bristled at the description.

'If you would, please.' She seized the sergeant's pen before he could offer it, scribbled briefly, and announced: '*Now*, I will go!'

The inspector rose to his feet feeling that he had been steamrollered, and opened the door. The virago swept by without so much as a nod, and he exchanged with his assistant a look of overwhelming relief.

'I could use a drink!' he murmured weakly and, as if in answer to prayer, the economus walked in with an expansive smile on his face.

'I passed Miss Melsdon in the corridor and thought that you might be feeling a trifle weary. She looked remarkably self-possessed, considering that she had been interviewed by the police in connection with a murder.'

'Who,' asked Morgan truculently, 'was interviewing whom?'

'Oho! Like that, was it? How very exasperating for you. I confess that I had rather guessed as much; there was an air of triumph... Would a glass of whisky help? Let us go to the van Dyck parlour.'

★   ★   ★

'Frankly,' remarked the inspector, after he had recovered somewhat, 'I don't know how you stand her.'

'We celibates have our crosses to bear, you know,' Dom Anthony chuckled gleefully, 'but I don't intend to endure this one longer than I can help. Could she have killed Matron, do you think?'

'I think she both could and would—but whether she did is anyone's guess. She seems very sure of herself and no amount of circumstantial evidence or cross-examination would shake that one easily. I formed the opinion that she is mentally unbalanced. On her own admission, she is both mad and jealous—and those evils are at the root of most murders. The only snag is that one would not expect an insane murderer to be aware of the former or to acknowledge the latter. On the

131

whole I don't think she did it.'

'Alas! Neither do I. It would be too simple.' He paused and added with a sigh of regret, 'her removal by the police would be such an easy solution to our difficulties regarding her contract! I don't wish anyone to be convicted of Matron's murder—although I suppose we shall none of us feel at ease until the scapegoat, or rather the actual villain, has been found.' He refilled the inspector's glass and murmured, 'If it has to be someone, then Miss Melsdon would have been such a very— er—unexceptionable choice.'

CHAPTER THIRTEEN

THE KNIFE

It was shortly after eight o'clock and Dom Erkenwald was still at his desk, trying to catch up with paperwork that had been pushed aside by the vicissitudes of the day, when a knock came on his door.

'Come in!'

Three boys entered on a wave of excitement—their eyes shining, their cheeks flushed with triumph.

'Sir! We've found it!'

'The knife, sir!'

'That killed Matron!'

Their joy, though understandable, was somehow shocking. Dom Erkenwald laid down his pen and contemplated them gravely, but he found it difficult to resist such enthusiasm and unbent slightly.

'Where?'

'In the book-room, sir.'

'Whereabouts?'

'On the table—where it always is.' Brancaster held out an object wrapped in a surprisingly clean handkerchief, and the headmaster was aware of acute misgiving. His knowledge of the boys told him that it should have been Hodges, the leader—or Peel-Llewellyn, his deputy—who handled the prize exhibit. It was out of character that Brancaster, the stooge in this particular trio, should be allowed to present it: the simple viscount was no match for the two astute commoners. Possibly the privilege was given as an amend for some low trick played on him by the others. Dom Erkenwald leant back in his chair and surveyed them from under lowered lids, instinct warning him that something was amiss. A thought struck him,

'Didn't the inspector ask the school not to touch any weapon, but to leave it where it was found and report to him?'

Their reaction to the question informed him that he was on the wrong track. They looked reproachful, mildly injured and a shade disappointed at the unworthy reception accorded to their successful sleuthing.

'We *thought*,' said Hodges, his eyes rounded in hurt surprise, 'that it would be *safer* with us. Someone else might have taken it or even used it to commit *another* murder.' The young blackguard managed to look sanctimonious and even to convey a suggestion of pained astonishment that his headmaster could be so casually unconcerned, and so unaware of the possibility of another disaster, as to expect anyone in his senses to leave—lying around!—an instrument that might have been expressly designed for blood-letting. Dom Erkenwald's phenomenal memory made a mental note that would have wounded Master Hodges still further, had he been privy to it— and he drew a deep breath before asking:

'Are your fingerprints on it?'

'Oh *no*, sir!' they chorused, and Peel-Llewellyn added that they had marked in chalk the exact position of the knife as they had found it.

'Remarkable!' said the monk, but excitement had dimmed the trio's powers of perception; they missed the irony and accepted the comment as a mark of approval.

'What made you look in the book-room?'—
they were not the sort of boys to have gone
there to slake a thirst for knowledge.

'We've been searching everywhere and we
worked backwards—down from the north
cloister. We thought of the knives in the
refectory—but they weren't the right shape.'

'Oh—so you knew what you were looking
for, then?' But they were not to be trapped
and exclaimed in genuine dismay at the
discovery that the headmaster did not enjoy
the confidence of the police enough to have
been informed that the murder weapon was a
long, thin knife.

'You see, the inspector told us exactly what
to look for, and we didn't really dream we'd
have such luck—so soon. I mean,' Hodges
explained kindly, 'you'd think the murderer
would have buried the knife, or thrown it
away, or hidden it in a *much* better place—so
we'd have had to go on searching for ages and
dig things up.' ('Heaven preserve us!' thought
the headmaster, appalled by the prospect of
Hodges and his friends attacking Ambelhurst
with pick and shovel.) 'You wouldn't think,
would you,' continued Hodges earnestly, 'that
he'd just leave it around somewhere obvious
where anyone—well, perhaps not *anyone*—'
he paused; modesty was all very well, but he
felt it was a mistake to denigrate their

efforts—'but *nearly* anyone, might discover it. We expected to have to go on looking for days.'

'Weeks,' corrected Peel-Llewellyn, and Brancaster—displaying, as usual, a somewhat limited intelligence—followed on with, 'Months and years!'

'I am relieved that your studies will not now be disrupted by the necessity of pursuing such an arduous search.'

Dom Erkenwald reflected that Hodges always spoke in italics—like his mother, whom the headmaster had last seen on Easter Sunday when she had driven up to the school at the wheel of a vast and shining estate car, wearing a new sheepskin jacket and with a matching yellow labrador seated at her side. She was extravagantly rich and enormously kind-hearted and longed to be allowed to smother people with care and attention. Dom Erkenwald had happened to be passing as she emerged from her vehicle in an expensive aura of scent and Russian cigarettes and he had witnessed her greeting of her healthy-looking son and his friends. '*Darlings!* What *have* they been *doing* to you? So *thin!* And *peaky!* Never mind! It's the holidays now—and we'll *soon* have you right again, *won't* we?' Here, she had directed a warm 'understanding' look at the headmaster who had never, afterwards, been quite certain whether he had actually heard, or only imagined that he heard her say, 'We *know* that you do your best—but men are so *hopeless*, aren't they?' Mrs Hodges was so clearly innocent of critical intent that it would have been unkind to take her up on the implication that the boys were starved and ill-treated. Simon was an only child and no doubt her attitude was the result of frustrated mother-love. Her son, thought Dom Erkenwald, seemed to be surviving the maternal excesses extremely well. There was nothing dependent about him.

'It really *is* a piece of luck, sir!' said Hodges, with the pleading air of a puppy yearning for admiration. The headmaster was beginning to wonder if he could have misjudged them after all. They were so thrilled with their discovery that it seemed unkind to cast doubts on the authenticity of the weapon; but a possibility was not a probability, neither was it a certainty.

'What makes you think that this must be *the* knife?' he asked.

Three pairs of shining eyes expressed outrage; but outrage of a sophisticated variety, without rancour or resentment. This, they seemed to say with unmistakable and unflattering clarity, was precisely what one could expect from grown-ups. They were not surprised; the headmaster's reaction was no more and no less than one would anticipate from an adult in whom cynicism, disbelief, doubt and an unwillingness to recognize the obvious, were unhappily combined. They had foreseen the lot!

With shaking hands, Brancaster held out the bundle over Dom Erkenwald's desk and his two acolytes gently unwrapped the handkerchief. With something approaching shame at his incredulity and unworthy suspicions, the headmaster gazed down at a paper-knife from which the dried blood stains had never been removed. There was a long silence. It was distasteful to him to stare at the weapon that, possibly, had been the instrument of Matron's death, but the three boys had no such feelings of delicacy in face of their discovery, and their sensibilities were in no danger of being offended. Serendipity, he mused: for them it *is* a happy discovery—but not for me.

'Wrap it up carefully,' the headmaster said huskily, 'and leave it on my desk, I will give it to Inspector Morgan, who will doubtless be more grateful and lavish with praise than I have been.' As an *amende honorable* it was not at all bad, and the sleuths were in a forgiving mood.

'That's all right, sir,' Hodges said kindly.

138

'We *quite* understand—you have to be careful.' He was magnanimous; he could afford to be. Dom Erkenwald wondered whether Hodges might not have a distinguished future as a diplomat.

After the trio had left, he sat and looked at the white bundle for some minutes, regretting—too late—that such a fantastically dangerous knife had been allowed to lie around the school for well over sixty years. Memory stirred, as he recollected the occasion when, as a young monk, he had first helped an old librarian to unpack a crate of books. He remembered having picked up the paperknife and made some comment about its sharp point and the old man had replied that it had been there as long as he could recall—on the long table that ran under the book-room windows—ready to slit pages or open packages. What, the headmaster wondered, would the Coroner say when apprised of the news that a potentially lethal weapon had lain conveniently at hand for generations of schoolboys and staff—just waiting to be seized upon by the first murderer in Ambelhurst history.

CHAPTER FOURTEEN

THE TRIO

Inspector Morgan knocked at the headmaster's door at ten minutes to nine on the following morning and advised him of a new development.

'The knife wasn't the murder weapon,' he said, 'and the bloodstains are not Miss O'Connell's. The pathologist suggests that one of the boys who found it may have added an artistic detail that he conceived to be lacking. I suppose you don't happen to have records of the blood groups of your "terrible three"?'

'We don't have blood tests done as a matter of routine but, as it happens, Brancaster is one of those unlucky people who gets blood poisoning if he so much as pricks himself—or so his parents believe. We were warned before he came here, and he certainly had a mysterious virus infection during his first term, so I'm pretty certain that we can produce some information on *him*. I'll ask Sister to turn up his records.'

With the commendable efficiency which Morgan had learnt to expect, the headmaster called up the school dispensary and made his request known to Sister Wilbraham, who agreed to check her files. The inspector drew a blue sheet of paper out of his pocket book.

'The blood group they've typed has been written down here,' he said, as he passed the laboratory form to Dom Erkenwald. Sister's voice came back on the intercom and the headmaster compared her reply with the paper in his hand.

'Thank you, Sister—that is most helpful. He flicked up the switch and looked at the inspector. 'I'm sorry. I had an inkling last night when those miscreants came to see me that something was amiss. I'm afraid the young crooks *have* been improving on their discovery—the blood matches Brancaster's exactly. I can only apologize. They were very wrong to try and mislead you, and—although it's entirely due to over-enthusiasm—I shall bring home to them the seriousness of what they have done.'

'Oh, dear! I had better not appeal to schoolboys in future. We'd better advise them to forget—'

'Do no such thing! They wouldn't want to lose the excitement of sleuthing, whatever happens. But they must play it straight. The sooner they learn to abide by the rules, the better. I only hope that Brancaster's blood was cleanly let; they *would* have to select a boy who is prone to every infection that is going.'

The inspector longed to say, 'Don't be too hard on them,' but he felt it would be rather impertinent and somehow unnecessary, so he merely sighed and withdrew to call on the economus and arrange for a further interview with the housekeeper. He thought he would ask the headmaster later when it would be convenient for him to see Charles Bolton.

*　　*　　*

The sleuths had no prescience of disaster when they received a summons to the headmaster's study. In fact they confidently expected to be rewarded by the sincere congratulations of the community and school—or, at least, of those members privileged, as they were, to be in the inspector's confidence.

'After *all*,' said Hodges, '*they'd* have been mucking about for *days*, but for us.'

'They ought to give us all gongs. D'you suppose,' asked Brancaster earnestly, '*we'll* be invited to Buck House—like those Duke of Edinburgh Gold Awards?'

'You really *are* a damn fool, aren't you!' Hodges exclaimed with withering scorn. 'They don't hand out *gongs* for the sort of thing *we* did! A certificate of commendation's the more usual thing—through the post. Or, if we'd recovered the knife in dangerous circumstances, *then* we might have been *presented* with more bumph. You're such a *half-wit*, Brankers,' he continued wearily. 'You don't seem to know *any*thing, *do* you?'

'Well, it was bloody well dangerous for me—having you sticking that knife—three times!—into my arm. I don't see why it had to be me—or why you couldn't get enough blood the first time. It's hurting like hell now—and I feel sick; like 'flu—all shivery and sweaty! And it's all your bloody fault!'

'God! You *are* a "wet"! Just ruddy well shut up! D'you want the whole *gallery* to hear you? And remember not to tell the Erk that we cut you. It was only a prick anyway. You're *imagining* you feel ill. My mother says it's the result of being neurotic.'

Peel-Llewellyn felt that Hodges was being somewhat harsh. After all, sticking Brancaster three times like that was a bit much; and the drawing of lots beforehand had been 'arranged' by Hodges and himself. If Brankers wasn't such an absolute drip he'd have guessed that they'd fixed things. And he *was* looking a bit green.

Unsuspecting of trouble, they hailed Mrs Macdonald, knocked at the headmaster's door

143

and, with a cheerful chorus of 'Good morning, sir!' ranged themselves in front of his desk. Alas, the atmosphere was frigid and one glance at Dom Erkenwald's face showed that all was not well.

'So!' he began in a deep voice, his head back and jaw out-thrust in a manner that boded ill, 'we have here three boys who think that they can deceive the police, and—' he paused with an awful impressiveness—'as if that were not bad enough, play a foolish game with a knife. To offer misleading and faked evidence to the police is nothing short of criminal lunacy; and to risk cutting an artery in an attempt to plant confirmatory evidence is deceit of a dangerous and unintelligent kind. Perhaps one should not expect common sense from Hodges—but I confess to being disappointed by Peel-Llewellyn's collaboration.' Each boy was fixed in turn by a penetrating stare. They stood as though rooted to the spot while the heinous depravity of their behaviour slowly percolated and destroyed all pride in yesterday's achievement. How on earth...! By what conceivable piece of misfortune could the Erk have discovered their deception?

The silence might have lasted longer had not Father Erkenwald observed Brancaster's unhealthy appearance and decided to end the proceedings swiftly.

'Brancaster, take off your coat—and turn up your sleeve, your *left* sleeve.' The headmaster had taken note of the way in which the boy was standing and this clearly indicated, to anyone with foreknowledge, which limb had been knifed. He was well aware that his special gifts of observation and memory were a by-word in the school, enhancing his reputation for omniscience, and he used them to the full. Surprise and dismay flickered on two faces but Brancaster merely went dead white and did as he was told. By this time he was feeling so unwell that he was incapable of any emotion other than fear that he might be sick.

'Give me your hand!' The stab wounds were angrily inflamed and red streaks ran up his arm. The headmaster handled it gently but he forced the conspirators to look upon their handiwork.

'Now, see what you have done. I trust that you are satisfied? Brancaster, go down to the infirmary, show your arm to Sister and tell her that I sent you. You will also tell her how you came by the injuries. Hodges, put his coat round his shoulders.'

Brancaster stumbled from the room and Dom Erkenwald, after a lengthy pause, said quietly:

'I suppose you realize that, through your

145

folly, he could lose his arm?'

*   *   *

When Hodges and Peel-Llewellyn had been
allowed to rejoin their classmates, the
headmaster called the infirmary and learnt
that Brancaster had been warded and the
doctor summoned. Sister was confident that
antibiotics and suitable dressings would do the
trick.

'No need to worry, Father. It's a good thing
that you got on to it so quickly.' The
headmaster was distinctly reassured and felt
that he could rely on Sister Wilbraham's
judgement.

CHAPTER FIFTEEN

CHARLES BOLTON

The inspector, as he had half expected, had a
depressingly unsuccessful second interview
with Miss Melsdon and he knew that he was
getting nowhere fast. She was a monstrous
woman and supremely confident of her ability
to handle any situation or suspicion. One
would, he thought, have to catch her with a

dripping red knife actually in her hand before she could be arraigned for murder. Morgan knew that he must be objective about his work and he was shocked to realize that Miss Melsdon was his 'favourite' suspect in the nastiest sense of the word and that he would be truly delighted if the crime could be laid at her door. The realization brought shame. He was, after all, a practising Christian—or tried to be. Disgusted with his self-discovery, he decided to divert his attention to Mr Bolton, who was reported to have returned from his day at Lord's. A telephone call to the headmaster elicited the information that the young man would wait upon him in ten minutes' time and Morgan settled down to re-read his notes while awaiting the advent of Ambelhurst's Don Juan.

Charles Bolton was all that he had been led to expect. Handsome, charming, self-confident, an extrovert—born with maximum physical gifts, average mental ability and a minuscule conscience. He would act first and think afterwards and, although not disciplined enough for the SAS or Commandos, he could be an asset to some units in wartime: in times of peace he was a menace. Born forty years too late, thought Morgan; a pity, and not really his fault. The fellow was fundamentally unreliable and one could assume that Dom

147

Erkenwald, a shrewd judge of men, must have taken the risk of employing Bolton with both eyes open.

Having made a quick assessment in the light of what he had guessed and what he had been told, the inspector abandoned the polite preliminary conversation concerning Bolton's return journey from London and explained that he proposed to question him concerning his reputed attitude towards Matron and his movements on the night of the tragedy.

'Fire away, Inspector. I'm used to police interrogation—though my crimes have so far been of the chamber-pots on statues, dud cheques in clubs and drunken driving variety—as you doubtless already know; I expect that MI5 has supplied you with my dossier? Murder in the monastery would be a new departure for me.'

'Mr Bolton! I am in no mood for your flippancy!'

'Oh Lord! You sound just like the headmaster. I fear I am beyond redemption, Inspector—didn't you know? Father Erkenwald has shaken his head over me for the last time and I'm here on sufferance—because the school needs me to improve the standard of cricket and athletics—and for no other reason. I've made mayhem among the maids—and it's curtains for Charles when the term ends.'

Inspector Morgan looked at him sharply; his quick ear detected a tinge of regret. The fellow was his own worst enemy, weak, silly and incapable of disciplining himself. Perhaps his schooldays had been the safest and best period of his life, when someone else had held the reins and kept him under control. The policeman had experience of these charmers who skimmed the cream off life for twenty-five years or so and awoke in their forties to delayed maturity, a trail of havoc, broken hearts and discarded friends left behind them.

'You don't *have* to slide down a slippery slope to disaster,' he said sternly, 'there are people willing and able to help you. It's nothing to do with me, but I should have thought that Ambelhurst suited you down to the ground.'

'It did—now it doesn't. I've had notice to quit. They don't want me any more.'

'Self-pity will get you nowhere. Is it really too late?'

'To stay on here and try again, you mean? I'm afraid so. I'm not reliable. I can't promise to be any different. I am—what I am. Driven by impulse—so I'm told.'

The man's weak acceptance of his limitations infuriated the inspector. He sat for a while in silence, controlling his irritation and

149

watching the sunlight dancing on the wall. Charles Bolton was hurt, but only in the most superficial way. He had enough insight and intelligence to appreciate a just assessment of his character; he could accept reproach without rancour, but he was incapable of taking positive steps to remedy his defects and he would always rely on his charm to see him through, or upon someone else to get him out of a mess. Morgan reflected that, without some self-respect or moral principle, a man had little incentive to restrain himself: for Charles Bolton the effort of achieving self-discipline was, unfortunately, too great.

The interrogation was not proceeding according to plan; it was no part of the inspector's duties to try and reclaim a recalcitrant Old Boy. All he had to do was to establish someone's motive, opportunity and guilt. Having overcome his annoyance and noted that the silence had done nothing to disturb Bolton's casual assurance, he began to question him.

'Did you get on with Matron?'

'Never! She loathed my guts. As a boy, I was always a menace at school—as far as she was concerned. She always had it in for me and when I came back on the staff the pattern persisted, with Matron reporting me to the headmaster at every possible opportunity.'

'I gather you asked for it?'

'I suppose so. All the same, I'm sorry she's gone—she wasn't a bad old stick. Quite a character, really—if you like cross-grained old witches! I don't. Sister Wilbraham is more in my line. Not that I go for vinegary virgins either; and perhaps she *is* a trifle austere. I once took a prehensile nip at her behind, and instead of ignoring me, she boxed my ear.'

'Mr Bolton! I have not asked for your views on anyone but Matron. Would you please stick to the point, otherwise we shall be here all day and I have other work to do even if you have not.'

'Too bad, Inspector. I was about to ask if you like cricket. We've got a good fixture laid on for today and I really *do* have to be up at the pavilion by eleven. I suppose you couldn't possibly continue this conversation, interrogation, cross-examination, or whatever, on the way up to the cricket field?' He was entirely unrepentant and the fatal charm was switched on full blast.

'Outrageous!' snorted the inspector and slammed down his notebook. Nevertheless, he rose to his feet, looked hard at his detective-sergeant, and declared, 'As a matter of fact, I do like cricket and I feel I've earned some respite after listening to your arrant nonsense. Sergeant Arrowsmith also deserves a break. But I would remind you that I shall still want to know where you were on the night of the twenty-sixth.'

'Inspector, you have been in too close contact with the Reverend the headmaster. You are beginning to sound like him and you have only been here for a day and a half. Someone told me that you are a Methodist.'

'I am.'

'Then this is ecumenicism gone mad. We can't possibly have you sounding like a papist priest! *Vive la différence!*—as I always say to that arch-hag Miss Melsdon. Have you met our hermaphrodite housekeeper?'

Charles Bolton's shout of laughter echoed right round the court-yard as they walked out towards the Kestrel gate.

CHAPTER SIXTEEN

CRICKET

The cricket fields lay in a broad open valley to the south-west of the school and the three flats were bounded by a running track, an outdoor swimming pool and a belt of magnificent chestnut trees. The pavilion was a two-storey stone building with a broad balcony at first-floor level, under which rows of spectators could stretch their legs in comfort, sheltered from the sun and rain and undisturbed by people passing along the front of the pavilion, or to and from the uncovered seats.

Morgan and Sergeant Arrowsmith settled themselves on a bench at the far end and watched the Ambelhurst elevens bring the visiting school's teams up to the changing rooms. There were two matches scheduled— between the respective First and Colts' elevens; and the flood of young players, plus their supporters, looked reassuringly normal as they drifted along, each side assessing the other's strength. The old hands were picking up the threads from last season's encounters; some of the newly selected were nervously preoccupied with their prospects. A few moved quickly and purposefully towards the nets and started loosening up and getting their eye in. It all looked so secure and unsensational. The inspector wondered if the visitors had been able to resist commenting upon the death of the school matron. The morning newspapers had been surprisingly discreet. Morgan speculated upon the identity of the man who had handled the public relations side so successfully—guessing that the headmaster and the procurator were both experienced diplomats. The veiled references to the police 'making inquiries into the tragically sudden death of the school matron', were vague enough to pass without comment. However, rumour and gossip have wings, and even if the visitors had been advised by their masters not to make any inquiries, it was unlikely that the Ambelhurst boys would resist the pleasure of discussing the tragedy.

Morgan relaxed, determined to push all thought of murder from his mind and to enjoy the scent of freshly mown and rolled grass, the sound of quick young voices and the click of bat on ball: even the thud of studded boots as the cricketers clattered down the stone steps or across the wooden balcony overhead was pleasantly evocative. Someone moved a sight screen, the captains tossed coins, the score box showed signs of activity, and the umpires in their long white coats moved out into mid-field. It was strongly reminiscent of the tuning up of an orchestra and the opening bars of the overture.

'Beautiful setting!' he murmured contentedly to Arrowsmith.

'About perfect, I'd say, sir. Lucky little bastards. Wonder if they appreciate it?'

'I should think so. If not now, then in the years to come they'll remember; there'll be summer days and scents and sounds that will recall the golden years.'

'And,' said a voice in Morgan's ear, 'someone will say, "Do you remember the wonderful summer—the year Matron was murdered?" Do you mind if I sit beside you, Inspector?' Father Paulinus sank down on the bench and stretched out his long legs. 'Taking a rest? Or is it a professional interest that brings you?'

'A bit of both, perhaps. I was in the middle of interviewing Charles Bolton, when he decided that he was needed up here. I don't particularly mind whether we continue during or after the match. On a day like this the opportunity to watch cricket is irresistible and, after all, I *might* overhear something—or interrogate someone in a casual fashion. At least I'm absorbing atmosphere and getting the feel of the place. I don't think that I could be accused of slacking—even if the Commissioner of Police arrived.'

'Take care, Inspector! You are over-eager to justify yourself—that denotes a guilty conscience! Furthermore, the present Commissioner is an old Johannine.'

'A *what*?'

'He is an Old Boy. The abbey is dedicated to St John the Less—hence 'Johannine'. Didn't you know?'

'I did not! Is Sir Henry likely to turn up?'

'Shouldn't think so. Though he does know

155

about our troubles. He was on the blower this morning and laughed like a drain about Brancaster's bloodstains. He thinks that we ought to have a school Police Cadet unit—with those three rogues forming the nucleus.'

'Indeed?'

'The First XI game has started. We've lost the toss—and I'm afraid it's a batsman's wicket.'

*   *   *

The morning wore on in leisured peace and the inspector's dormant conscience was further lulled when Bolton leant over him and whispered:

'Don't worry! I'm still around and will make myself available later. At present it wouldn't be fair; it's a perfect batting wicket with a very fast outfield, and our lot are fielding like a bunch of giraffes. I'm so bloody bad-tempered, I could murder the entire team. If I'm not put inside before then, they'll spend the whole of next week on fielding practice. Fortunately our Colts XI *is* batting—and the two openers have knocked up sixty between them. Oh! Shot!' The visitors' captain had lifted a six right out of the ground. 'He'll be picked for the Public Schools XI—or I'm a Dutchman. Best batsman Downworth's

156

ever had, I reckon.'

At midday, the abbey bell tolled suddenly and with startling clarity. To Morgan's astonishment, the ball went out of play and the entire game came to a halt, while caps were removed, the spectators stood, and all Catholics present were apparently lost in prayer.

'The Angelus,' explained Sergeant Arrowsmith, as he made an elaborate Sign of the Cross. More, thought Morgan irritably, for his inspector's benefit than the Almighty's.

'A bit shattering for the visiting teams, isn't it?' he commented as play was resumed.

'Oh, very,' answered Dom Paulinus. 'One of our secret weapons, you know! Gravely disconcerting and really rather unsporting. However, unless our fielding improves and Vaughan takes off that slow bowler, the visitors have nothing to fear and we shall continue to be knocked all over the place. I should warn you that the muezzin ritual occurs again at six o'clock this evening, Inspector. By then—' he smiled maliciously— 'Sergeant Arrowsmith will have had time to write out for you a copy of the prayers we say when the Angelus bell rings.'

Morgan found that the interruption had temporarily disturbed his absorption in the game and he allowed himself to take note of the panoramic view supplying a background to the First XI pitch. Above and beyond a screen of silvery grey Atlantic cedars, of larches and beech trees in early summer leaf, the monastery and school buildings stood out against a china blue sky. To the left soared the tower of the abbey church, a sturdily impressive reminder of the reason for Ambelhurst's existence. Morgan had spent the past thirty hours absorbing information and he now knew that the abbey's influence extended beyond outlying parishes and church schools to university chaplaincies, Oxbridge halls of residence, and to poor city parishes throughout the United Kingdom and overseas. The dynamism generated from the monastery could involve the most casual visitor and uncommitted parent: it could influence scholars, saints and sinners alike. Murder was alien, a scar on the peace, but it could not disrupt the essential harmony. The wound caused by Matron's death might even be—not so much excised—as transmuted, metamorphosed into something good.

Morgan felt that the sun and peace were in process of transforming *him* and that his Celtic sixth sense was operating once more.

★   ★   ★

Just before three o'clock, Downworth declared at two hundred and thirty-eight for seven, and Ambelhurst went in to bat. Their opening pair made eighty-three in even time, but after tea three wickets fell in quick succession. Another three fell for a mere ten runs. But then a young batsman promoted from the Colts for the first time that season set about the bowling to such effect that an hour and a half after he had gone in, Ambelhurst were one hundred and fifty-three for seven and into the last over. Then, on the first ball, the man at the other end was bowled. Number nine missed the next ball and spooned the third easily into mid-on's hands. Somehow, number ten managed to survive the last three—and the match was a draw.

'Too close for comfort, Inspector,' said Charles Bolton. 'Let me see these people away, and I am all yours.'

Morgan found it difficult to slip back into the role of policeman after such a relaxing interlude but, as he and the sergeant and Charles Bolton walked up from the cricket field together, he managed to ask with almost casual indifference:

'Where *were* you on the night of the twenty-sixth?'

'Do you really want the whole sordid

story—minute by minute?'

'Most certainly. Had you an appointment to keep?'

Charles Bolton shot him a quick sideways glance. '*Now* who have you been speaking to? Mary Burke?'

'I have spoken to several young ladies who seem to know you quite well,' Morgan replied primly.

'I get it. Well, I did have a date with the lovely Irish rose; but, as it happens, I ditched her.'

'Any particular reason?'

'You won't believe me, but it was a case of conscience. She's an innocent—and I only seduce the sophisticated. Rosie Beale is one thing; a simple Irish peasant girl who still thinks the Ten Commandments were given for her to keep is quite another.' Morgan was impressed, despite himself—but his cynicism was restored when Bolton spoilt the effect by adding, 'I could have had her any time these past two weeks, had I wanted, but I don't take unfair advantage.'

'It's a pity you're so damned conceited!'

Bolton let out a shout of uninhibited laughter. 'Inspector! You're jealous! and I'm irresistible! I'm not so much conceited as dead honest. Now, if you had said, as Dom Erkenwald did, that it would serve me right to fall heavily in love with some girl who wouldn't have me at any price, I'd agree with you.'

'The sooner it happens, the better, as far as I'm concerned,' said Morgan, 'and believe me, I am not jealous of your reprehensible successes. You've thrown away talents, opportunity and a pleasant career here for the sake of a few cheap victories.'

'Oh, dammit, Inspector! Not you too! I have to take this from "the crows"—the monks,' Bolton amended, 'but *not* from the police, surely? Spare me the lecture or I shall refuse to cooperate.'

'Very well. But get on with the recital of your misspent evening. With whom did you spend it? Remember, please, that I shall check every word.'

'Cissie Sheridan.'

'How long were you with her?'

'Half past seven until—well, I suppose it must have been after half past eleven when we got back to the infirmary door. It was short of midnight when I reached my room.'

'How can you be so sure of that?'

'Because I usually listen to the midnight weather forecast on steam radio—and I noticed that there was time to kill, so I got down to some work on the athletics training schedule.'

'Witnesses?'

'Well, Cissie, of course, and Sister Wilbraham must have seen me when I left Cissie at the foot of the maids' staircase, because she was coming down from the dispensary then.'

'At that hour?'

'Why not? The hags often work long hours; some of our bright lads wait until after "Lights Out" before developing gangrene or stepping on broken glass.'

'Anyone else?'

'Divil a one, as Rosie would say.'

'Then, for your sake, I hope that both Cissie and Sister Wilbraham will corroborate your statement. When Sergeant Arrowsmith has typed out a summary, I shall want you to sign it.'

'Stick to the factual bits, cut out the moralizing, and I'll sign.'

They had arrived back at the Kestrel gate and Morgan left the Sergeant in their temporary office and went down to the infirmary.

CHAPTER SEVENTEEN

TOWARDS EVENING: SATURDAY

Sister Wilbraham was writing up her Report Book when Morgan arrived at the open sitting-room door. It was a gracious room with white walls and ceiling reflecting sunlight upon dark wainscotting. A bowl of mixed flowers stood on a low table and a tall, urn-shaped vase holding an arrangement worthy of a Dutch Master filled the empty fireplace.

'What a nice room, Sister! I hope I'm not disturbing you at an inconvenient moment?'

'No, indeed, Inspector. I've just finished the Day Report and the insurance records can wait. What can I do for you?'

'Mr Bolton has made an informal statement and mentioned that you may have seen him on the night of Matron's death. I only want confirmation.'

'Of course. Do sit down. May I offer you a cigarette? I was expecting you to ask me for a statement at some point!' She settled gracefully on a sofa covered in faded chintz, handed him a tortoiseshell case and lit herself a cigarette. The action drew his attention to her beautiful, capable hands and, as she leant forward over her lighter, to long golden hair which she wore swept up into what he believed was called a 'french pleat'. The severe hairstyle suited her classical features and enhanced her elegance. She put down the lighter and offered him an ashtray and he noticed that she had clear blue eyes with long silky lashes and that her mouth was firmly chiselled. At most parties she would have attracted attention and she was quite the best-looking 'hag' he had seen in any school; they hadn't come like this in his day.

'I was gradually working around to you, Sister, but there have been more obvious people to question first. I am afraid that most of the morning and all this afternoon have been taken up with watching cricket. Perhaps it's an odd way to go about a murder investigation but my sergeant and I had been hard at it since early yesterday morning—and we didn't get much sleep last night. We were late to bed and then the abbey bell seemed to wake us as soon as we'd shut our eyes. I can't think straight if I get overtired, so I regarded today's break as an unexpected bonus that will, eventually, pay dividends.'

'You're absolutely right. In any case, I expect whoever killed Matron got clean away before her body was discovered.'

'I don't think so. This was an inside job—if

my instinct serves me aright. But—no need for you to consider the matter. Your job is to heal and I somehow don't imagine that you have a morbid interest in death. To change the subject: I didn't see you up at the cricket pavilion today?'

'I couldn't make it. We are short-staffed for the moment; but the Nurses' agency says that they have someone to send up for interviewing tomorrow—she sounds suitable and could start at once—so I'm just hoping.'

'Will you take over as matron here?'

'The headmaster has asked me to.'

'Is it what you want? You could have your pick of appointments, I imagine.'

'I believe I could. But this is where I want to be. I can find peace here.'

'You look serene enough *now*! Or do still waters run deep?' Morgan smiled quizzically; an image of Sister Wilbraham, ruffled and distraught, was incongruous.

She shrugged expressively. 'Schools do have their mad moments: Matron's death has thrown several people into disarray—or given them an excuse for incompetence. But at Ambelhurst I can do all sorts of things that would not be possible if I took up a hospital nursing officer's appointment. I can read, write, study, garden—oh! many things— including work for an Open University

165

degree. Where else could I make use of the library and the audio-visual equipment, and plague the staff for advice or coaching?'

'Do you?'

'Do I what?'

'Plague the staff. I should think they would rather like to help you.'

'My nickname is the Ice Maiden—does that answer your question? But, yes, Claude le Mesurier has been very kind. I have not had to ask anyone else, as yet.'

'But why a monastic school?'

'I'm a relatively new convert to Catholicism, Inspector. God—prayer—the liturgy—religious life—they fascinate me.'

The Ice Maiden, he thought—cool, yes! But surely, hidden fires, the tightly wound spring of coiled energy beneath that calm exterior? She was restful to be with: she did not fuss or move around. His much loved wife had died ten years previously and he had never ceased to miss her warmth and companionship. There was always his work—and television—but nothing compensated for the deep loneliness, the price one paid, as a widower, for having had a happy marriage.

Sister Wilbraham wore no wedding ring. He wondered whether he dared ask her why she had not married. It could be construed as gross impertinence; nevertheless, he found himself asking her that very question. She looked a little surprised but answered frankly. 'My parents were getting on when they married and quickly produced my elder brother, myself, and then twin sons. My father was a General at the end of the Second World War, and he had pretty rigid ideas about women's place being in the home. My brothers were sent to Winchester; I went to the second-rate, local independent girls' school. I stayed at home to run the house for my mother who became an invalid and when my father died I kept things going until she followed him. By that time my brothers had all married and had their own homes. There was nowhere for me and in any case everything had been left to them. So I took up nursing and was excused A-levels because I had years of practical experience, nursing my parents.' She spoke with a trace of bitterness and Morgan felt it to be understandable. The useful 'daughter at home' could be safely discarded by her brothers and sisters-in-law when she had served her purpose.

'You don't—' he hesitated. 'Forgive the impertinence and please don't answer unless you wish, but—you don't feel called to become a religious yourself?' He had learnt this rather Catholic phrase from Sergeant Arrowsmith.

'No!' She was definite—but then she hesitated and he could see her deciding to speak. 'At least, I did consider it. But I like my independence. I like to decide for myself what I will do, when and how. I've never been free before.'

'I know,' he agreed sympathetically, 'it's one of the advantages of getting on in my own profession. One can choose, make decisions, plan a timetable, set one's own pace. Which reminds me—I'm due to meet Sergeant Arrowsmith for supper in the parlour and I have not yet asked you to confirm Mr Bolton's statement that he believes you saw him on the night of Matron's death. The night before last, in fact. It seems so long ago.'

'Supper-time! May I offer you a glass of sherry, Inspector? I have some reasonable Amontillado.'

'Thank you. That would be pleasant.' He watched her unlock a cupboard in the wainscotting and bring out a bottle and two glasses.

'I don't yet run to a decanter. My brothers inherited everything and it is taking me time to get together the bare essentials for a home of my own.' There did not appear to be any self-pity in her voice; merely a cool acceptance of the lot of an unmarried and perhaps under-privileged sister.

'Reverting to Charles Bolton, if I may? Could you tell me about your own movements on Thursday evening, so that I can check them against his informal statement?'

'Of course.' She handed him a glass and pulled a Georgian wine table forward. 'I suppose you mean from the infirmary supper-time onwards? Matron and I had ours at seven, as usual, and then I took the evening surgery from eight o'clock. I had intended to go up to the abbey for Compline at eight thirty-five and sometimes she would carry on for me—rather under protest,' she added wryly, 'but there was a racing programme on TV and she particularly wanted to see it. She studied form very seriously! Some of the boys were late coming up for their t.d.s. medicines—they often are in the evenings.'

'T.d.s.?'

'*Ter die sumendum*—three times daily. We give out those drugs after breakfast, midday dinner and supper, you see. If we didn't issue the medicines from the dispensary the boys would never take them.'

'What did Matron do? Would you know?'

'She was racing mad and used to spend her evenings picking out winners for the following day. She always had coffee in her sitting-room after supper and liked to read *Sporting Life* and the *Leader* and the *Daily Telegraph* racing

169

correspondent and so forth. It occupied a lot of her time.'

'Was Sister Hanlon with you?'

'No, she had a day off. She is an Agency nurse and they have different terms of service from the regular school nursing staff.'

'I see. What time did the evening surgery end on Thursday?'

'It must have been after nine o'clock by the time I had cleared away and locked up. I came to this room and—well! that was that! It was too late to go up to the abbey.'

'You didn't join Matron for coffee?'

'No. She liked to be quiet when studying form—and Sister Hanlon and I usually make our coffee in the infirmary kitchen and bring it up here. I didn't bother on Thursday.'

'Did you go out at all? For a walk, perhaps?'

'No. I read and wrote letters and did some sewing until bedtime.'

'What time would that be?'

'Around half past ten. I went to the infirmary chapel, had my bath and went to bed. We get up at six-thirty, take any temperatures at seven and attend Mass—if we wish—in the infirmary chapel, at seven-fifteen. The maids get the breakfast trays ready and we sisters take it in turn to superintend the serving at quarter to eight—

before having our own breakfasts. Then it's time for morning dispensary, bed-making, treatments, the doctor's surgery—and so on.'

'Did you see Mr Bolton at any time on that particular evening?'

'On Thursday? No, I can't recall having seen him. But he could have passed the dispensary door when I was taking the evening surgery.'

'He says that he saw you coming down from the dispensary at a much later hour. Is it possible that you went back for something?'

'No. I returned the keys to Matron's office soon after nine o'clock. They are kept on a hook behind her office door, so that if any of us is called to an emergency—day or night—we can find them and open up the dispensary quickly.'

'I see. You've been most helpful and that is all I wanted to know. Now I must allow you to complete your insurance records and I suppose it's almost your supper-time—and mine, incidentally. Thank you for allowing me to interrupt your work.'

'Not at all, Inspector.'

★　　　★　　　★

So! thought Morgan as he walked back towards the van Dyck parlour, either Charles

171

Bolton is lying—or he perhaps confused Thursday with some other night. There was still Cissie Sheridan's evidence to check. But whether she supported Bolton's story or not, that young man would require further investigation. Sister Wilbraham's statement had been quite definite.

He turned off and stepped through a side door into the courtyard in order to confirm the time by the school clock which, so he had been told, had never been known to gain or lose a second—unlike his wristwatch which was due for attention. He emerged through the door leading from the south-west corridor just as the headmaster left his house on his way to the refectory for the boys' supper.

'Well?' they greeted each other simultaneously, and with one accord retired to Dom Erkenwald's study.

'*Not* so well, I'm afraid, Headmaster. I have taken an informal statement from Mr Bolton and he gave Sister Wilbraham's name as a witness; he claims to have seen her coming down from the dispensary after eleven-thirty on Thursday night and thinks that she must have seen him parting from Cissie Sheridan at the foot of the maids' staircase. However, Sister says that she went up to her sitting-room just after nine o'clock and stayed up there—and never saw Mr Bolton at all.'

Dom Erkenwald looked thoughtful.

'I have never known Charles Bolton to lie to me. Would you like me to have a word with him in the morning?'

'I would indeed.'

With nods of mutual understanding they separated and went to their respective suppers.

CHAPTER EIGHTEEN

SUSPECTS

The headmaster led Inspector Morgan into his study and, crossing the room, he threw open two casement windows, letting in the warm brown velvet smell of the wallflowers planted directly beneath.

'Phew! Lovely smell!' drawled the inspector, giving his Welsh vowels full play.

'Better than incense?'

'Much. Incense seems for-eign to me, e-eastern' (again the long vowels) 'like—joss-sticks.'

'Our incense is supplied by Cistercian monks who make it in a remote monastery off your Cambrian coast.'

'Caldy, I suppose. I've been to Tenby, but

I've never ven-tured...' The Welsh lilt was left suspended in mid-air.

'Too Roman for you, is it?' inquired Dom Erkenwald—and realized with horror that he had mimicked the inspector's intonation. 'I do apologize. Your attractive national lilt is infectious. What brought you so far north?'

'Chance of promotion—years ago. I like it up here. Lots of lovely, unspoiled Pennine country; wild fells and crags outside the moorland mill towns. Lucky so few people have discovered the beauty of rural Lancashire. When you get away from the M6 and the M62 and out of the big cities it is remote, unspoilt. I like Cumbria, Northumberland and much of Durham, too. The South Country is too obviously pretty for my taste. And the—well, *some* of the people who've always lived round here are very like the Welsh—small, dark hill-men. They're the real British; with maybe a dash of Roman blood from the Lost Legion.'

'Blast!' said Dom Erkenwald loudly and leant from the window calling out, 'Come here, you cur!' He brought his head and shoulders back inside and laughed. 'Sorry, Inspector, but just *look* at the Irish setter. Someone should have held it in leash. Why do people slip their dogs off the lead if they can't control them?' There were loud squawks of alarm and then the clap-clap of ducks' wings as several rose from their nesting places below the sunk fence bordering the right-hand pond. 'Oh, well! at least they're safe now—and I see some woman arriving to call her animal to heel.'

They moved away and sat on either side of a Chippendale partners' desk. 'What can I do for you, Inspector? You mentioned reviewing and revising the list of suspects.'

'I did. I haven't fully con-sidered' (again the long-drawn-out vowels that sounded so attractive to the headmaster's ears) 'what might have made it desirable—to someone—that Matron should be killed. What was it in her that roused the murderer?' He paused and continued gravely, 'It may sound far-fetched but perhaps we should look at the possibility of a political motive.'

'Political?'

'Well, you've mentioned that she was fiercely proud of being Irish—'

'Indeed she was and she had a very soft spot for the Irish boys here.'

'I saw the display of photographs and prints of Irish leaders—everyone from O'Connell to Garret Fitzgerald—on the walls of her sitting-room.'

'Umm. She hadn't any time for Haughey or Sinn Fein or the Ulster Defence Volunteers—

nor for the IRA. But she was certainly a loyal Irishwoman. She went home every holidays and planned to retire there. But she was, after all, a British Army nursing sister during the war.'

'There were also Irishmen fighting alongside the Brits in the Second World War—and since—who are now supporting one side or the other in Northern Ireland. They don't see any inconsistency. There's the apocryphal question: "Is it a private war—or can anyone join in?" and I suppose the war provided an opportunity for practical training in guerrilla warfare if one got into the right unit. But I really can't think that anyone would come over here to murder the matron of an independent boarding-school. Can you?'

'Not really. You were right to raise the possibility, but—it's too remote. A non-starter, I'd say. What else?'

'There are too many around who had the opportunity and the ability—and, frankly the temperament! Motives are not lacking once one starts asking questions.'

'Shocked are you, Inspector? To find—in a Christian community—so many sinful people with tempers and aggro, spite and lasciviousness in their make-up? Think what they would have been like without the restraints imposed by the teaching of the

176

church! Pity there aren't more born—like Our Lady—transparent to grace. But the Lord saw fit to create only this one person without the tendency to sin. His mother had to be born perfect—or "conceived immaculate", as we say. I don't begrudge her the privilege, do you?'

'Er—not at all.' The inspector thought, not for the first time, what unusual conversations one had with these Catholics.

'So your major suspects are—?'

'Young Juan-Pedro McCreaghane-O'Riordan, Charles Bolton, Ms Melsdon, Claude le Mesurier—whom I have yet to meet—'

'He's gone away for the weekend to Oxford.'

'So I understand. Charles Bolton saw fit to assure me that he has gone to dine some of his old chums and thus ensure that they look kindly upon the Ambelhurst candidates seeking places at Oxbridge.'

'Most improper of Charles—but typical. Boys and girls from state schools now stand a better chance of getting any available places. The government put on pressure, as you know. Money and influence don't buy this sort of privilege any more.'

The inspector nodded in acknowledgement and, consulting his list, added, 'And—Colin

177

Winter.'

'Colin Winter? Who is he?'

'A long-haired, skinny lad in Miss Melsdon's department. He was engaged as a kitchen porter and has ambitions to become a *sous-chef*! Miss Wilbraham saw fit to send me a note advising me that he'd conducted a vendetta with Matron. Apparently he had some form of scabies when he arrived at Ambelhurst—also a fungal infection between the toes.'

'Doesn't sound very desirable in kitchen staff!'

'Precisely what Matron said. She and Miss Wilbraham treated his condition but made strong representations to the housekeeper. They both considered that he was undesirable and tried to enlist the support of Dr Patterson. However, he insisted that—as the infections were responding to treatment—the boy would, eventually, be able to return to duty. Miss Melsdon, somewhat predictably, saw the attempt to get him dismissed as gross interference in her department and Colin became her special protégé. I've checked the story with Dom Anthony.'

'Ah, now I remember the episode. It was about a year ago: I'd forgotten the lad's name. Matron also tried to enlist my support.'

'It appears that he never forgave Matron—

178

not only for endangering his job (he'd pr_viously been unemployed for a year) but for certain humiliating and stringent remarks she made about his infections; and he was one of the prime movers in stirring up dissension between the kitchen department and the infirmary. Matron tried to insist that he should have his long fair hair cut to a respectable length—a "manly length", she called it—and he refused point blank. Miss Melsdon backed him up.'

'I suspect that if the suggestion had not emanated from the infirmary she would have been the first to seize a pair of scissors and cut it!'

'I'm sure you're right! I interviewed the lad this morning and he steamed at the nostrils at the very mention of Miss O'Connell's name: no conventional "*de mortuis nil nisi quod est bonum*". For that very reason I don't think he is a prime suspect—though of course it could be a blind. If he is clever enough to murder her and cover his tracks, he could be our man.'

'Anyone else?' They were interrupted by a brisk knock at the door. 'Come in!' the headmaster sang out, and Dom Anthony eased his considerable bulk round the door. 'We're discussing suspects. Join us—if that's all right, Inspector?'

'Oh, certainly.'

'Are you plotting or planning?' inquired Dom Anthony.

'We're considering possible suspects. Five so far: Juan-Pedro, Charles, your Ms Melsdon, Claude, and Colin Winter.'

'We were also looking again at Matron herself,' said the inspector. He turned to Dom Erkenwald and said, 'You have praised Matron highly, Headmaster, and yet, as the investigation proceeds, it emerges that not a few people found her—abrasive. You found her admirable.'

'I did. Trustworthy, shrewd, discreet, reliable, professionally competent.'

'Sister Wilbraham does not altogether support the view.'

'She trained at St Thaddeus, a famous London hospital; Matron at an old, former voluntary hospital in Yorkshire. They were poles apart in outlook and Matron had years of practical experience in two boys' public schools. She adapted well to the great changes in treatments and to the current availability of hospital services which means that seriously ill boys are no longer nursed in the school. *Ceteris paribus*, I would think Matron's professional judgement and competence to be the equal of Sister Wilbraham's.'

'When I first met you, the impression I

received was that Miss O'Connell had been a popular Nightingale, pursuing her amiable activities admired by all. It doesn't now look as though this was quite the case.'

The headmaster pursed his lips and flushed slightly. 'I'm sorry, Inspector, I had no intention of misleading you. I was aware of some disagreements and I thought I had indicated that there is no one who is totally acceptable in any school. Perhaps I underestimated the animosity. We all incite resentment and irritation in others. Christ Himself did no less. Why should Matron be different?'

'I take your point. But several people seem to have threatened to murder her—or had scores to settle. Reverting to Colin Winter: I gather that in addition to the nurses' objections to his employment in the kitchens, he was at the time paying assiduous attention to one of the maids on Matron's staff: Siobhàn Murphy.' Morgan consulted his notebook and continued primly, 'In Miss Melsdon's inelegant phrase, "the young madam drew him like a bitch on heat"! Later on, he found Cissie Sheridan more to his taste.'

'That I didn't know.'

'Sexual attraction,' boomed Dom Anthony, 'though important for the continuation of the race, is a tiresome element in a boys' public boarding-school when there are lusty lads and seductive girls around. Remember that, Headmaster—' he waved an admonitory finger—'should you be tempted to fall in with the modern zeal for coeducation. What is *your* philosophy of education, Inspector? Should immature adolescents be subjected to—'

'Dom!' protested the headmaster. 'If you intend to embark on philosophical discussions, may I suggest that you and Inspector Morgan continue elsewhere. I have a great deal of work clamouring for attention.'

The inspector was all contrition. 'Indeed you must have. I do beg your pardon. I have taken up far too much of your time—and in any case it is high time that I returned to the parlour you have so kindly put at my disposal to meet up with my assistants.' With an apologetic smile he withdrew, quickly followed by Dom Anthony, who was not disposed to abandon any discussion about coeducation.

The headmaster groaned as he picked up a file and brought it over to his desk. 'I'm tired, Lord,' he announced to the ever-attentive deity, 'and there's a devil of a lot of work to do before Compline. Help me!'

CHAPTER NINETEEN

COMPLINE

The inspector and his staff might dislike Miss Melsdon as a person, but they had no complaints to make of her catering, which was a vast improvement on that of the police canteen at divisional headquarters. The cooking was excellent and the supply of wine and spirits which Johannine hospitality made available was still more acceptable. Father Henry, the guest-master, flitted in and out in his quiet, friendly way, ministering to their comfort as required by the Rule of his Order—in fact, as Constable Gray tersely expressed it, 'they had never had it so good'.

On Saturday evening after supper, Arrowsmith and Gray declared their intention of sampling the beer at the Black Swan while the inspector set out on one of the walks essential to the functioning of his sixth sense. He wandered through the monks' wood appreciating the birdsong and the scent of wild garlic and, returning by a different route, found himself outside the public entrance to the abbey church. Inside the small square porch a well-stocked bookstall relied upon the honesty of the public and he could have lingered happily for hours, browsing through doctrinal, philosophical, and liturgical tomes, spiritual treatises, hagiographies, scriptural exegeses and books of cartoons by a certain Brother Choleric which at first shocked him by their irreverence, then captivated him by their draughtsmanship and wit. There were also children's books, books of poetry and postcards of Ambelhurst and he had made a small selection and was counting his money into a cash box when a bell began tolling overhead. In a short time people started pushing past him on their way into the church, and each time the inner door sighed open or softly shut, it allowed the now familiar smell of incense to assail Morgan's nostrils. On an impulse, he turned to a young woman who was adjusting her headscarf and asked:

'What service is this?'

'Compline,' she answered in some surprise, pointing to a framed timetable fixed to the wall. Then, as if recollecting the need to help an inquiring stranger, she added, 'It's the official night prayer of the church. Used to be in Latin but everything's in English now. Here—' she thrust a book into his hands— 'take this. You can leave it behind in the porch when you've finished with it. I'll pick it up sometime.'

184

The beautiful day had clouded over and the church was dark and full of shadows when they went in but he could just see a handful of schoolboys and a dozen adults scattered above the nave. Morgan sat on a rush-seated chair near a pillar and allowed the welcoming peace of the place to settle like a cloak about his shoulders. Nothing stirred—apart from a tongue of red flame flickering in a lamp hanging in the dim distance beyond the choir. The bell ceased its deep tolling and in the stillness he could hear the swish of the bell rope as it swung to a halt. A door in the south aisle opened and a silent procession of monks entered, wearing widespreading cloaks with flowing sleeves, which he knew were called cowls. With their faces partly concealed by their raised hoods they seemed to have strayed from a mediæval Book of Hours. No sound of footfall disturbed the quiet as they moved in silence to the choir, where, throwing back their hoods with a flick of the head, they separated to right and left and filed into the stalls. Looking at these men, young, middle-aged and old, Morgan marvelled at the spirit of dedication and self-sacrifice which had drawn them away from the world, from careers, from the joys of family life and the intense pleasure of recognizing inherited characteristics in one's children and grandchildren: legitimate pleasures, all—for some compelling reason—voluntarily abandoned. The inspector had seen, on the bookstall, a Johannine Almanac—a handbook listing the names and academic qualifications of the Ambelhurst community. He had been surprised to find among the arts graduates and scientists, the doctors of divinity and philosophy, one who was a doctor of medicine, another who was a surgeon and still others who were lawyers and engineers. A few held awards for gallantry and there were two with the Territorial decoration—presumably for service with the school's Cadet Force.

The monks stood still in their places, just visible under the soft pools of light thrown by the lamps above the choir stalls and over the lectern. Softly the cantors intoned a heart-raising chant, someone near Morgan switched on a light attached to a pillar and he could just make out the English words in his borrowed prayer book: they were the old and comforting psalms he had known since his boyhood. The monks tossed the words towards God, first from one side of the choir, then from the other. Morgan found it immeasurably soothing and reassuring; if this was opium for the people it was certainly good opium and he believed that Marx had admitted as much. Even he, a Christian of another denomination—in many ways opposed to and distrustful of Roman Catholicism—rejoiced to think that wherever his work might take him, whatever sordid task might fall to his lot, always—at this time of night—there would be some whose duty and vocation brought them here to commend the world and all mankind to God.

The chanting died away, the choir lights were extinguished. Up and down the nave shadowy figures turned and switched off the pillar lights. Morgan thought the service had come to an end and stood with the others, straining through the gloom to see the monks' sombre shadows drifting up to the High Altar and beyond it, out of his sight. No one stirred. Quite suddenly, out of the total stillness, the men's voices rose again on an unearthly note of sheer beauty. *'Salve regina, mater misericordiæ...'* He could no longer see the translation in his book but he had enough knowledge of Latin to realize that it must be a prayer to the mother of God. He longed to follow the monks up to the Lady Chapel from which their anthem floated back so eerily, but no one else moved and he stood stock still until long after the last note had died away.

One by one the laity left the church and a monk, after a glance of recognition at the inspector, went down and locked the door of the outer porch. Morgan knew that he could regain the school by the leather-studded door high up in the south aisle which would lead him back into the north cloister down which Matron had walked to her death. He was not alone, however, and as he reached the heavy door it was opened for him by Father Knox-Wesley. In silence they walked down the flight of wooden steps; then the Christite spoke softly and musingly, in tones very different from his usual cackling croak.

'It's the Greater Silence, but you and I are guests. How do you like Compline, Inspector?'

'Very much. Most soothing.'

'Encompassing and enfolding. As a boy, I lost both parents in a cholera epidemic; my father was serving in India and I had no brothers or sisters. I was really too young to be allowed to come up to Compline but my housemaster was an understanding man and turned a blind eye. Night after night I came up and released my sorrow until peace came and wrapped me in a mantle of protection and comfort. As you say—most soothing. I was too proud to ask any man for help—my father had been of the old school, stiff upper lip and all that. It was years before I learnt that my housemaster stood every night, concealed behind a large pillar, waiting—just in case I could bear human sympathy. I never could. I was far too vain, and Compline was my safety-valve and solace. The Church is an understanding Mother. Goodnight, Inspector—God bless you.'

'Well, really!' exclaimed Morgan to himself. 'Who would have thought it! The man's an enigma. I don't suppose he often allows his heart to show.'

The Christite had disappeared beyond the door leading to the Petit Cloister and the inspector continued on his way down the north cloister, turning by the lay masters' refectory to enter the gallery. The last of the senior boys were leaving the Assembly hall after bidding good night to the headmaster with what was evidently a traditional handshake. Morgan fell into step with Dom Erkenwald and they walked on slowly through the throng of boys drifting away to their rooms. A tall youth, oblivious of authority at his heels, broke into a spontaneous song and dance act and, strumming an imaginary guitar, sang out cheerfully:

'If you can't get a Rocker, Punk! Punk!
You can always knock a Rozzer, Punk! Punk!
By the sea-side—by the sea!'

It was a catchy tune and the boy's performance would have earned him a place in many pop groups—but the headmaster interrupted smoothly:

'I only hope, Fellowes, that when you go up for your Oxford interview, you will succeed in conveying as good an impression of an educated public school boy with a future before him as you undoubtedly give of a moronic Mod with a past behind him. Good night!' The boy grinned appreciatively and stepped aside to let the two men pass. 'They used not to be allowed to talk after nine o'clock,' explained Dom Erkenwald, 'the young ones go to bed and the upper school can read or study and have hot drinks in their rooms until "Lights Out" at ten-thirty.' They crossed the courtyard and stood in the gathering dark beside the Kestrel gate.

'Anything I can do for you, Inspector? Or are you turning in now?'

'I think I will do just that. It's time I hit the hay. I seem to have taken things rather easily today—but I feel sleepy none the less.'

'Fresh air on the cricket flats—in combination with Charles Bolton—sometimes makes *me* feel old and weary! Good night, Inspector—and God bless!'

'Good night, Headmaster.'

CHAPTER TWENTY

THE ABBOT COMES HOME

The prior made every effort to contact Abbot James before he reached London on Friday for a conference of major religious superiors, but the flight from Peru was re-routed and when, many hours late, the abbot arrived at Heathrow he failed to see the notice asking him to telephone Ambelhurst. He went straight to the conference and since his report on a four-month tour of the South American missions was followed by group discussions and a plenary session, it was late evening when he learnt of Matron's death. His experience of life in shanty towns was recent and raw and jet-lag further blunted perception, so he had difficulty in switching from Peru to the Pennines and only slowly grasped the horror of the situation.

Next day he was met at Carnforth by the prior, who drove him through the green valleys of the foothills where the fells were streaked with waterfalls and rills ran into burbling streams alongside the roads, providing music for his ears and delight for his tired eyes, but a reproach to his memories of barren lands where water was more precious than gold.

Ambelhurst looked confident in the afternoon sun and the Father of the House learnt that he had been much missed. He made brief appearances in choir, calefactory and staff common room and was encouraged by the apparent normality and impeturbability of the place. References to Matron, to the gap she left, to the nuisance created by the mass media and sightseers were counter-balanced by consideration of the cricket season at home, at Old Trafford, and in Australia; by forecasts of examination results and by comments on the quality of Common Entrance candidates. Rehearsals for Speech Day events, the choice of sites for the annual camp for handicapped children and plans for the Lourdes pilgrimage received at least as much attention as speculation about the murder and arrangements for Matron's funeral. Balance, order, routine! he thought: three useful key-words in time of crisis. Ambelhurst was not easily thrown out of its stride.

On Sunday morning Inspector Morgan discovered that the choice of service in Ambelhurst village was limited and entirely catholic, Anglican or Roman. He was not drawn to either but, since there was no

Methodist Chapel available, he decided that High Mass in the abbey church would at least give him further insight into the life of the school and accordingly made his way there. He drifted peacefully through the service and was roused from a reverie at the end when the school rose, with a vigorous scraping of chairs on the parquet floor, and with loyal abandon roared out a Latin prayer for the Queen. '*Domine, salvum fac,*' they sang, '*Regina nostra Elizabeth, et exaudi nos in die, qua invocaverimus Te...*' The exultant shout nearly split his eardrums and his neighbour commented drily, 'There would seem to be some Empire Loyalists here.'

The congregation moved out into the sunshine and Morgan watched cheerful reunions taking place between parents, boys and masters. Old Boys and their girlfriends, lay masters and their wives. It was evident that some girls were being trotted out by Old Johannines for the benefit of contemporaries and, where the attraction was serious, for the approval of former Housemasters. He wondered how the pretty creatures liked the inspection to which they were subjected and what impressions they would carry away of Ambelhurst: and he wondered how many unsuspecting persons became entangled in its silken web woven of kindness and genuine interest. Against this background the Old Boys could assess their potential life-partners and, if they dared, measure themselves. Here success or failure could be gauged and the truth admitted by some. Here, if they wished, the Old Boys could be sure of finding someone ready to listen and advise and, in a world where people are in a perpetual hurry and appeals for sympathy and personal concern go often unheeded, this was valuable.

A knot of older men engaged in earnest conversation attracted Morgan's attention and, hearing the words 'matron' and 'murder' he had no difficulty in persuading himself that it would be expedient to eavesdrop. It seemed that they were discussing some form of memorial to the dead woman in recognition of her thirty-five years' service and Morgan's sense of the ridiculous was captivated by the impossible suggestions put forward. The guest-master, who had detached himself from a cluster of parents, appeared at Morgan's elbow and nodded towards the group.

'Old Johannines,' he said, 'in unofficial committee.'

'They're coming up with some pretty appalling suggestions,' whispered Morgan.

'Doubtless. I gather, from what I overheard, that they're considering a mark of appreciation of Matron's work here. They

194

came down from London last night, very upset by the whole business and anxious to show proper respect for her. The present mood must be a reaction!'

The last of the sports cars, driven by a man who thought he was at Brands Hatch, roared away, the chattering groups dispersed and the inspector and Father Henry strolled slowly past the modern classroom block and round by the nineteenth-century academy room and school library.

'What weird and incredible recommendations have been put forward so far?' inquired Dom Henry.

'A racehorse, presumably a filly, to bear Matron's name and to carry the newly registered Ambelhurst colours; a statue for the infirmary garden intended to be a monument to Haggery, and a new infirmary wing. But some contend that a new building wouldn't smell right. They're nostalgic about leaking gas and old linoleum.'

'Oh well! The headmaster will cope in his tactful way and with due deference paid to the intelligence and generosity of the Old Boys. This year's President is a racing man. I suspect he has a two-year-old to sell.'

They were intercepted by the headmaster who announced that he had a favour to ask of the inspector. During the night all the sporting cups had disappeared from the school refectory and, given the level of excitement, this could be the first of a series of mysterious occurrences. Would it be possible for the police to use their expertise and recover the missing trophies, preferably before supper-time?

Ten minutes later, armed with a photostat plan of the school, Detective-Constable Gray stood before the empty cases in the Great Hall from which twenty-nine shields and cups had vanished.

'Eh, them blasted boys!' said Connolly, the school butler, with a mixture of pride and loathing. 'They've not pulled this one afore, least not in my time. Must 'ave done it in the night. They've likely sacked them in duffel bags or rugs so's not to make a noise moving round, like.' But Gray, having formulated his own theory, was disposed to pour cold water on amateur suggestions.

'Given a team of boys,' he began impressively, 'they could take two or three cups apiece to the place of hiding—' But Connolly interrupted with an irritating assumption of knowledge born of more than forty years' experience.

'Ah came 'ere as pantry boy, nobbut fifteen—me fayther were butler afore me—an' I reckon as there'd not be more'n three or four on 'em in on the game. Sacks, rugs or duffel bags, you mark me word!' As he spoke the housekeeper erupted violently into the hall and, recognizing the police officer, shrieked:

'Constable! if you've nothing better to do than keep my staff gossiping, I'll thank you to get out of my refectory!'

'Her refectory indeed!' snorted Connolly, who knew it to be his domain. 'She's a one, an' all! Eh, I reckon it were she as did Matron in, with one of 'er own skewers like as not.'

'D'you really think so?' asked Gray with interest. Being bawled at by a woman was enough to ally him instantly with Connolly.

'Sticks out a mile. But we'd best clear out of 'ere. Or 'appen I'd best. If you wants to stay an' 'ave a look round afore them boys come in, you just do it. *Her* staff indeed!' Connolly had seen several housekeepers come and go and had no liking for this one. Experience told him that Miss Melsdon's reign was nearly over. 'Pity they 'as to 'ave these women 'ousekeepers,' he confided. 'Nought but trouble comes of introdoocing women into schools like this 'un. Leastways in positions of authority.' He could be pompous when he chose. 'Dormitory maids an' cleanin' women are one thing and—' with an air of importance—' I 'as to take me quota of parlourmaids ter supplement the men. But in charge? Nay!' He sniffed and added darkly, 'Ah reckon it's the moothers' faults.'

'The mothers?'

'Of the boys. They're shown round 'ere, there an' everywhere—takin' an interest in food an' 'ygiene. Yer wouldn't believe 'ow they come around, peering into *my* pantry an' sniffin' the air an' askin' if we always serve cabbage an' do the windows open, an' are the boys well fed. Mothers used to know their proper place—an' that were outside; but not any more! An' the fathers—they just gives in to it. Pandering!' he added in deep disgust.

'You mean the fathers of the boys?'

'I mean the Fathers,' said Connolly with emphasis. 'Them monks. Beer an' swipes was what them Old Boys 'ad—an' they looks well enough.' He marched off down the refectory, flicking his napkin at invisible crumbs on immaculate tables.

Gray remained on the dais looking down the Great Hall and noticing how the sunlight threw brilliant patches of heraldic colours from the stained glass windows filling the oriels and depicting the coats of arms of founder families. Then he moved down towards the minstrels' gallery at the far end, admiring the portraits of headmasters and of distinguished Old Johannines and thinking how lucky the boys were to have such a dining

198

hall. The school's electric bell warned him that a ravenous horde would soon flood in and he climbed the stairs and conducted a fruitless search before the first boys arrived from the servery with their trays. From his vantage-point he scanned their faces, but no one so much as glanced at the empty cases and no looks of triumph were exchanged. They had probably congratulated themselves at breakfast-time. He descended and went from the buttery to the assembly hall, becoming more depressed as he observed the many doors in the wainscotting hiding stone staircases leading down to the cellars. It would take years to search this place and the little bastards could run circles round six policemen. They were on their home ground and capable of humping sacks of silver to the other school houses in the grounds and bringing them back to the main building just as they pleased. The prospect of assisting with a murder investigation and possibly earning a commendation vanished as he considered the unrealistic search for school property in what was not even a case of larceny but merely a stupid schoolboy escapade. In fury he aimed a kick at the base of a stone pedestal beside which he had come to a halt.

'Venting your ill-temper on a statue of the mother of God will do nothing to advance your promotion, young man,' said Father Knox-Wesley who had emerged from a dark passage. 'You look a trifle put out. Do you want help?'

The policeman felt foolish and incapable of replying but the old priest rumbled on. 'Have you heard of the marriage feast of Cana? She—' he stabbed with an arthritic forefinger—'asked her Son to help the host who'd run out of wine and *He* said, "What's that got to go do with Me? My hour's not yet come." But His mother knew He couldn't refuse her anything, so she told the waiters, "Whatever He says to you—do it," and, well, I expect you know the rest? Vintage wine, made out of water!' He laughed in genuine delight as at a joke that had just been perpetrated. 'Vin ordinaire would have been good enough! But if He gives, He gives handsomely. One can't outdo Him in generosity.'

Gray didn't feel like laughing and Knox-Wesley asked, 'What's your problem?'

'The cups, sir. The sports trophies— missing from there.' He jerked his thumb in the direction of the refectory. 'The Headmaster thinks the boys have whipped them.'

'He's undoubtedly right. Now, let me see ... You ask *her* and I'll start thinking.' The embarrassed policeman had never prayed to 'the Virgin' in his life and was unaccustomed to asking inanimate objects for anything, but he stared stonily into the carved eyes while the priest hummed for what seemed a very long time. Suddenly, a raven croak escaped him and he seized Gray's arm and propelled him down the gallery towards the academy room.

'Of course, of course,' he chortled triumphantly, 'we shall see ... I could be wrong, but I well remember—' He broke off, climbed some steps to the stage and crossed to what was evidently a trapdoor. 'Help me, boy!' he commanded and together they lifted an iron ring and pulled. 'In you go, Constable!' he said as the trapdoor opened wide. 'If there isn't enough light to see by you'll just have to feel. Got 'em?'

Gray had lowered himself through the gap and almost stepped on to a knobbly bundle. The butler's hunch had been right. He lifted up a duffel bag, followed with two more clanking loads wrapped in tartan rugs tied with string, and then brought up a sack and a cardboard box. Meanwhile the old priest bobbed around as excited as a child with his neck waving from his collar at a surprisingly reptilian angle. 'You can forget that you met me,' he said. 'Just go back to your inspector and tell him your mission's accomplished.'

'Thank you very much, sir.'

'Don't thank me, young man. Praying to images isn't in your line, I know, but next time you see a statue of the mother of God—think twice before you kick it! Let's put these behind the curtains until the refectory's clear, then we'll put the trophies back in their cases. Oh, it's a long time since I was a boy here, a very long time. But I haven't forgotten everything. Oh dear no! No, indeed!'

CHAPTER TWENTY-ONE

THE INFIRMARY

It was two o'clock on Sunday afternoon before Dom Erkenwald had time to see Brancaster in the infirmary. He was accustomed to visiting sick boys at any hour of the day or night convenient to himself and was well aware that this practice disconcerted new, untried staff and kept the nurses on their toes. 'Father! You did make me jump' was a protest with which he was familiar, but he continued to make his rounds wearing sandals or house slippers—not in order to catch anyone out, but simply to avoid disturbing any patient who might be sleeping; the infirmary floors were of old, creaking boards, innocent of modern, sound-deadening covering.

On this occasion he met Sister Wilbraham in the infirmary passage and asked, 'How is Brancaster this afternoon, Sister?'

'Much better, Father. His temperature is coming down and he's responding well to the antibiotic. The doctor's pleased with his progress and thinks he should be back in school within days.'

'Good. I'm on my way up to see him.'

The headmaster tapped lightly on the door of Room 6 and went in. Brancaster lay listlessly on his bed and, judging by the tray which was still in evidence, he had scarcely attempted to eat his midday dinner. He stiffened slightly but did not speak.

'Still feeling rotten?'

'Yes, sir.'

'Did you sleep well, last night?'

'I—I think so.'

'Is your arm still hurting?'

'A bit.'

'I see. Well, if it's any comfort, I think you've suffered enough for your part in the business and we'll consider the matter closed.'

'Oh—er—thank you, sir.'

'I don't see any books or puzzles. Have you nothing to do? I'll get some sent in. What do you like? Jigsaws? Bloods? Desmond Bagley?

Dick Francis? Or is it John le Carré and any of the James Bond novels? ... Maybe science fiction?'

'Anything, sir. D-don't bother.'

'No bother. There's plenty around the infirmary. I'll come in again. Or perhaps you'd rather see your fellow sleuths? I'll send them.' He raised his hand in salute and was gone, leaving Brancaster considerably more cheerful.

Sister Wilbraham tried to disguise her annoyance but the headmaster knew that she did not relish being told that her patient needed occupational therapy. He wondered whether she had been punishing the boy or had simply forgotten to provide any distractions for him. Hag O'Connell would never have had to be told a thing like that; her professional techniques might be old-fashioned but she had nursed with her heart. Sister Wilbraham, he thought anxiously, nursed with her head. She might spend more time in church than the old matron, but he would have expected a nurse to show more feminine compassion for a boy as sick and unhappy as Brancaster. But no doubt she'd been busy—and taking over Matron's job and the shock of her death were excuse enough.

Turning the corner by the dispensary, he encountered Hodges and Peel-Llewellyn who, clutching an extraordinary assortment of boys' treasures, were tiptoeing towards the infirmary. From their furtive air he guessed that they were visiting without their housemaster's permission and he doubted whether they were likely to get Sister's.

'Are you intending to visit Brancaster?' A strained silence, accompanied by an 'out of luck, again' expression on each face, gave him his answer. 'Well, you'll find that his arm is recovering fast. You may tell Sister Wilbraham that I sent you.' He knew when to show mercy.

★   ★   ★

On the way back to his study, the headmaster was waylaid by Inspector Morgan,

'May I have a word with you, Headmaster?'

Dom Erkenwald could have groaned aloud but Johannine courtesy, allied to strict self-discipline, enabled him to control his feelings. Work was piling up on his desk and the extra demands on his time and attention seemed unending; behind it all lay an uneasiness which he could not define but which involved the wellbeing of the school. The inspector was doubtless as concerned as he was himself at the delay in discovering the author of the crime; meanwhile, speculation among the boys was rife, the inevitable Book had been opened with long odds offered on Charles Bolton, and with Claude le Mesurier and Miss Melsdon quoted as hot favourites. The sooner someone was apprehended the better, thought the headmaster—just so long as the murderer was not one of his boys.

The two men walked in silence across the courtyard, conscious of the fact that in a school the very walls have ears, and that a casual sentence overheard could form the basis of a superbly embellished rumour which would in a very short time be circulating among boys and staff alike. In his study, Dom Erkenwald dropped into the swivel chair behind his desk and motioned the inspector into a deep leather-covered armchair.

'Well—at least,' said Morgan, 'we've recovered the cups! I expect you've heard?'

'I have and I'm grateful. I also wonder what will be the next move. The younger element shows signs of getting out of hand and the sooner the whole business can be cleared up— the better. I feel as if this crisis has been lasting three weeks instead of a mere three days.' He smiled to show Morgan that he was not holding him responsible for the delay, but he rubbed his hand wearily across his forehead. 'The parents and the Press are becoming a problem and whatever drama has disturbed our monastic peace, I've still got a school to run. Murder on the premises is not conducive to serious study and there are examinations ahead; *and* the preparations for the Academies—Speech Day. It's actually a long weekend during which we are on show to the parents, scheduled for mid-June.'

'Dear me!' said the inspector, 'I'd forgotten. Interrupting your routine is bad enough, but of course the GCE and Speech Day just ahead make it so much worse. I wish I could hold out some hope of an early dénouement, but it's all so indefinite at the moment. Too many people might have murdered her *and* had every opportunity, there's little enough to go upon, I'm afraid. Really, I came to ask if you had been able to have a word with Charles Bolton.'

'I *am* sorry, Inspector! I'm afraid I haven't—but I promise you that I will. I'll catch him this evening and let you know how he reacts.'

Inspector Morgan rose. 'I'm not going to trespass any further upon your time. I am most grateful for your help.' He slipped out quietly and Dom Erkenwald sat for a minute, thanking God that He had seen fit to send a gentle and charming policeman; a blustering detective-inspector would have danced on his nerves, just now. He felt old and tired and a nagging worry was tugging at his mind.

There was a false note somewhere. It wasn't just that murder was evil, and premeditated murder still more so; there was something— he cast around for a word that might express his growing unease—sub-human, inhuman ... devilish ... no, not quite that. What was it? Why was he afraid at this juncture—and of what? It must be reaction. After all, he'd had no premonition before the murder—so why was he so apprehensive now? Earlier in the day a reporter had thrown out a stream of speculation and innuendo and disturbed him with the word 'unnatural'. The man had only been doing his job but he had contrived to be somehow unpleasant and suggestive of an unspecified evil that would never have occurred to the headmaster in the context of his beloved Ambelhurst.

He tried to shake off the ominous cloud, realizing that he was tired and that—of all things—he could do with a solid hour of uninterrupted prayer. Or even, he smiled briefly, a not too arduous game of squash. It's off key, he thought; something's out of tune, not quite right or not as simple as at first it seemed. Murder is never simple; there have to be undercurrents. He shook himself and pulled a pile of letters towards him; his clear duty was to tackle these before the Monday morning letters engulfed him—

The buzzer rasped insistently on raw nerves and his secretary recognized a harsh note of exasperation in his voice,

'Yes, Mrs Macdonald?'

'The Agency has sent us a nurse, Father. I didn't know how long you would be with the inspector so I took her over to the Infirmary and Sister Wilbraham is showing her round. I've got Mrs Barnes's papers here. She's free to start at once. Shall I bring them in?'

'Yes, do.' He groaned inwardly. To have to interview a nurse at this juncture seemed the last straw—yet without Matron, it was important to get the right team—even as a temporary measure. The fact that this Barnes woman was free immediately could be a bad sign; though the agencies had a quick turnover. However, they really needed a third woman in the infirmary—especially as Sister Hanlon was rather young and silly and what old matron had scornfully described as a 'poor law nurse'. It was quite out of date, of course! An absurd concept carried over from the old voluntary hospital days when Matron had trained. 'Clock-watchers! working to rule and keeping Union hours!' she would say. 'They're not *nurses*— they're bedside-orientated technicians!' He visualized Hag O'Connell's imperious flick of the head and the memory made him smile. Thank heaven for Mrs Macdonald, who had voluntarily given up her Sunday off duty to cope with the extra secretarial work produced by this tragedy.

A gentle tap on the door and Jean Macdonald came in with a sheaf of papers and stood patiently while he skimmed through Mrs Barnes's curriculum vitæ and references. All very satisfactory—excellent qualifications and testimonials. He hoped that she was not all technical efficiency and precious little else; another superb surgical nurse like Sister Wilbraham, with ability but not much 'heart' was not quite what he was looking for. He was rather wishing that he had not rushed into asking her to take on Matron's post. One did not want sloppy women nursing schoolboys, but they must possess some vestige of maternal instinct. The thought of Brancaster lying in bed for a day and a half, feeling sick and guilty and expecting further punishment, worried him. Any woman ought to have had enough compassion to see that the boy was unhappy—'to comfort always ... to cure sometimes'—how did it go? The infirmary was important and he must be able to feel confident that the sick would be served with love and understanding.

'Oh Lord! I suppose I'd better see her, we

don't want the wrong woman there—however competent she is. Better ask her to come over.'

'Very well, Father.'

He sorted out some papers, irritated by the delay during which Mrs Barnes was being conducted to the headmaster's house. Usually he would have been able to get on with his work and give it his full concentration, but this obscure worry was causing him an uneasiness that he had not known in eight years in office. Something was brewing up . . . and he wished that he knew what it was.

The intercom buzzed again.

'Mrs Barnes is here now, Father.'

'Thank you. Please show her in.'

The woman who entered the room was in her late forties, short, well-built and with a cheerful smile and easy manner. He conducted her to an armchair facing the light and with customary headmaster's cunning, took a chair opposite that left him in shadow.

'I gather that Sister Wilbraham has shown you round the infirmary—and I expect you know of our present predicament?'

'Yes. I'm sorry, Father—my family was fond of Matron.'

'Your family?'

'My husband was at Ambelhurst. He was killed climbing the Matterhorn a year after we married.'

'Not Johnny Barnes? I taught him classics.'

She smiled warmly. 'Yes—Johnny. We had a son who would have come here, but he died of leukæmia when he was eleven—and then I trained as a nurse. They were so good to him in hospital and if he could have been saved, he would have been. So, I did my general and children's training.' She spoke simply; there was no self-pity, no regret for what might have been. This looked decidedly promising; but he must be sure, before he began to look ahead.

'With your qualifications'—he looked down at her papers—'you could hold a senior position in the hospital world.'

'I could. But it wouldn't be what I want. I'm tired of institutional life.'

'But Ambelhurst *is* an institution.'

'Oh *no*, Father!' She did not hesitate to contradict him flatly. 'It's a family—and it's home from home to me. All my brothers were here and I used to come over for Academies weekend with my parents. Ambelhurst is a family!'

His spirits soared. They were going to be all right.

'I stand corrected, Mrs Barnes.' He bowed ironically, but she was quite unabashed and gave a contented laugh. 'And who were your brothers? I don't know your maiden name.'

The conversation ranged around people they both knew and it confirmed Dom Erkenwald's impression that all would be very well. A thought struck him.

'What are your views about keeping sick boys occupied? When would you think that they should rest—with absolutely no books or games at hand?'

'I have strong views on that subject, Father—but it's rather a long story.'

'Indeed?' he looked at her in mock alarm. 'Just the same, I'd better hear it. It is, perhaps, as well that I should know what orthodox—or unorthodox—views are likely to be promulgated from the infirmary.' Mrs Barnes looked demure enough but a dimple in her cheek revealed that she enjoyed being teased.

'I could read before I was five,' she said, 'but our nanny believed that we should rest on our beds after lunch, with nothing to read or do. My sister and I shared the night nursery but for our rests we were separated—as otherwise we were bound to scrap—and I was put into an empty bedroom where, luckily for me, there was an old copy of the *Garden of the Soul*. It was sheer disobedience, implicit if not explicit, but the moment I was alone I would creep off the bed, seize my precious book and

213

read through the epistles and gospels for Sundays. Inevitably, the personality of Christ came alive for me—a most undeserved consequence. I knew that I wasn't meant to be reading and hid the book whenever I heard anyone coming. Very deceitful! But, perhaps it's in keeping with Christ's sense of humour that I should nevertheless benefit.'

'A case of the Lord drawing straight with crooked lines, I suppose?'

She laughed. 'That's about it. Anyway, I would never leave a sick child without *any* occupation or form of distraction.'

'I'm glad to hear it. Well, I suppose we'd better go down to the infirmary—or, since you are already at home here, perhaps you would be good enough to find your own way back?'

*　　*　　*

Dom Erkenwald was conscious of a vast relief and thanked his Maker. He called in his secretary and told her that he thought they had got a winner in Mrs Barnes; and he dictated twenty-eight letters before the bell rang for Vespers. Just in time, he recalled his promise to the inspector.

'Mrs Macdonald, could you get a message to Mr Bolton and ask him to come and see me immediately after supper?'

He realized as she left the room that he had never thanked her for giving up her day off—but she was a sensible woman and probably took his acceptance as a compliment.

CHAPTER TWENTY-TWO

SUNDAY EVENING

Charles Bolton was always conscious of unease and vague apprehension when summoned to the headmaster's study. He knew well enough that his cricket and rugby Blues, unsupported by a degree, were not enough to have earned him a place on the Ambelhurst staff, and when Dom Erkcnwald had given him a chance to redeem himself and some of his debts, he had been aware that this was a matter of grace and favour and more than he deserved. It was unlikely that he would find such a post again, because all that he could offer was a trail of unsatisfactory references from an assortment of second-rate preparatory schools at which he had distinguished himself by his casual promiscuity and irresponsibility. Dom Erkenwald had never had any illusions and had made it clear that Charles need entertain none: the appointment was offered on Dom

215

Erkenwald's terms and Charles had the choice of accepting it or of confronting implacable creditors infuriated by bouncing cheques. Unfortunately, penitence and gratitude had not long survived and only a series of rather unpleasant interviews, at which Charles accepted without rancour a flow of well-earned invective, had kept him in any sort of check. The headmaster's patient persistence amazed other members of the staff who had no knowledge of Bolton's unsatisfactory childhood: they could see in him little but a born crook; irresponsible, entirely charming—but quite impossible.

Charles's conscience, however quiescent at ordinary times, began to trouble him as soon as he passed Mrs Macdonald's office, and his casual grace had deserted him by the time he had knocked on the door and sidled into the study. The headmaster did not invite him to sit down—which was, he knew, a bad sign—and he continued to write for a further two minutes, which was ominous indeed. Charles's apprehension grew and his spirits sank. It was almost a relief when Dom Erkenwald laid down his pen and looked up.

'Your indiscretions and reprehensible behaviour have already earned you dismissal from Ambelhurst. I understand that you recently uttered threats against Matron and this has been reported to the police.' He paused and asked softly but forcibly, 'Did you murder her?'

'No! Of course I didn't! I threatened her, I admit—but I swear I never killed her. I wouldn't—surely you know that?' Charles sounded hurt. There was a long silence while Dom Erkenwald fixed him with an unwavering and penetrating stare from which there was no escape.

'This is the truth?' he asked.

'I've never lied to you, have I?' Charles' voice expressed all the indignation of one who admits to many vices and is affronted when the single virtue to which he lays claim fails to attract the appreciation it deserves. Almost too quickly his volatile temperament reasserted itself and, with the engaging grin which was one of his more endearing charms, he added, 'I'd never have got away with it, would I?'

Satisfied at last, the headmaster leant back in his chair and barked, 'Get—Out!' and in his immeasurable relief, he uttered a laugh of pure joy.

★   ★   ★

Inspector Morgan decided that he might just as well go the whole hog and attend the abbey evening service at six twenty-five. The Scarlet Woman had him properly in her clutches, he thought sardonically—or so it might appear to his colleagues. The truth was that he found the church an oasis of peace, and he was so much at a loss as to the next step to take in this case that it was quite pointless to hang around the van Dyck parlour. Furthermore he was not in the mood for a walk.

Vespers, with the school present, had not quite the power to soothe that he had discerned at Compline the previous night; but the Benediction service which followed was another matter. There was a majestic certainty and power about it which impressed him deeply. These people believed; had faith in God to a tremendous degree and their conviction was communicated to him with absolute assurance. One did not need to prove the existence of God—one *knew*. Someone lent him a book and he joined in the final hymn—contented, as were other non-classical members of the congregation, to sing the unfamiliar Latin words. They all knew what they meant to express and the triumphant joy gladdened his Welsh Methodist heart.

'*Te laudo Dominum*
Te laudo millies
O manna coelitum

218

Quia benignus est.
Te laudo Dominum
O esca hominum
Laudabo te absconditum
Per omne saeculum.'

On the way out, the inspector met Father Knox-Wesley, who, rather to Morgan's surprise, informed him that he intended to take a long walk after supper—it was such a lovely evening. The thought of the 'turtle' taking strenuous exercise was faintly risible.

'I wish I could join you, Father, but I've got to see the headmaster at a quarter past nine. He's had a hectic day and he's keeping this appointment free with some difficulty.'

*　　*　　*

During their evening meal the inspector and Sergeant Arrowsmith decided that there were altogether too many suspects and that their most sensible course would be to find out more about the dead woman and see what had so far been overlooked. One needed to discover why hostility had built up to crisis point and precipitated an almost certainly premeditated execution.

There are at least two people involved in every murder; what the police needed was a

219

lead towards the person who not only had the opportunity to kill Matron, but had what seemed to the murderer an unassailable reason for doing so. One had not expected to find in a school run by monks so many who could be suspected of committing such a crime. But then, witch hunts in Salem, the killings in Northern Ireland and, above all, the betrayal of Christ by Judas, suggested that even 'religious' people can be tempted beyond endurance. It would seem that Browning's poem of hate in a Spanish cloister had been matched here at Ambelhurst.

★   ★   ★

'Tell me about Miss O'Connell, Father,' Morgan invited as he settled himself into one of the headmaster's leather armchairs. 'Everything you can think of—even at risk of repeating what you or others have already told me. There's got to be some special animosity that we haven't yet grasped. There's got to be an—apparently—justifiable reason.'

'I will, Inspector. But I've been given a bottle of Dry Fly and this seems a good moment for opening it. A glass of sherry will improve my recollection and sharpen your attention.'

'Splendid! I want to see her as a person and

not as a bloodstained corpse. You've all helped to present the living Hag O'Connell—now go on, please.'

'She was sixty-four,' said the headmaster, handing him a glass. 'She punted mildly and, I think, successfully—probably breaking even at the end of a season. Though one never knows: people who back horses tend to see their hobby through rose-coloured spectacles. She certainly had a good winner last week when she backed Irish Dancer at thirty-three to one.'

'Attracted by the name, breeding or previous performance?'

'Actually, a tip from an Old Boy who trains on the Curragh.'

'Did she encourage the boys or the staff to gamble?'

'Possibly. Her enthusiasm was infectious. But she knew the school rules: she would never lay a bet for a boy.'

'And her bookmaker didn't have it in for her because she'd made him bankrupt?' They both laughed. 'I think not,' said Dom Erkenwald. 'She had no private means and I would think few savings. We didn't pay on the Whitley scale for a long time and the rates recommended by HMC are scarcely princely.'

'What sort of people did she dislike?'

'The malingerer—the lazy layabout who

was trying to get out of games or "off corps". I've passed by the dispensary when she was in full cry: "I'll not have ye working yer ticket, Howard!" and "Smith minor! If ye'd take more exercise ye'd not be asking for No. 9s! Get along with ye now! I prescribe three times round the building at a jog trot. That'll put paid to yer constipation!" or: "That's the abbot's wall ye're kicking, Myles Stapleton! Ye're not at home now and if yer parents allow it—*which* I beg leave to doubt—I don't. Stand up straight, you boys! 'Tis a pity they've all but abolished the Corps. Ye're a sloppy lot of layabouts, so ye are!"'

'Ah yes! You told me that she'd served in the Army.'

'She had, with one of the nursing services, I'm not certain which.'

'What about the monks?'

'I believe she classified us in the same way: energetic people pulling their weight or geriatric malingerers. Luckily for me, I was one of her favourites; though she often treated me like one of the boys, while scrupulously addressing me as "father"!'

'And the lay staff?'

'Armed neutrality as a rule. She could be dismissive and fiercely intolerant of what she regarded as interference in her department. A coach who tried to get a boy off the sick list and back into a team before she deemed him fit and free from infection was likely to be confronted by a virago.'

'What about her relations with other women?'

'When she came to Ambelhurst there were very few women on the staff. One matron, a number of maids—mainly Irish in those days; cleaners who lived out, a cook-housekeeper and not even one woman on the teaching staff. The headmaster's secretary was a monk. Gradually things changed. The school grew in size, so we added a professional housekeeper or catering officer. Then we added more trained nurses—always addressed here as "Sister" if SRN and "Nurse" if SEN; and women teachers, lab assistants and secretaries arrived —plus a woman librarian. Maybe Matron was a little jealous. In the old days a woman about the place was fairly unusual— and correspondingly conspicuous. A stray visitor once pointed out Miss O'Connell to her friend as "the abbot's wife". Perhaps her army square suggested a nun's coif!'

'Your Infirmary Sister, Miss Wilbraham—' He hesitated then went on, 'I asked her if she had thought of becoming a nun.'

'Did you indeed?' The headmaster looked amused.

'She said she valued her independence.'

'She's drawn by the religious atmosphere but not, perhaps, enough to give God everything and enter a convent.' He was silent for a while, then added: 'There's a *noli me tangere* air about her. Difficult to define: it's a withdrawal from contact. Physical, certainly—and maybe mental contact. I don't think she has any close friends here and she's not exactly cosy when a boy's sick and has dirty feet and bad breath. She sometimes makes *me* feel unwashed! I remember Matron saying piously: "Far be it from me to criticize a saint in the making—but . . ." and then she launched into a three-minute diatribe emphasizing the virtue of service—her own particular forte—as opposed to the practice of prayer, on which—in Miss O'Connell's opinion—Sister spent too much time.'

He rose to top up their glasses. 'Matron was a great walker and exercised Scampi, her yappy little terrier. Which reminds me, I must get someone in the village to take him on. I don't think the two nurses care for the little brute.' He made a note on the pad on his desk and continued: 'Matron liked to give the impression that she was almost a "country member" where the Church is concerned. Quite false. She never missed Mass on Sundays and Holydays—but she had a distinct loathing for the sort of women who take a job

224

in a monastic school simply because it offers exceptional opportunities for religious exercises. Matron was a practising Catholic but not what you'd call fanatical about religion.'

'How did she get on with parents?'

'They either doted on her or detested her: as with headmasters! I suppose some may have been indifferent. I met those with more positive reactions.'

'The domestic staff?'

'Most of the old guard liked and admired her. The young ones resented her discipline and complained of her as a battle axe or, to use their expressions, "a withered hag" and a "bloody old bitch".'

Inspector Morgan was surprised that a monk should repeat such phrases, but then Dom Erkenwald was a schoolmaster and in daily contact with the young.

'She was discretion itself and kept her lips tightly closed. Sister rarely lost an opportunity to hint that she was not honoured by Matron's confidence and that this made it difficult for her to gain the information that would have been helpful to her in her handling of boys.'

'You seem to manage to see quite a lot of your nursing staff,' said Morgan, and then he added quickly, for fear of being misunderstood, 'You seem to have made time for them so that they could—as it were—cry on your shoulder.' He did hope that he had not, by implication, suggested any impropriety.

'Priests have to be careful, especially with lonely widows and spinsters, but one has a duty to see that members of the staff are happy. I learnt from my own headmaster to respect nurses and to consider the inevitable isolation and loneliness of school matrons in particular. They are more free nowadays, of course, and they have television. But in most schools they are not welcomed in the staff common room—unless they have strong personalities and an easy social grace. They can feel left out. Of course it's easier when there are two or three trained nurses in the infirmary; but one can't rely on them getting along together.

'Another nice feature of Mary O'Connell's character was her kindness to old matron—known as Maggie—who, for years, lived on in one of our cottages. When she retired Maggie thoroughly approved of her successor and they developed a mutual admiration society—deploring the march of time and the advent of the permissive age. They disapproved intensely of modern domestics wearing overalls instead of cap and apron. I think Matron was lonely after Maggie's death. Her only friends were Dr Patterson's wife and a former infirmary sister who has married and lives locally.

'Our normal complement of nurses is two—if there is a 'flu epidemic we usually call upon the local Red Cross VADs and in return we help them with fund-raising for their ambulance and welfare work. Recently we've had two very elderly and ill monks down in the school infirmary because they need skilled nursing and don't want to leave home. That's why we have had a third—an agency nurse—Sister Hanlon. Despite this adequate cover, Matron was of the old school and reluctant to take more than a few hours off duty, never mind a half-day.'

'What's Sister Hanlon like—apart from being blonde, fluffy, silly and whatever else she's been labelled?'

'Matron considered her as merely adequate, professionally, and tiresome socially! And Sister Wilbraham, who trained at St Thaddeus and regarded any other hospital training school as underprivileged, would agree with that assessment. Even Mary O'Connell's highly respectable and ancient provincial hospital was classed as not *quite* up to the "Thad" standard.'

'Did Matron ever strike you as worried or apprehensive?'

'Far from it! She put a report through the office letter-box every day and notified me at once of a boy's admission to the infirmary or to hospital. Once a week she would drop in to see me—and she would telephone if she was concerned about a boy or member of staff. I enjoyed her Irish wit and perspicacity. She had a refreshingly direct view of life and of people and was extremely shrewd. I am confident that she had no foreknowledge that her life was in danger. I hope she died without knowing she had been attacked.'

'What about the other nurses? Did either of her colleagues ever hint at some hidden threat? Could there have been mistaken identity involved?'

There was a long pause. Then the headmaster shook his head. 'No. Sorry, but I can't recall the least indication. I used to see Sister Wilbraham here about twice a term, at the beginning and the end, and of course about the school. She had really taken over all the sick nursing of the boys and ran the dispensary—but not the doctor's daily surgery which was held in the dispensary and supervised by Matron. Sister had taken over the boys' health records and the store-keeping of medical supplies. Matron wrote to parents and she used to do health and safety tours of the school buildings. Another job that was particularly hers was the supervision of lunches and teas in the cricket pavilion. Traditionally, because it was nearest to the infirmary, Matron's maids had always laid tables, served and washed up for the cricketers and their visitors and it was one of those habits that continued long after the centralization of catering. The time and motion men would tell us that it is uneconomic of time, effort and everything else to have the infirmary maids doing a job that should more logically be covered by the housekeeper's department; but irrational time-honoured custom is the very stuff of school life, and though I'm prepared to be an iconoclast where necessary, I'd have hated to upset Mary O'Connell over a small matter that meant so much to her. It would have been seen as an affront. Miss Melsdon will now be able to have it her own way—and if I know anything about schools she will probably start belly-aching about the imposition of extra work!'

'So, the violent Ms Melsdon conducted a running battle with Matron throughout the summer term?'

'She did indeed. I've told you earlier about the nonsense over the infirmary meals. Whether served to the sick or the nursing staff, opportunities for being bloody-minded are endless. The economus had been driven to the expedient of buying in and distributing to the infirmary all the dry stores like sugar, tea, coffee, cocoa, Horlicks and biscuits—because the housekeeper made it so difficult for Matron to replenish her stock. There are plenty of time-consuming and humiliating ways of keeping busy people standing around waiting with their begging bowls!'

'Don't I know it! I did my national service in the army and as a raw recruit learnt all about the tedium of a QM Stores run by a bloody sadist.' The inspector stopped short in the confusion proper to a practising Methodist who subscribes to the Christian teaching about letting your 'Yea' and 'Nay' be unembellished, and calling no man 'Raca'.

'I do apologize, Father. The memory has quite carried me away!'

'Not at all. I am sure that your mind could recall far worse words if you let it: and as I make occasional descents to the boys' level of language, in a way that would appal my poor mother, I owe *you* an apology.'

CHAPTER TWENTY-THREE

THE CRICKET PAVILION

It was after nine o'clock when Father Knox-Wesley, shoulders hunched and neck out-thrust, walked with brisk short steps through the monastery garden and out towards the cricket flats. Once away from the school, he slackened his pace and with arms folded and hands hidden in his sleeves, slowed down to a tortoise crawl while for over an hour and a half he lost himself in contemplation of the Almighty. He circled the cricket fields in an anti-clockwise direction and was about a hundred yards from the pavilion when a scream of pure terror slashed violently through the night air and awoke him to the realization that darkness had descended. Hysteria took control of the female larynx responsible for the noise; as the terrified yelps succeeded one another, Father Knox-Wesley emerged from his stunned horror and—breaking into the nearest thing to a run that he was ever likely to achieve at his advanced age—plunged across the grass towards the sound. Blood pounded in his ears and his throat was seized in a grip of pain, but he struggled on and almost fell as his left foot struck a block of stone. Stumbling, he stretched out for support and realized that he had reached the pavilion steps. Someone brushed past him—jeopardizing his balance once more—and ran off into the night. From the deep shadows created by the overhanging balcony and sloping roof of the building came a man's deep groan.

The woman who had screamed was now sobbing and, as the priest stood still, gasping for breath and straining to see through the fitful darkness, he could make out the shape of a huddled figure in the corner beyond the entrance to the visitors' changing room. Clouds that had obscured the moon must have passed over, for a shaft of moonlight suddenly lit up the scene.

Charles Bolton, alternately groaning and making a rasping sound as though struggling to get air into his lungs, was slumped on the fixed bench, his hands clasped across a dark stain spreading over his white shirt. Blood oozed and trickled from between his fingers. The girl standing beside him was frozen into immobility: her fists were thrust against her mouth as if to hold back the obscene sounds she was making.

Walking tremulously up the last step and along the stone deck, Father Knox-Wesley spoke as crisply and authoritatively as his breathless condition allowed.

'Get the inspector, he's with the headmaster.' The girl stood as if transfixed but she had stopped keening; two seconds passed—then she shuddered, turned suddenly, and with a gasp ran down the steps and made off in the direction of the school.

Out of his pocket the priest produced a none too clean handkerchief and with shaking hands tried to staunch the flow of blood. 'It's—no—good,' said Charles, each word uttered with immense effort. Recognizing that he was beyond first aid and that time was short, the old man set about his professional duty of reconciling a dying man to his Maker.

* * *

Dom Erkenwald and the inspector were concluding their somewhat inconclusive review of Matron's life when Cissie Sheridan—wild, distraught and almost incoherent—burst into the headmaster's study. Both men jumped to their feet, knowing that something terrible had happened.

'The pavilion!' she gasped, eyes glittering with terror. 'The cricket pavilion. Oh, quick! he's dying!' Neither wasted a second on reassuring the girl or attempting to discover who 'he' might be: afterwards Dom Erkenwald realized that he had known without asking. He pressed the intercom button connected to Father Robert's room and said urgently:

'Get Sergeant Arrowsmith to the cricket pavilion—and send an ambulance; someone's badly hurt. I'm going up there with the inspector.'

'My car—it's the nearest,' he said to Morgan, and then as they passed the girl standing in the doorway, he ordered, 'Go down to Sister—in the infirmary. To the *infirmary*,' he repeated as the frightened creature gazed at him with wild, uncomprehending eyes.

★   ★   ★

It seemed like hours before they arrived at the pavilion and faced Father Knox-Wesley across Charles Bolton's dead body. The Christite answered an unspoken query in the headmaster's eyes. 'It's all right: he's at peace.' He paused and as the detective leaned forward to examine the corpse more closely, added over his head, 'He got a last chance—and took it. One might have known after all your pr—'

Inspector Morgan broke in imperatively. 'What happened?'

'I heard the girl screaming when I was about a hundred yards from here. By the time I got to him he was coughing up blood and losing it fast from a chest wound. But he just manged to speak.'

'Who was it? Who struck him?'

'I—I've no idea! There's been no time to think.'

'*Think!* Didn't he *say*?'

'No. There were more urgent matters—'

'More *urgent*?' Morgan was aghast.

'I'm a priest—not a policeman, Inspector—' Knox-Wesley's voice shook with fatigue— 'and administering sacramental grace takes precedence over detection. There was no time for trivialities.'

'Trivialities!' exploded Morgan. 'Two murders—and you speak of trivialities!'

'It's all relative. Your job is to protect the public and see that the criminal gets his deserts. Mine is to help the sinner and prepare him for eternal life.'

The inspector shrugged dramatically in a gesture of despair. 'You realize that a third murder could well be perpetrated before we catch up with this—*lunatic*?'

'Inspector, I'm truly sorry. If it's any help,' the old man said consolingly, 'there's a

wicked-looking kitchen knife down there—'
he pointed to the second long terrace step
provided for deck chairs. 'It's one of those
Sabatiers. I haven't touched it. That girl must
have dropped it. I didn't see it, of course,
when I sent her down to fetch you. It's a
wonder she did what I asked. D'you think—'
he stopped as Morgan and the headmaster
looked at each other, appalled.

'I hadn't thought of Cissie being more than
a witness,' said Dom Erkenwald shakily.
'We'd better get back—'

At that moment the sirens and lights of two
police cars and an ambulance came up the
slope on the far side of the mound between the
swimming pool and the cricket flats.

CHAPTER TWENTY-FOUR

THE NIGHT WATCHERS

Hodges and Peel-Llewellyn, as was not
unusual for them, were breaking a strict
school rule. At eleven-thirty on Sunday night
they were together in Hodges's cubicle in the
top dormitory of St Aldhelm's House and in
order that their voices should not be
overheard, they were hanging out of the

window and carrying on a conversation in whispers. With the forethought that came naturally to a born leader, Hodges had already worked out a line of defence in case they should be caught, and he judged that injured innocence would be the wisest attitude to adopt. He knew exactly how to open his eyes wide in pained surprise that anyone could misinterpret his motives. It was true that the touch of artistic realism which on his recommendation had been added to the knife, had proved to be a mistake, but he did not often misjudge a situation and he was pretty certain that the incident was now closed; 'the Erk' might be hard—but he was not unjust and the fact that they had been allowed to go up to the infirmary to see Brancaster was a sign of forgiveness. This present breach of regulations could be explained away on the grounds that they were responding to Inspector Morgan's request for alertness and that it was imperative that they should meet to discuss in private the list of possible suspects. Juan-Pedro had been dropped from first place and although Constable Gray had told them that—in his opinion—Charles Bolton seemed the most likely murderer, the boys admired him greatly and preferred to regard Miss Melsdon as prime favourite in the murder stakes.

'She's the most *godawful hag* of all time!' said Hodges, 'and she could *easily* have stabbed Matron.'

'Of course, everyone knew that she and Hag O'Connell hated each other's guts, so she was taking an awful risk. I mean, we'd all be bound to think of her.'

'Agreed. But then—she's *barmy*. You've only to *look* at her and hear her screeching. They'll put her in Broadmoor.'

'I don't think they send women there.'

'Well, wherever they *do*. Don't be so literal. You always get *lost* in detail.'

'Huh! Who was it who added detail to the knife?'

'All right, all right! I botched that, I agree. But you *never* make a mistake, do you? And shall I tell you why? Because you never have a single *original* thought in your *head*.'

'God! You are the most pompous ass—'

'Keep your *voice* down! D'you want the monitors—'

At that moment, a distant scream was carried on the still night air. The boys craned further out of the window and froze into immobility. It seemed to come from the direction of the pavilion and the sound continued in a series of yelps that struck terror into their hearts.

'It's a vixen,' said Peel-Llewellyn

238

doubtfully, as though seeking reassurance.

'Never!' whispered Hodges, 'it's a woman.'

'Vixens *do* sound like damned souls. My father always says—'

'That's *not* a vixen. Shut up and listen!'

Their fingertips became white through pressure on the sill as for several minutes they stood on tiptoe, straining to hear and to see through the darkness. Then they saw movement within the blackness; they heard nothing, but a shape detached itself, drew nearer and nearer and, silhouetted against the gravel by a shaft of moonlight, a slender figure crossed the path with long strides. They heard stones scuttering, then the sound was lost as the runner raced down the grass slope towards the infirmary.

'It was a boy,' said Peel-Llewellyn. 'Wearing rubber-soled shoes.'

'But what was he doing out at this hour? ... The screams have stopped.'

Again they strained to hear. Nothing happened for a few minutes, until another person—labouring slowly on sandalled feet and sobbing as though with the effort—passed beneath the dormitory window. The clouds scudding over the moon gave them an intermittent view and Hodges, pleased to have been proved right, hissed, 'It was a *girl* that time!'

'Lord!' said Peel-Llewellyn, awestruck, 'D'you think—'

'I don't *think*,' Hodges stated emphatically, 'I *know*. There's something up! Something awful's happened. I feel it.'

'What shall we do?'

'Wait a while and see if anyone else has heard. If lights go on, then we'll know it's safe to admit that *we* heard, too.'

But there was no other sound and St Aldhelm's remained in Stygian darkness. After a long pause, Peel-Llewellyn asked doubtfully,

'D'you think there's been another murder?'

'I shouldn't be surprised.'

'W-well—oughtn't we to do something?'

'*What?*'

Peel-Llewellyn took the initiative for once. 'We could go and look.'

'Where?'

'The pavilion f'r instance.'

'And be murdered?'

'Oh!—I h-hadn't thought of that. You mean—he might still be there?'

'He—or she.'

'But someone ran away.'

'Umm. Two people.'

'P'raps they were running away from each other.'

'In the same *direction*? The girl ran *after* the

boy.'

'Then—there isn't anything—or anyone—up at the pavilion.'

'You don't *know* that.' There was a long pause before Hodges added, 'If you're so *keen*—why don't you go and have a look?'

Peel-Llewellyn thought that this suggestion was in poor taste. His dignified and resentful silence at length drew from Hodges a more attractive alternative.

'We could go and *tell* someone.'

'Who?'

'The Erk.'

'But—what if it was a boy meeting one of the maids? Or—Charles Bolton?'

'Not *him*. Not big enough.'

'Well, one of the boys then?'

'I don't think it was *like* that—meeting one of the maids, I mean. Something *terrible* happened up there; and the girl came down the *same way*—towards the school.'

'Well, she would. If she lives in.'

'I don't think so. Girls would run *away* if a man attacked them.'

'You seem to know a lot about it.'

'It's common *sense*, you creep!'

Another long silence ensued and then they heard a car coming up the gravel sweep that led from the avenue to the cricket flats. A shaft of moonlight momentarily allowed them

241

a clear view.

'Good Lord! It's the Erk's car!' said Peel-Llewellyn.

'Then he *knows* something is up—and the people who ran *down* must have gone to tell him!'

'I think there was more than one person in the car.'

Excitement had taken fresh hold of them and in breathless whispers they discussed the possible meaning of this new development.

'P'raps someone's hanged himself in the pavilion!'

'*Murdered* more likely! It's becoming a habit round here.'

'Two murders are quite something! We ought to get a half-holiday to—to recuperate.'

'Good idea! Let's write to our people and say we feel *nervous*.'

'Can you imagine the Erk's face—if he got a letter asking for you to be sent home as you were suffering from nerves!'

'I *bet* you I could put it across! After all, it's what—what you might call a—a—' Hodges paused, searching for a phrase—and brought out triumphantly, 'a *traumatic* experience.'

'Wherever d'you learn such expressions?' asked Peel-Llewellyn admiringly.

'Well, *actually*—I had a private tutor once, cramming for Common Entrance, and he told my father that teaching me was "a traumatic experience from which he doubted that he could ever recover".'

'What had you done?'

'Oh, I let my ferrets loose and—one or two other things. Anyway, I think we could get a *weekend* off, if you do *just* what I say.'

'We did what you said—about the knife. "Misguided" was what the Erk called us. That's what he said we were—"misguided"! And who guided us?'

'Please yourself. *I* could *do* with a weekend at home.'

Again a long pause, whilst Peel-Llewellyn weighed up his chances and struggled with his conscience. The proposition was tempting and, to give him his due, Hodges was usually successful in his projects. Father Robert had called them 'nefarious projects'; Peel-Llewellyn was not sure what 'nefarious' meant but thought it might be another word for 'successful'.

'All right. What do you suggest?'

'Stop eating. Go off your food. You'll have to go around looking pale and vague—slow in the uptake. Should be easy for *you*; it's called "being listless".'

'We'd be sent to the infirmary!'

'Not if our *mothers* wrote—or came up.'

'Hag O'Connell would have seen through it.

And the Erk certainly will. I don't think my mother would dare to tackle the Erk.'

'Then mine will have to work it for both of us.'

'I say! Would she really? That's jolly decent.'

'She'd love it. Eyes misted with tears and all that sort of thing; right up her street!'

'Well, if you really think the Erk will let us go—? I'm on.'

'He *will*. And glad to see the back of us and of my overpowering mama. *This* time, anyway! He's not on a very good wicket, allowing dangerous knives to lie around the school and *inviting* murders to happen. The day will come, of course, when my mama will put on her act once too often, but *this* time I think we're on to a cert.'

'Suits me!'

Having planned his campaign, Hodges lost interest in the scheme and reverted to the current mystery, his curiosity overcoming his previous reluctance to investigate.

'Wonder what's happening up at the pavilion?' he mused. 'We could go and look.'

'And meet the Erk?'

'Perhaps not. But, after all—' he hesitated—'we *did* see and hear people running down *past* here.' He looked at Peel-Llewellyn challengingly, 'They woke us up!'

244

'No one else woke.'

'*We* were only half asleep—tossing and turning; worried and anxious! It'ud prepare the ground for the long weekend off.'

'A *long* weekend, now!'

'Why not? Don't interrupt—I'm *thinking*! Anyway, we *were* woken up in time to see the two people running past. Why should *we* be left out of whatever's happening?' He was beginning to warm to his own theme and his courage always tended to mount in hot pursuit of his flights of fancy. It was this that assured him of an unchallenged leadership. Peel-Llewellyn, however, was still a little dubious.

'Let's just say—that *you* were woken up.'

'OK! And I called you. I saw *both* these characters; you only saw the *second* person.'

'You're an awful liar, you know!'

'I'm a *good* liar—and it's in a good cause—as my mother would say.'

Peel-Llewellyn snorted with laughter—but quickly suppressed his mirth and they stood transfixed, listening for any reaction from the sleeping dormitory. No one stirred. But, in the stillness they heard another vehicle approaching and could see a light-coloured ambulance, blue light flickering, climbing the slope towards the pavilion.

'I *told* you!' said Hodges triumphantly.

'Good grief!' Peel-Llewellyn was again

awestruck. 'It *is* another murder!'

They watched, in tense silence, and ten minutes later saw both vehicles returning—followed by a police car which, presumably, had approached the pavilion by another route.

'We'll give the Erk a chance to get back to the school and then go down and see the inspector,' Hodges declared firmly, 'I'm *not* going to be left out of this.'

'Right! I'm feeling shivery—even in my dressing-gown. D'you think the inspector would give us a hot drink?'

'*Anything* could happen tonight! Let's count up to three hundred—very slowly—and then we'll go down to the van Dyck parlour.'

'How'll we get in?'

'We *could* tap on the window. But I think the infirmary door is left open until quite late and with all this business going on there's a good chance it's been forgotten. Anyway, we can try it and if not, there's lots of easy windows.'

'Suppose the inspector's in the Erk's study?'

'Then we wait till he comes out. We'll soon know—there'll be lights on. Now, let's start counting. One . . . two . . .'

*   *   *

Shivering with excitement, the conspirators stole out of St Aldhelm's House and crept stealthily over the grass towards the infirmary. They were less than a hundred yards away when the door opened and the girl whom they had seen earlier slipped out. She caught sight of Peel-Llewellyn's lanky figure, hesitated, and then with a stifled gasp, turned and ran back.

'Quick! After her!' breathed Hodges, sprinting ahead of his friend and through the infirmary door. The girl had vanished. They cast around, searching in dead silence, and wondering in a confused way whether they were looking for a murderess or for a terrified witness or potential victim.

An unspoken conviction bolstered their determination. She could not have gone far. It was unlikely that she would have slipped up the maid's staircase since her object had clearly been to escape and hide. Hodges' brain worked fast.

'The tunnel!' he whispered, clutching at Peel-Llewellyn's sleeve, 'That's where she'll be!'

She was. They found a light-switch and, in the flash before the fluorescent tube flickered on, saw a woman cowering against the wall. The neon light flickered again, went out, then came fully alight, blinding all three. When the boys could see again their eyes widened in horror. Cissie Sheridan, her light dress splashed with blood, stood with blood-streaked arms and hands raised before her face, shielding her eyes. She moaned softly; then yelped like a terrified animal and slid down on to her knees, whispering hoarsely, 'No! No!' With the chase at an end the two sleuths experienced a sudden reaction and terror invaded them—perhaps communicated from the creature huddled against the side of the tunnel. In a shaking voice, Hodges stammered,

'Y-you stay here with her. I-I'll get the inspector.' He stumbled away, leaving a trembling Peel-Llewellyn to stand guard over the petrified girl.

CHAPTER TWENTY-FIVE

NEW ADMISSIONS TO THE INFIRMARY

On returning from the pavilion to the school, the headmaster went straight to the infirmary in search of Cissie Sheridan whom he had sent there earlier, with instructions to find Sister. But Mrs Barnes, the newly engaged nurse, who had agreed to go on night duty and whom he met emerging from Brancaster's room, had neither seen nor heard her.

'I'm quite sure she's not been here, Father. I've been on this floor the whole evening and would have been certain to hear her. She can't have come over.'

'Poor kid! She was terrified. Something—' he hesitated—'unpleasant has happened. She must have run away and hidden herself somewhere—or gone up to her bedroom to be with her friends. But I'd better have a look round the infirmary—just in case.'

Without asking questions, Mrs Barnes joined him in a quick search conducted in a silence that Dom Erkenwald appreciated. Cissie was nowhere to be found.

'I'll go and tell the police. Call me at once, Sister, if she turns up. By the way—is Brancaster all right? You were with him when I came up.'

'All right now, Father. He was a bit restless so I gave him a hot drink.'

'And the others?'

'Fast asleep.'

'Good.'

Dom Erkenwald had joined the other police officers and Father Knox-Wesley in the parlour before Hodges and Peel-Llewellyn had left St Aldhelm's.

*   *   *

Gathered around the table in the van Dyck parlour were Father John Knox-Wesley, several police officers, including Dr Gibson the police surgeon, and Dom Robert who had appeared with a welcome bottle of whisky, given to him that day by a grateful parent. They were in process of restoring themselves when the headmaster joined them with news of Cissie's disappearance. Father Robert looked grave.

'Does this confirm things, Inspector?' he queried.

But Father Knox-Wesley interposed slowly and thoughtfully, 'I don't think she did kill Charles Bolton. They were lovers, I should think. Someone else attacked him. Possibly they were so engrossed in each other that they never saw the murderer approach.'

'What makes you say that?' The inspector turned on him in sharp inquiry. 'Did you see a third person?'

'No. At least—not consciously. But I've just remembered that someone brushed past me as I mounted the pavilion steps, and yet the girl, Cissie, was still standing there, screaming, beside Charles when I got to him; and her hands were over her mouth.'

250

'What sort of person? A pity you've only just recalled it!' grumbled the inspector in acute irritation. He felt that his brief honeymoon with the Catholic Church was coming to a disappointing and unsatisfactory end. These priests had appeared to be so helpful and cooperative from the police point of view, but in the last half-hour he had become grievously dissatisfied by their scale of priorities. It was quite infuriating to receive vital information too late to be of any value.

'I'm sorry, Inspector. I'm an old man and in the confusion and excitement—with Charles groaning and struggling for breath, and the girl screaming and hysterical, I—'

'Yes, yes,' Morgan interposed testily. 'No one's blaming you. But what *sort* of person?'

'I'm not sure. A youth, perhaps. Long tight trousers, jeans, longish hair—that sort of thing.'

'Tall—or short? Broad or slim?'

'I wouldn't know about the height. I'm not tall myself and I was bent almost double trying to get up the steps. I could hear the noises coming from the pavilion and was concentrating on getting there; I knew that I mustn't delay.' The old man was trembling violently; he had survived a ghastly experience surprisingly well until this moment. The headmaster thought it time to intervene.

'I think, Inspector, that Father Knox-Wesley must be exhausted. If Dr Gibson—' he turned and raised an inquiring eyebrow at the police surgeon—'would be so very kind as to ensure that he has a good night's rest, perhaps he would be able to give you further assistance in the morning.'

'Yes, of course. I'm most exceedingly sorry.' The inspector was contrite. 'I'm afraid that I've allowed my professional enthusiasm to carry me away and have discounted *your* professional zeal. I am anxious—as anxious as you are—that there should not be a third tragedy, and time is on the side of the murderer. He may be well away by this time and have covered his tracks; worse, he may have got hold of the girl. I've had extra men drafted here, but checking is difficult with so little to go on and so many involved.' He stopped and looked at Father Knox-Wesley and back again at Dom Erkenwald in an agony of apprehension; the last thing he wanted to do was to draw from anyone an admission that would distress the headmaster—and yet he knew that he must put the question. Facing the old priest he asked deliberately:

'Could the youth—could it have been a boy from the school?'

The Christite father hesitated. 'I don't know. The impression I received was so vague. I may recall something later. At present—I—it's so bewildering. I felt rather than saw this figure rushing past me down the steps ... quite slim, I think, and—of course—above my height—and just to my left. I don't know how I got the idea that he had rather long hair.'

'Do you let your boys wear their hair long, Headmaster? I've not noticed it!' The inspector sounded aggrieved—as though, whether permitted or not, such slackness implied a grave lack of discipline which hitherto he would not have expected.

'No, Inspector.' The headmaster was conscious of a reprieve and the lines of his face relaxed. 'It sounds more like one of the village boys. The Corps commander is even more insistent upon "short back and sides" than are the housemasters or myself. At this stage of the term, we've managed to persuade the long-haired to see the barber.'

'I *thought* it was long—but I may have been mistaken,' said Father Knox-Wesley miserably, not wishing to add to Dom Erkenwald's problems but anxious to be scrupulously honest. 'It was—as I say—all so vague and quick.'

'I'm afraid we must assume that the murderer is someone from inside Ambelhurst,' said the inspector, and he added with a troubled glance at the headmaster, 'The murderer is so obviously conversant with school life—and the two deaths are linked; of that I'm convinced. The same stab-wound method, though not necessarily the same weapon. *Colin Winter!*' he said suddenly. 'Sergeant! Will you—?'

At that precise moment Hodges burst in upon them. There was no need for him to put on an act; his eyes were almost starting from his head, his hair stood on end and his face was deadly white.

'We've found a girl!' he announced. 'One of the maids.'

'Alive?' asked Morgan and Dom Robert together.

'Yes.'

'Thank God!' The headmaster's exclamation was heartfelt.

'Where?' demanded the inspector.

'In the tunnel. Peel-Llewellyn's guarding her. She's crying. There's blood—'

'Will you come too, Headmaster?' asked Morgan—and made for the door.

'I will. Robert, go and get the new night Sister, Mrs Barnes. Hodges, you stay here—with Father!' He nodded towards the Christite and followed the inspector out of the room.

'What's been happening, sir?' asked Hodges. But Father Knox-Wesley evaded the

254

question with a faint smile, and the greyness of his face and his total exhaustion were obvious enough to quell even Hodges.

'I think you'd better ask the headmaster that. What brought you down here? Suppose you tell me how you came into this affair?'

★   ★   ★

In the tunnel Cissie sobbed hopelessly and uncontrollably and Peel-Llewellyn felt that he had been standing over her for hours. He was chilled to the bone and scared of the darkness that lay beyond the pool of light; he was quite sure that Matron's murderer was about to jump out at him. When he saw the inspector, followed by the headmaster and another man, his relief was immense.

'It's all right!' Dom Erkenwald addressed the remark to both young people in his most reassuring manner—and bent over the frightened girl. 'Come on, Cissie! You've nothing to be afraid of. You're quite safe. Come on, now! Stand up, there's a good girl!' But the poor creature was temporarily out of her wits and, although he persuaded her to look up, she gazed at him unseeingly and seemed incapable of movement and bereft of speech. Dr Gibson conducted a swift examination but he could get no response.

When Sister Barnes arrived, she took in the situation at a glance and decided to try other tactics. Speaking sharply, she managed to rouse the girl and, with the doctor's help, raised Cissic to her feet and led her away.

'I'll put her in an empty bedroom, Father,' she said, 'it's no use talking to her now. Father Robert has told me what's happened and I can see she's in a state of shock.'

'You're absolutely right, Sister,' agreed the police surgeon. 'I'll help you get her to bed and we'll give her a sedative. We won't get anything much out of her for hours yet.' Inspector Morgan sighed. All his witnesses seemed to be useless tonight.

The headmaster took a considering look at Peel-Llewellyn and remarked, 'I think, Doctor, that we could do with your help here, also.' He turned to Mrs Barnes and said, 'I'd like to bring two more boys into the infirmary, Sister, but you get Cissie settled first. Come on, Peel-Llewellyn!' The boy stared but did not move; his teeth were chattering and he was shivering violently. 'Come along! We'll get you into bed. Robert, bring Hodges, will you?'

In silence, the procession emerged from the tunnel into the infirmary passage, with Dom Erkenwald propelling Peel-Llewellyn while Sister and the doctor supported Cissie

256

between them. She had stopped sobbing but looked barely conscious. Very quietly, they mounted the stairs; there was no point in arousing and alarming any more people that night and the other nurses would have extra work to face in the morning.

*　　*　　*

In a small unoccupied ward, Dom Robert and the headmaster lit a gas-fire and turned down two beds. They made hot drinks and filled hot-water bottles and, when the boys were tucked up, the monks settled themselves in the shabby, army surplus armchairs and Dom Erkenwald asked:

'What brought you over here?'

Hodges's prefabricated story had vanished without trace and, reacting against an overdose of excitement, he was incapable of attempting anything but the truth.

'We were looking out of the window by my bed,' he began huskily, 'and we heard someone scream. Then—a boy, I think— came running down from the pavilion, and later a girl. It must have been Cissie. We—we saw your car go up—and then an ambulance. And then—we saw you come back and a police car with a blue, flashing light: though we hadn't seen that going up to the cricket field.'

'It went by the top lane. Go on!'

'Well—then we thought—I mean ...' he faltered and looked helplessly at Dom Erkenwald.

'I expect you couldn't bear to be left out of everything,' the headmaster supplied encouragingly, and the boys noted with relief, that his mouth turned up at the corners in a reassuring manner.

'We thought we ought to tell the inspector what we'd seen and heard,' corrected Hodges. He was beginning to feel that he was on safer ground than he had dared to hope. The headmaster knew the exact moment that Hodges registered security, and he was amused by his resilience. With difficulty, he suppressed a smile and took a deep breath.

'Go on!' he commanded.

'When we were just near the infirmary door, Cissie came out—and when she saw us—she ran back. We couldn't find her at first, but then—we thought of the tunnel— and there she was! In the dark!' His pupils grew large with the memory. 'W-when we put the light on—she s-sort of—fell down and moaned. She was frightened.'

'I'm not surprised. Your appearance would frighten anyone. I must find you a hairbrush.' The atmosphere was distinctly friendly and

Hodges warmed to his story. His voice became stronger and more confident.

'I told Peel-Llewellyn to stay with her and came for you.'

'Or—for the inspector?' Dom Erkenwald raised an eyebrow and watched Hodges flush and his eyes become wary. 'How fortunate that Father Robert and I were there. The inspector alone would have had his hands full coping with you two *and* Cissie!' Both boys looked sheepish and there was a short silence while they sought for something to say.

'Thank you for the cocoa,' Peel-Llewellyn ventured politely.

'Not at all. Any time!' replied the headmaster in equally civil tones. 'Cigarette, Dom?' he held out a packet to Father Robert. 'I expect Sister Barnes will be able to supply some biscuits and possibly another drink, when she comes. Do you think you'll be able to get off to sleep soon? I must telephone your housemaster before he discovers that you are missing. How strange that no one else in St Aldhelm's seems to have been disturbed!'

There was an immediate tensing of the atmosphere. The boys looked at him from under lowered eyelids but made no comment and they were thankful that Sister Barnes chose that moment to walk in. The peaceful scene reminded her of a night nursery.

259

'Thank you, Father,' she said approvingly, taking stock of the restored appearance of her new patients. 'You seem to have done my job very well. Cissie has had an injection and is almost asleep and Dr Gibson has prescribed for the boys. He asks me to tell you that he has gone back to the parlour to see Father Knox-Wesley. But the doctor will come up again if you would like him to see these two.'

'I hardly think it's necessary—do you, Sister? But they would like some biscuits and possibly another hot drink when you have time.'

'Certainly, Father. They can take their tablets with it.' She turned to Hodges and Peel-Llewellyn, 'What's it to be? Horlicks, Ovaltine, chocolate—or just hot milk?'

'We'll leave you.' Dom Erkenwald rose and signalled to Father Robert who was half asleep in his chair. They had reached the door when Hodges—greatly daring—asked, 'Sir! What *did* happen tonight?'

'I think we'll discuss that when you've had some sleep. Goodnight and God bless.'

★　　★　　★

It was almost one o'clock when the two monks returned to the van Dyck parlour. Dom Erkenwald noted with concern the shocked

260

and shrivelled appearance of the old Christite who sat huddled in his chair.

'I think,' he said firmly, in a voice of authority that none would dare gainsay, 'we should take Father Knox-Wesley up to bed and I should be obliged, Doctor, if you would prescribe something to make him sleep.'

'Hang on a minute!' said the police surgeon. 'How far away is his room?'

'I was thinking of taking him up to the *school* infirmary. It's a good deal nearer than the monks' infirmary and we can't leave him unattended in his guest room. The excellent Sister Barnes will cope admirably with one more patient.'

'If,' warned Dom Robert, 'she doesn't give notice in the morning! She may well be thinking that Ambelhurst has changed since her husband and brothers were here, that patients are habitually admitted after midnight, and that murders are commonplace.' He was glad to have made the headmaster smile. 'Ought we to call Sister Wilbraham?' he went on. 'Being newly in charge, she may not take kindly to the fact that there have been four new admissions, *and* a murder committed while she slept.'

'Maybe you're right. But, on the other hand, she'll need all the sleep she can get if life carries on at this rate.'

'I was wondering,' interrupted the police surgeon, 'whether you have a wheelchair handy? We could carry him—but I expect you have a chair somewhere.'

'Several,' answered the headmaster, 'for accidents, old monks and handicapped visitors. There are two in the infirmary gallery—I'll get one.'

Walking down to the infirmary, he reflected upon something else that should be done. The abbot was, he hoped, sleeping off the effects of jet-lag and it seemed a shame to disturb him or the prior; but one or other ought to be told of the latest development. He decided to wait until first light. The abbot would be up in good time for Matins and there really wasn't much point in disturbing him before then.

*　　*　　*

Once again a small procession set off for the infirmary: Dom Robert pushing the chair with Dr Gibson and the headmaster as escorts. Sister Barnes greeted them cheerfully and showed quiet concern for John Knox-Wesley's condition.

'There's plenty of room,' she said. 'There's a warm room next to Brancaster's. You monks look all in. Can't you get some sleep between now and dawn? Here, if you like.'

262

'Not a bad idea,' said Dom Erkenwald. 'I don't feel like undressing: I'll have a shower later: could you possibly call me at twenty to six, Sister?'

CHAPTER TWENTY-SIX

LIGHT ON DARK PLACES

The monks were allocated separate rooms and Dom Robert fell asleep at once but the headmaster could not relax. He got up and went down to the infirmary chapel on the half-landing, raising his hand in silent salute to Sister Barnes and to the police constables he passed on the way. The chapel was dark and the red sanctuary lamp flickered gently, casting shadows on the ceiling and striking fire from the shining brass candlesticks. He recalled his night nursery in an old country house and the giant shadows that had wavered on walls and ceiling, thrown from a coal fire in the grate. It was peaceful and safe here and the Source of all power and energy, the Uncontainable, was localized in the tabernacle: a focus for the concentrated anxiety that Erkenwald now released. Above his head an Umbrian crucifix hung in the shadows, symbol of the murder of God Incarnate. The monk knelt at a prie-dieu and pleaded in silent agony.

'Please, Lord, no more murder; no more nightmares. Father, forgive us and show us what to do next—how to guard against the evil that stalks by night.' He prayed for the dead victims of the murderer's hate—both of whom he had really liked and loved. He prayed for the murderer and for Cissie Sheridan, Mary Burke, and all the other women in whom Charles Bolton had aroused passion and, sometimes, love. He prayed for Inspector Morgan and thanked the Almighty for troubling to send such an exceptionally nice and unabrasive police officer to take charge. He prayed for an early solution and realized that it would be easier if one knew whether the murderer was motivated by anger, revenge, jealousy—or insanity.

What was the connection between the two murders? Why did the murderer take such a chance when Charles was in the company of his girlfriend? Girlfriend? Was that it? What about Colin Winter, the long-haired kitchen porter? Had he been driven by jealousy? If so, there was less reason to fear another violent death since he would have disposed of the two people whom he thought to come between Cissie and himself. But that would mean he was mad—and the insane stop at nothing. He would go for any witnesses, and all were concentrated in this part of the house.

The headmaster was profoundly uneasy. More than that, he was apprehensive. Something was menacing Ambelhurst. There was danger in the air, danger close at hand. The chapel clock struck four on silver chimes and as the sound died away the door behind him opened letting in light from the landing. The sanctuary lamp flickered wildly in the draught and he stiffened as a shadow fell across the floor and then moved forward, stopping at the prie-dieu next his. He did not stir.

'Father,' whispered a gentle voice and he looked up to see Mrs Barnes standing over him. 'Sorry to disturb you—but there's something I think you should know. Cissie's injection is just wearing off. I heard her cry out and when I went in she was sitting up in bed flexing and contracting the fingers of her right hand. Then she suddenly shook it and began to sob. It's difficult to understand what she's saying but she seems to be talking about a knife. Shall I call the police? She's in an awful state and she needs another injection. The police surgeon has written her up for a strong sedative. I thought I'd tell you before giving her anything.'

265

'Quite right, Sister. I'll get the inspector and, meanwhile, see if one of the police guards can listen and write down or tape what she's saying. You stay with her.'

He rosc and hurried out of the chapel and down to the parlour where the inspector, Sergeant Arrowsmith and Constable Gray were examining photographs that had just been handed in by a despatch rider. They were of Charles Bolton's body and of fingerprints. Morgan and the sergeant followed Dom Erkenwald back to the infirmary where he left them with Cissie and Mrs Barnes.

It took the inspector only three minutes to extract useful information from the frightened girl and it confirmed Father Knox-Wesley's belief that there had been a third person up at the pavilion: presumably the one who brushed past him as he mounted the pavilion steps. Cissie had been able to tell them that she had been standing with Charles's arms around her when she had felt him jerk violently as though he had been hit, at waist level, on his left side. Her arms had been round his neck, her hands behind his head and she had seen nothing because her face was against his. She recalled a second violent spasm and Charles's sharp intake of breath ... Someone had seized her right wrist and forced her hand down. A hard object had been thrust into the palm of her hand and her fingers were wrapped round it. Then Charles fell, sideways and backwards, on to the bench that ran along the pavilion wall and Cissie had fallen on top of him. She had pulled herself up and remembered the sound of metal striking stone before she started screaming.

'She said,' added Morgan, 'that her eyes were closed when she was in Charles's arms. After the second spasm she felt a smooth hand grasping her wrist and then her fingers. I asked her if it was a gloved hand and she hesitated, then said, "Not exactly a glove—not wool or leather—it was—silky, clammy—but dry." I think that's a fair description of a surgical rubber glove, don't you?'

'The boy could have bought a pair or stolen them from the surgery—or waste-bin,' said the headmaster slowly. 'I mean the kitchen porter—Colin—if it was he who murdered Charles.'

'It's interesting,' said the inspector, 'to see how near this murder came to being laid at Cissie Sheridan's door. A crime of passion. But for Father Knox-Wesley's walk round the cricket fields the evidence would have pointed to her. Her fingerprints all over the hilt of that wicked-looking butcher's knife—long, narrow and well-honed; but easy to conceal on a ledge at the back of the seat where they were standing. She could have detached herself from Charles's arms, picked up the knife with her left hand, transferred it behind his back to her right hand—and driven it in as he leant over her. Quite easy to manage.'

'But she didn't. There's no shred of evidence against her now, is there? Apart from the fingerprints.'

'No. Father Knox-Wesley and our two night watchers all witness to a third person. The murderer is unlikely to know that the boys saw him. But we can't be sure. He may know that they were chasing Cissie and found her in the tunnel.'

'Four of them—and all together under one roof,' said Dom Erkenwald, his face ashen. 'They are all at risk and I've made it easier— bringing them together in the infirmary.'

'Don't worry. It makes them easier to guard. We've got two constables up here and all windows are closed. Apart from the fire escape and the internal staircase there seem to be no other ways in or out of the infirmary at this first-floor level; or up on the second floor. We've done a careful check earlier in the night. I take it you have no secret passages or priests' hiding holes?'

'Not in this part—that I know of. Matron's flat is locked up and to go to or from the sisters' quarters one has to go down to ground-floor level, along the infirmary gallery and upstairs. With Matron's keys, or a pass key, one could go from her flat to the sisters' dining-room and kitchen—but one would still have to come up the staircase. Have you got men posted around the outside?'

'Yes—five. Guarding all approaches—and I'll now double that until we've caught the murderer. I've sent two constables over to the menservants' quarters. Trust us, Headmaster, and get some rest. You look all in. My sixth sense is stirring and I'm going off alone to think. Sister Barnes has given Cissie her second injection. It's twenty past four—she'll be out for another four hours or so but we've got the information we wanted and we've taken her fingerprints for confirmation of the knife story.'

'Four-twenty! I'll go and rouse the abbot. It's time he knew what's afoot. Will you be around if I bring him over?'

'I shall be—by the time you've been up to the monastery and returned.'

'If you want to think in peace—may I recommend the infirmary chapel? It's down those three steps, turn left, and the door is in front of you. Lights just inside the door if you want them. Or there's the sisters' duty room if you don't want to go back to your parlour.'

'Thanks. The chapel will be just right and I'll be back in the parlour in quarter of an hour if you want me.'

*   *   *

On the way to the monastery Dom Erkenwald tried to picture the young kitchen porter getting back to his room after this second murder. He must be cunning, thought the monk: Rubber gloves; a butcher's knowledge of anatomy—of where ribcage, heart, lungs and spleen could be found; casting suspicion on Cissie by getting her fingerprints on the knife and then throwing the murder weapon away where it would easily be found. Colin could have been activated by wounded vanity and desire for revenge.

Cissie's almost incoherent babbling had been believed only because it confirmed what John Knox-Wesley had said earlier. But for his meditative stroll, and the evidence of the night watchers up in the top dormitory of St Aldhelm's, Cissie could have been convicted of both murders—or one of them anyway. Tried on account of the second, of course, but neatly framed for both. The headmaster shuddered. This murderer was clever, cunning. Jealousy impels people towards great evil, he thought: but so does insanity.

Walking softly down the Haydock cloister and up the turret staircase towards the abbot's room, Dom Erkenwald heard the first faint twitterings and chirps of the dawn chorus. The dark night was nearly over.

'*Dominus illuminatio mea*,' he whispered aloud and his tired kaleidoscopic brain recalled Daniel's description of the Lord walking on the wind, and then the wonderful words of Jesus Christ to Martha, 'I am the resurrection and the life. If anyone believes in Me, even though he were dead, yet shall he live.' Matron lives, and Charles—for all his faults—lives also in the peace and glory of the resurrection. Even a *murderer* can be reclaimed by Christ and brought to everlasting life. His heart was more cheerful than it had been for the past forty-eight hours but, as he knocked on the door, a new suspicion disturbed his mind.

★   ★   ★

The abbot shook off the remains of sleep and decided that he would meet Inspector Morgan in the parlour before going up to the abbey church for Matins.

'I'll go back to the infirmary,' said Erkenwald. 'I want to settle one or two points with Sister Barnes. And then I must telephone

Charles Bolton's next of kin. We'd better not wait until full daylight—just in case there has been a leak. I hate to disturb them—they ought to be at their best to receive such a shock, but Charles's parents have a right to know. Poor things, they haven't known how to help him in recent years.'

'I suspect,' said the abbot sadly, 'that his early death may be something of a relief.'

'Hell bent on a disaster course, poor lad!'

CHAPTER TWENTY-SEVEN

HIDDEN DEPTHS

At four forty-five the abbot and Inspector Morgan were seated in winged armchairs on either side of a blazing fire in the van Dyck parlour. Constable Gray brought in mugs of hot coffee and, having seen the inspector's weary face, the abbot rose and added a dash of whisky to the policeman's drink. 'You must have had a terrible night,' he observed.

'It's been worrying,' replied Morgan, 'but everyone has been most kind. Incidentally, we've not kept your domestic staff up. Constable Gray has a magic touch with fires, as you can see, and he found a pile of apple

272

logs stacked up in a courtyard. I hope it was in order to use them? We were rather concerned about Father Knox-Wesley initially—and then it seemed a pity to let such a fire die down before the sun comes up.'

'It's splendid and I shan't want to leave its warmth and go up to the church!'

'But we shall need your prayers. It's been a bad night—full of death and shadows and stalking evil.' The abbot was surprised to hear a police officer, well used to violence, speak in this way. Perhaps he did so only because he knew that his comment would fall on sympathetic ears. Abbot James gazed into the leaping flames and quoted softly,

'Have you been shown the gates of death—
  or met the janitor of shadowland?
Tell me about it if you have!
Which is the way to the home of light
  and where does darkness lie?'

'*Job*,' said the inspector, 'Chapter thirty-eight, verses seventeen to nineteen. I don't know the translation you're quoting from—but your choice is apt.'

'Jerusalem,' replied the abbot.

'I like it. It's unfamiliar—but I like it. I wish I knew "the way to the home of light" and could see into the mind of our murderer and "the source of his darkness". Do you know Today's English Version? We must hope for—

"the dawn to seize the earth
and shake the wicked from their hiding
    place . . .
the light of day is too bright for the wicked
and restrains them from deeds of
    violence."'

'You have quoted verses thirteen and fifteen and I think I prefer your TEV—at least in this instance. It seems that we share a fascinating pastime. Used you to quote from King James—as I from Douai?'

'I did indeed—and still do. It teases my middle-aged memory to play the one against the other. How long have you been at this game?'

'Since the noviceship. I sharpened my wits on a brother novice who's been serving for a long time in Peru. I was out there until last Thursday—and we revived the game. I thought how much I should miss it when I returned home—but now I meet another addict. May we keep in touch when this nightmare is all over?'

'May the Lord complete the work that He has begun,' said Morgan, smiling. '"Those who live as the Spirit tells them to, have their minds controlled by what the Spirit wants!"'

'*Romans* eight—I think it's verse five,' the abbot responded with a wide grin. '"No wonder that men fear Him and thoughtful men hold Him in awe".'

'That's *Job* thirty-seven, verse twenty-four!'

'It is indeed. And look through the window—a golden glow is seen in the east—I've taken the liberty of altering the direction.'

'Absolutely right! We can't claim that morning comes from the north. You know, Father Abbot, I'm feeling happier... The night is ending.'

'"Visit this house, we pray you, Lord,"' murmured Abbot James, '"drive far away from it all the snares of the enemy."'

★   ★   ★

While the abbot and the inspector were getting to know one another the headmaster went up to the infirmary, surprising Sister Barnes who was preparing three extra breakfast trays in the brightly lit kitchen. She jumped slightly on seeing the dark-robed figure, but greeted him with relief.

'All's well. I'm only setting up six trays—Cissie will be out for the count until about ten o'clock. I've just done a round. Hayden and Butcher have slept through the night's dramas; Father Knox-Wesley is snoring gently; Hodges and Peel-Llewellyn are dead to the world and Brancaster has had a good night after all. He seemed over-excited earlier on—he'd had long visits from his friends.'

'Touché!'

She looked at him in surprise—and then laughed. 'Oh, of course! I believe you visited him last evening and then sent the two boys along. I'd forgotten. Anyway it did him good; he was in great form by the time they left. But as he was still wide awake and tossing around at ten o'clock last night, I sponged him down and gave him a hot drink. He fell asleep almost at once and never heard our new admissions arrive.'

'Good.'

Mrs Barnes went on with her work and because she was searching a cupboard for honey and marmalade, she did not notice that the headmaster looked out on to the landing and listened carefully before closing the kitchen door.

'Sister—' He hesitated. 'Did Sister Wilbraham go out for a walk last night?'

'Yes, Father. She's feeling the strain of Matron's death and she needed exercise and fresh air.'

'What was she wearing?' Mrs Barnes had an open face and did not hide her astonishment.

'Shirt and jeans, Father. And a sweater—and shoes with crêpe soles.'

'Was her hair pinned up?'

'No—she wore it loose like a page boy. It made her look younger.'

'You're observant.'

'Nurses' training.'

There was a pause and across Mary Barnes's expressive face the headmaster saw slight confusion as though she had been taken unawares. 'Do you—' she began hesitatingly, suspecting an unexpectedly narrow attitude towards the off-duty wear of the nursing staff—'do you prefer us not to wear trousers? I'm not really the right shape for them, myself—but Sister Wilbraham certainly is. However, if you don't wish us to—'

'You can wear what you like, Sister! Shorts, slacks, tracksuits—anything! Useful garments and they suit some women admirably. You've misunderstood the purpose of my question—which is not at all surprising.' He smiled reassuringly and added, 'I had a theory which you've confirmed. I'll explain later. Thanks for your help.' Turning swiftly on his heel, he was gone.

The headmaster walked down the infirmary staircase determined to risk his reputation for perspicacity. Suspicion was not certainty and he had no proof. But too much was at stake. The murderer had proved capable of cool premeditation and swift action. Despite their dramatic and bloody boldness, the two deaths had been skilfully executed. There were now four important witnesses in bed in the infirmary, and even with police officers posted all around, he could not rest until he had passed on to Inspector Morgan the strange conviction that was hammering in his brain.

★   ★   ★

Down in the parlour the abbot and inspector looked like two men at ease in their club, thought Dom Erkenwald, as he walked into the firelit room redolent with applewood. He hated to withdraw them from what was evidently mutual admiration but he knew that any risk of further deaths must be forestalled.

'Forgive me for intruding,' he said—and, looking from one to the other, added simply, 'I think you should know that Sister Wilbraham was out in the grounds last night—wearing jeans, shirt, sweater and crêpe-soled shoes. I've just checked with Sister Barnes.'

There was silence in which the clock ticked, applewood crackled and spluttered and ash

278

fell.

'It fits,' said Inspector Morgan, at length.

'Oh dear!' whispered the abbot. '*Poor woman!*'

'Mad?' queried the headmaster.

'She could be a psychopath. Probably schizophrenic,' replied Morgan.

'In which case she would have little or no appreciation of guilt. Defective conscience.'

'That is so,' said the abbot and inspector together and despite their physical dissimilarity, the headmaster thought that they had much in common.

'I'll take the necessary precautions and make preparations,' Morgan said decisively. 'We can't wait until she's expected to wake up. She may be up and dressed already—for all we know.'

'And she has proved herself cunning and clever,' the headmaster intervened. 'The possibility only struck me as I walked up to your room, Father. I had been thinking of Colin Winter—until then. The description of a young boy—and the Sebatier knife.'

'Perhaps she meant us to do so,' responded Morgan. 'We shall need a confession—in my sense of the word, not in yours! Circumstantial evidence isn't enough. The important thing is to secure this without— alarming her. If at all possible.'

'I think, Inspector,' said the abbot with due diffidence, 'I might just be able to help. I believe Eleanor would talk to me. Or perhaps the headmaster? Or maybe Claude le Mesurier: though he would find "trapping" her too distasteful, whereas I must put the needs of Ambelhurst and the danger to others first. There is no question of a breach of confidence or breaking the seal of sacramental confession: I'm not her confessor and I doubt that she's yet faced reality. It will be some time before she can cope with truth and contrition. I had some dealings with schizophrenics and psychopaths when I served as chaplain to a mental hospital.'

'Thank heaven for that!' Morgan said devoutly. 'They're tricky people and need kid glove handling.'

The headmaster thought of Cissie's description of the gloved hands clasping hers and forcing her fingerprints upon the knife handle ... and Morgan's comment about surgical rubber gloves. The inspector's sixth sense had been stirring even then and, judging by the calmness with which he had accepted Dom Erkenwald's report on Eleanor's evening walk and her attire, he realized that Morgan— even without Mrs Barnes's evidence—had been reaching the same conclusion.

'You had already begun to suspect Sister

Wilbraham?' he asked.

'I had. It was just a feeling that motive, opportunity, ability were all there. I wasn't sure about her temperamental qualification. Perhaps I didn't want to know. I found her—attractive.'

'She is,' said the abbot. 'Poor girl! She must have been very unhappy; driven to desperation.'

'I have the feeling,' said the headmaster, 'that she'd already set her sights on the matron's post. When I offered it to her she didn't hesitate: not for one second. It was as though it came as no surprise to her. But I'm speaking from hindsight. It is only now that I realize that she was—'

'Waiting for a dead woman's shoes,' said the inspector. 'Father Abbot, I think we should waste no more time. May I accept your offer to lead Miss Wilbraham along towards the necessary confession? I'll come up with you as far as the police cordon and set things in motion. Take all the time you want.'

'I will. And will you please both pray.'

Left behind in the parlour, the headmaster returned to the resurrection and reconciliation prayer that he had been praying on his way up to the abbot's room. 'Though she be dead—yet shall she live. Lord, be her light—her light and her salvation ... her good shepherd.

Lord, Your servant is sick—save her from the power of evil. Rescue her from the sin of bitterness—from the pain of rejection—from fear and the feeling of worthlessness. Let her discover how much she means to You.' He realized that he had acquired an understanding of her condition during and since his brief vigil in the infirmary chapel. '*Dominus illuminatio mea!*' he marvelled.

CHAPTER TWENTY-EIGHT

SNARES OF THE ENEMY

Sister Wilbraham, her hair swept up into a French pleat that enhanced her tiny ears and high cheekbones, was graciousness itself.

'Welcome home, Father Abbot. We've missed you.'

'You've been lonely,' he replied, accompanying the words with a look full of sorrow.

Her face registered surprise.

'How did you know?' she asked. 'How *could* you know what I feel?'

Gently he took her hand and said, 'Shall we sit down? You must want to talk.'

'Yes.'

'You thought you had come home when you arrived at Ambelhurst?'

She nodded. 'I came, full of joy, wanting to give of my best and I met with indifference. Matron didn't want the infirmary modernized. She and Sister Hanlon were boring company. We nurses were not acceptable to the masters' common room.'

'But Claude le Mesurier appreciated your wit and intelligence. I know because he told me so: and he enjoyed helping you with your Open University course.'

'That's true. But working with women whom I found incompatible—'

'And with the monks inaccessible,' he said apologetically. 'They're all so busy with their monastic and professional duties, and though I'm Father of the House, I have little time for courtesy visits.'

'In any case, you've been away in South America for the past four months. Was it wonderful?' she asked in a warm, deeply interested voice. But the abbot was not to be deflected. He was skilled at keeping penitents and troubled novices to the point once they had touched on their problems.

'Whatever rejection you have suffered, Eleanor, is as nothing compared to the rejection suffered by Christ. He came among us, arms outstretched, and men spat in His face. Imagine it! Ultimate Goodness and Truth burning with all love's desire to serve and to give—and he was despised and rejected.' He paused, looking at her with compassion and choosing the right moment to continue. 'Most of us have committed sins which merit punishment and rejection. Christ never sinned; not once. Sinless and incorruptible, driven by the longing to help the unhappy—even sinners—to love and—to love again. Can you imagine what that means?'

She nodded slowly and after a pause he went on. 'You and I, and many others called by Christ, have a great urge to give. We start out full of longing to serve . . . but sometimes those we want to help reject us.'

'Yes.' She paused. 'It is—as it has always been.' Bitterness twisted her mouth and narrowed her eyes and her low, musical voice became harsh as she continued, 'My three brothers had everything lavished on them: public school education, university and professional training. They had allowances, holidays overseas, help with their first homes.' She paused for a long minute, struggling for control; then, with a voice so painfully constricted that the words were forced out in short, jerky phrases, she went on: 'I was sent to an indifferent private day school.'

The abbot did not as a rule find people suffering from self-pity at all attractive but he was wrung by her evident grief.

'My mother became an invalid—or semi-invalid, the doctor said she was a hypochondriac; but when I was just seventeen I had to leave school and go home to act as—as—maid-companion to her. I helped her to dress and undress: I took over the housekeeping, nursed her, drove her wherever she wanted to go . . . and there was no let-up, not even a brief holiday away from my parents. People said I was so lucky to have such a beautiful mother, such handsome brothers, and such a wonderful home—with all one could want.' Her control began to crack and she sat silent, twisting her long fingers together as she struggled for calm. 'My brothers and their wives never cared about me. They had full and interesting lives. I walked the dogs, gardened, did the flowers . . . Not even a hack hunter remained for me when my brothers married and the stables emptied. Life left the house when they went. Then my father fell ill: he lingered on for four years, querulous and autocratic. He was a major-general and accustomed to being obeyed, but at the end there was only me to fetch and carry for him. His soldier servant grew old and retired. The maids left and couldn't be replaced. I managed with daily help and a gardener's boy. When he died suddenly my mother was frightened of life without him. She couldn't cope with the obvious fact that I'd already taken over everything, financial affairs included. She believed—wanted to believe—that my father and my brothers had always controlled things ... and when my father was dead and my brothers were still serving abroad, then—' her voice became loud and vicious—'I made her see that she and my father had depended on me, fully, for the previous five years.'

'You felt triumphant?'

'Yes.' Again the pause, 'But they won in the end. I had no foreknowledge of my father's will—or my mother's. She died three months after him and I discovered that they had left me *nothing*!' She spat out the word with venom. 'They had assumed that I would look after them to the end. I was twenty-four when the solicitor explained that I had no home, no possessions, no money. My brothers sold the house and garden I had worked in since I was seventeen. They allowed me to choose a very few small pieces of furniture, a picture or two, a set of china and glass. Not the best,' she added bitterly. 'And the solicitor persuaded them to settle some money on me. He was ashamed of what my parents had done. He

286

and his father had tried to persuade them that unmarried women are not necessarily exploited by fortune-hunters and that I had proved myself capable and a good manager ... My brothers agreed, for the sake of peace, to the purchase of a small annuity and that has given me the only independence I have ever known.'

'Did you feel resentful always? From the time you had to leave school?'

'I suppose so. I bottled it up and tried not to see or hear about the good time other girls had. Fortunately, they didn't like me. That helped.'

'Why didn't they?'

'I was said to be clever—and—' she stumbled.

'And?'

'Sarcastic.'

'Understandably.' She looked up momentarily—and then away. Compassion was unexpected and hard to bear.

'My mother wanted another boy. She liked having handsome young men around her. She was dark and Spanish-looking—and she deplored my "mousey" fairness.'

'Hardly mousey, would you say?'

'I was—until I took myself in hand.' She did not smile. 'The local chemist understood. Without any explanation from me, he wrote

287

up our accounts in such a way that my mother didn't realize that I got cosmetics under the heading "medical supplies".'

'Did the deception worry you? Did it feel wrong?'

'No. Why should it? I was cheated. I had to ask for money for books, periodicals, shoes—everything.'

'I see.' He paused. 'Have you thought that your parents may not have realized what they were doing to you?'

'They knew. But I didn't count. "Poor Eleanor",' she mimicked.

'Surely you know that you are very good-looking? Didn't you know then?'

She shook her head. 'When they died I took up the only profession I was fitted for. Nursing!' She made it sound distastful. 'With my record of devotion—getting into Thad's was easy. I did well. Nursed with my head.'

'But not with your heart?'

'We were exploited. Long hours for little pay. The patients as well as the hospital management had cheap labour at their disposal.'

There was a long pause before she continued: 'There was a hospital pantomime. The make-up woman made me look stunning. Told me I had good bones, beautiful eyes and a decent figure. Showed me how to smile; how

288

to "produce" myself—as she called it. She used me as a model for her dress shop. Gave me elegant clothes. Taught me how to stand, walk, dress. My mother had always made me feel gauche. She sighed for the days when she was a débutante and sought after—and she shook her head over "poor Eleanor"!'

'She gave you a beautiful name.'

'I hate it.'

The abbot changed tack. 'When did you become a Catholic?'

'At the end of my training. "Roman" Catholics were distrusted at Thad's. I took an interest to annoy them.' She smiled grimly. 'Then I felt—different.'

'God had called you by name?'

'If you like.'

'How would you put it?'

'I was special—at last. God had singled me out, I was something my family loathed and detested—and I was *glad*!'

'Yet you came here full of the longing to repay God for singling you out? Wanting to serve?'

She sat as though carved in Carrara marble: upright carriage, the head bent forward; hands clasped tightly on her lap. She fought for self-control and evaded truth.

'To serve—yes.' Truth struggled for mastery. 'And to show them what I could do.'

'Show who?'

'My family.'

'Are you in touch?'

'No. But—one day—they will know.'

He wondered what tortuous scheme she had in mind. 'Are you ambitious to be a saint? To achieve a degree? To be accepted as an important person at Ambelhurst—loved by the community and Old Boys—as Matron has been?'

'Do you have to make it sound so selfish?'

'I did not intend to hurt you. You must have found it disappointing. Wanting to give generously.' She stirred slightly and he knew that he had touched a nerve. Any giving she had planned was to have been on her own terms and calculated to earn rewards. 'You heard no word of praise or thanks,' he said. 'The brethren take themselves and others for granted. "Love is all."'

'I know what your Latin motto means!' she snapped in irritation.

'I'm sorry. Of course you do.' He felt genuinely distressed at having appeared condescending and ashamed of his insensitivity.

'You must,' he said gently, 'have found it lonely working with colleagues unable to share your interests. We religious can be blind to lay people's needs because our own desire for friendship is usually met within the community. My generation was taught to keep custody of the eyes—but some of us avoid temptation by keeping custody of intelligent understanding as well! We can develop an insensitivity that is akin to monumental indifference. I'm sorry,' he said with heart-felt contrition, 'very sorry that you have suffered from the absence of companionship and lack of encouragement. You are not, in fact, as secure and self-sufficient as you seem on superficial acquaintance?' He managed to put a note of inquiry into the last sentence and left it suspended in the silence that followed; but she did not respond.

'Perhaps,' he continued as though musing aloud, 'perhaps you have been challenged by someone—or some standard—that you admired and could not match?' He saw her flinch and knew that he had touched another nerve. Her eyes were lowered, her face impassive, but the muscles of her shoulders and mouth tightened. That was all—but it was enough for an experienced priest. He changed tack and began to speak more quickly, circling the danger area and moving in, closer and closer to obtaining a confession of murder.

'Christians ought to be aware of the need of others to be accepted and drawn, as far as

291

possible, into a family community. But we are all selfish. Many religious men and women fear encroachment and intrusion. We don't want to encourage developments that we can't control; relationships that could become too personal. In the past we've been too fearful— more by training than by instinct—but psychologists have taught us that total isolation and the avoidance of human relationships is dangerous, or can be. It was not a danger that Christ feared or avoided. He didn't feel threatened when people moved instinctively towards Him. He allowed Himself to suffer all the invasions of privacy, and the suffocating contacts with vast crowds of people, that some religious seek to avoid. Over the last four months I've had the opportunity to reflect, especially in Peru, on our fearfulness. I've realized that modern monasteries are poised between two hazards: that of encouraging an invasion of our silence and of the total dedication of our lives to the *worship* of God: and the alternative hazard of remaining apart, private and privileged— instead of sharing in the *service* of the people of God.'

'Does it have to "either—or"? The destruction of sound monastic foundations and experience *or* the preservation of complacency?' She was interested and also eager to distract attention from her particular case to something more general, but the abbot was too shrewd to be deflected for long. He allowed some digression to give her breathing space but would move in when it was expedient to do so.

'The effect of so many religious leaving their communities to seek God elsewhere has made us afraid,' he began. 'In some monasteries and convents the drawbridge has been lowered and almost total invasion allowed. In others, the doors have been triple locked and, metaphorically speaking, there has been a withdrawal from contact with "the world". And school life has changed. Once it was possible for a matron to live a happy and fulfilled life, feeling wanted and involved for twenty-four hours of the day. Now, with shorter hours and better, self-contained living quarters she may well feel isolated. There are also more women involved in the life of the school; a matron is no longer unique.'

He paused and, after a while, she looked up inquiringly. Speaking more slowly, he said, 'We have not, at Ambelhurst, accepted women as true equals: we don't welcome them as full colleagues. People in some professions—particularly teachers—can be arrogant in their approach to others and too certain of their own superiority.' Again he noticed the merest ripple of distress and he pressed home with the observation. 'Perhaps you found it hard to be classed as non-academic and to be excluded from the staff common room where you would expect to find more stimulating conversation than you enjoy in the infirmary.' It was a statement rather than a question; yet until that moment he had not been aware that Sister Wilbraham had been so excluded.

She straightened up, looking proud and disdainful, and murmured that she had found some of the teaching staff 'farouche' and had no regrets at being excluded. Her cool manner might well have distanced people and tempted members of the teaching staff to relegate her to a 'nursing and domestic' category. He wondered how the housekeeper and the headmaster's secretary felt. The latter was married and able to hurry home to a warm welcome, but Miss Melsdon, displaying aggressive and domineering behaviour, could also be feeling isolated.

'Mary O'Connell,' he said, 'represented the old regime. She regarded herself as set apart and superior to many other members of staff—including, I sometimes thought, several of the monks.' He smiled briefly. 'She had access to the physical and mental health records of pretty well everyone at

Ambelhurst; she was privy to intimate secrets and her discretion and integrity were bywords. She became a legend in her lifetime. With hindsight, I can see how her style has stamped and to an extent limited the involvement of the nursing staff. Open-ness and collegiality have characterized all departments other than that of the school infirmary which is still based firmly in the nineteenth century. In two years, you never joined in the local village life: it swept along without you. Isn't this so?'

'I didn't want to become involved in the *village*.'

'No. But neither were you involved in discussions with the brethren.' He turned and gestured towards the theological books and periodicals filling one shelf of her bookcase. 'Isolation is not healthy. You came expecting companionship and shared interests and met with blank indifference, compared to which the Berlin Wall looks like the netting on a fruit cage.'

A brief musical laugh escaped her and the abbot took heart. All was not destroyed: one may build on signs of humanity.

'You've never taken part in school discussion groups, in liberal studies, or in debates, have you?' the abbot asked. 'Were you involved in the pastoral congress or in commission work in your home diocese?'

'No one asked me! I was—I *am*—a convert; one waits to be invited.' Her voice was venomous. 'I came here full of hope: full of warmth for what de Lubac called "the Church, my mother"—and *nobody* cared. Polite social noises were the last thing I expected in a place like *this*: a power house of prayer, a fountain of dynamic thought. I read your Johannine periodicals and they mouthed theology. They spoke of the love of Christ for His Church and the love that exists between the People of God. I read your founder's rule and his chapter on hospitality—but there was no place in his family for me.'

'You could have become a lay Associate.'

'I had heard some amusing comments on your Associates. I did not wish to be identified with women solacing their frustrated maternal instincts by sewing buttons and patches on monks' habits, knitting them sweaters and inviting them to "boring meals with ill-chosen wines": any more than I wanted to be associated with your male oblates who seem to be religious manqués and merely aiming to be, at the end of their lives, buried in the habit.'

'But there is so much more to our lay Association than that! It is a living, loving, dynamic family. It really cares.'

'I have not noticed.'

'Could your initial feeling of disappointment have prejudiced you? You expected a warm welcome—'

'I got it. For perhaps three weeks; maybe only for three days. Then I realized that it was superficial interest. There was to be no real involvement. I overheard caustic comments about spinsterish associates and confraters; snide remarks about choir oblates. All very funny—but I felt disillusioned and betrayed. This was not the warm, loving community that I had anticipated. There was no Holy Spirit brooding over the bent world "with warm breast and with ah! bright wings".'

Silence—deep silence. The abbot sat stunned as the whole of 'God's Grandeur' passed through his mind. Eleanor had not shared Hopkins's discovery of 'the dearest freshness deep down things.' The very reason for the existence of the abbey of St John the Less had not been evident to her. His vision of himself as father of an extended family, a caring community, had received a vicious swipe. Her onslaught had been unbalanced and there was ample evidence of her unsound mind: nevertheless, he recognized just cause for her criticism.

Eleanor had subsided once more into the marble-like tranquillity that—until this morning—had been characteristic of her.

Artemis, the moon goddess, he thought. This woman, scarred by life, had human needs deeply enmeshed with her love of God. We have to love ourselves before we can believe in the love of God; she had expected that in her new church she would be welcomed for herself; had entertained legitimate expectations of the support and spiritual refreshment she might receive—and she had not found it. Matron's matter-of-fact, Irish brand of the faith, with its Lourdes and Lough Derg overtones, had been alien to Eleanor. The beauty of the monastic liturgy had sounded hollow to her, because she had not experienced the love of Christ which should have flowed from it to those with whom and among whom she worked. Cradle Catholics had been indifferent to her longings.

The abbot sighed, accepting this belated revelation of the truth as it appeared to one who had come to live at Ambelhurst and had known distress. Something needed to be done. In future there must be a definite attempt to integrate all lay members of the staff, men and women, so that they had a sense of belonging. It was not enough just to run a club for the resident domestic staff, to organize dances in the village hall, and to celebrate Masses in their vernacular for Spaniards, Italians and other nationals. We can never do enough, he thought, for the people of God entrusted to us here in England—never mind those far off in Peru. He had not realized that to an intelligent woman convert, looking for human support and shared delight in her new-found faith, the apparently impregnable north front of the monastery that she observed from the nursing sisters' quarters was symbolic of religious life as seen by an outsider.

Everyone had assumed that Eleanor was content to attend the conventual Mass and as much of the divine office as her duties allowed. She had chosen to be present at the Masses in the abbey rather than at the Catholic church in the village—so she had not been drawn into parish life. In any case, timetable difficulties and Matron's intransigent attitude towards the mingling of school and village life would have deterred her. She had not realized that some association of 'town and gown' was acceptable to the monks. The abbot saw the inconsistencies in Eleanor's profession of faith, but he knew that her murderous behaviour originated in rejection and frustration. The headmaster had been right when, six months previously, he had suggested that hot molten lava coursed through the Ice Maiden's veins. That nickname—the Ice Maiden—had surfaced soon after Eleanor's arrival and both monastery and school had adopted it, finding pleasure in its accuracy. For the monks it had implied chastity and dedication; to the lay staff it had suggested disdain.

As though reading his thoughts, Sister Wilbraham said in a hard, tight voice, 'I know my nickname. I've known it since the beginning of the second term after I arrived. I overheard people discussing the school pilgrimage to Lourdes and the need for a trained nurse to replace Mrs Perkins when she fell ill. My name was proposed and the response was, "That Ice Maiden—with the frozen halo? Spare us!"'

'Through such wounds are we hammered and shaped,' the abbot murmured into the silence of her grief. 'Sometimes we are able to go all out to prove the opposite—turning a malicious hurt into positive good. And sometimes we are too vulnerable—as you were at this important juncture in your life. Perhaps you could think only of what you had given up—for God and for Ambelhurst; and of your gifts which had been slighted. It became impossible to recognize the great, surging, living warmth of others and to notice their self-giving.'

'Oh, I agree. I became preoccupied with the snub of rejection.'

'And with the pursuit of self-perfection?' The abbot surprised himself by the swiftness of his attack and saw Eleanor wince.

'If by that you mean—' she began hotly and then hesitated. He decided to probe further. 'Don't let a sinus heal, Sister. Probe it and let the evil matter drain away. Never seal up poison: let it come pouring out. Healing takes place from the depths.'

'I wasn't aware that you have a medical training,' she said, adding sarcastically, 'We use antibiotics a great deal nowadays.'

He let her gain some breathing space before he answered, 'I had just qualified as a doctor when I felt the compelling urge to become a priest. Unlike the former Jesuit General, Pedro Arrupe, who used his medical training after the bomb fell at Hiroshima, I'd never done more than patch up a minor wound until I went out to Peru and was able to give outdated and clumsy help.'

'I wish I'd known,' she said. 'You might have understood—but now it's too late.'

'It is never too late with God,' he said quietly, 'and I am His unworthy servant. Please tell me—' He paused, then continued: 'When did you begin to lose your temper with Matron? What was it that pushed you past endurance?'

Her head went up, her eyes blazed and the

abbot thought that anger gave her face a beauty that icy calm had concealed.

'What did Matron know of sacrifice?' she demanded. 'Her prospects—coming from a large bog Irish family were richly fulfilled; and no doubt the people back home were proud of her achievement in becoming matron at Ambelhurst.'

'One of the most distinguished and brilliant women I know—the Mother General of an internationally famous congregation—started life as a barefoot child "off the bog", as people say. She has all the marks of a saint.'

'Oh, I'm sure! But Matron wasn't of that calibre. She was narrow, obstinate, pig-headed and just clever enough to string me along with her talk of retirement. She did less and less work and took credit for improvements I made.'

'We did realize that the changes began after your arrival,' he said humbly.

'What a pity, then, that you said nothing! Not one word of encouragement. Maybe you monks don't need such a spur—though I doubt it from what I've heard! But we women—even Matron—would do so much more and give unstintingly, if only you could bring yourselves to utter those two words "Thank you". Even Christ wanted to be thanked by the lepers He cured. Yet you seem to think that we nurses should work solely for the love of God—without acknowledgement—without praise! Suppose such praise did feed our vanity and self-esteem—wouldn't it be worth the risk?' She was swept along by anger and the abbot sat back and let the torrent pour out of her.

'Matron was a nosey, prying old bag and you all—or most of you—sanctified her. If you had shared her company at mealtimes, at recreation and at work, you would have a very different impression. She cast me as a "spoilt nun"—to use her unpleasant phrase—and made several attempts to find out whether I had tried my vocation—'

'And had you?'

'No! I wanted *freedom*. I'd been tied up for too long—with my parents and then in hospital—'

'Did you think that this institution would be any more free?'

'I didn't know. I certainly didn't expect it to be circumscribed by the walls of the infirmary and the church—or that I'd be confined to the company of two rather dull women, to whom I seemed like a women's libber—or even, where Matron was concerned, like a would-be priestess!'

'Did Matron taunt you with that?'

'Certainly. She was a reactionary,

schismatic schemer—rooting for Lefebvre and totally pre-conciliar. Baring her ill-fitting, plaque-stained teeth and talking with food in her mouth. It was obscene!'

'So you killed her?'

'Yes. I killed her, and Charles Bolton—not just because he saw me in the cloister but because he was promiscuous and evil, and treated women as sex objects.'

It was out. The boil had burst in a spate of fury and what the abbot's professor of surgery would have called 'laudable pus' poured forth. The abbot reflected that free discharge from a mental wound is possibly even more essential than free discharge from a physical one. Slowly, as though from a great depth of suffering, Eleanor began to cry. He made no move as shuddering sobs racked her—resisting his instinct to interfere, and soothe her like a child. Even children have to come to terms with suffering. Acknowledging resentment, hatred was half the battle on the road to recovery. This woman had endured much and her vivid imagination had fuelled actual grievances; but she had closed in on herself and pent-up frustration creates a more cruel havoc than sudden outbursts of anger ever do.

'I killed twice.'

'Yes.'

'God does not forgive the same sin twice.'

'Who are you to question the mercy of God? Are you privy to His inmost counsel?' The abbot reflected that he sounded like Job.

'But I planned Matron's death—and Charles's. And I meant to implicate that alley-cat Cissie.'

'God has forgiven us for killing His Son. Your thinking is distorted.'

'But I am not *mad*. That would be some excuse—if I were!' She spoke in passionate bitterness and hopelessness.

'No, you are not mad. You did not, however, behave in a normal and balanced way. You expect too much of yourself. Your vision is fixed on your own self-perfection and you have to learn to look beyond that self—in order to contemplate the glory of God. For you, a number of slights and wounds have led to tragedy. It could—but *must not*—remain a sterile tragedy. God can heal anything: renew anyone. Rely on Him—look at Him and His great power—and not at yourself. All things can be restored in Christ: recast by Him to His greater glory.'

'Even murder? Two murders.'

'Even two murders. The *evil* caused by sin may be, naturally speaking, irreparable: but it is not, therefore, irreparable by Christ. If a murderer repents, this makes it possible for him to begin to share in Christ's universal and timeless sacrifice. Those are the words of a fine Jesuit, Bernard Leeming. When you have recovered from the shock of realizing what you have done you will be able to understand. And I shall remind you, if I may, that you *are* able to join your sorrow with the sacrifice of Christ. In unity with Him, you can even begin to love those whom you have murdered. Nothing is lost forever—or it need not be. *Everything*—even the effects of sin—can be united together in Christ, with His love enfolding you all.'

He watched the dawning hope and saw her crush it in self-mockery. 'Murder is a mortal sin, Father Abbot. Or didn't you know?'

'A grave sin. But you can break free. You are not tied forever to the guilt of what you have done.'

'How can you say that? I killed someone I despised and hated. But—' her face crumpled—'when she was dead, and I had—*come into my inheritance*—'she spoke the words harshly and emphatically—'it was too late. No one cared who was running the infirmary as long as it ran smoothly. I was still the Ice Maiden. Adequate—but not acceptable. She at least had been a character and people loved her; though goodness knows why! She was a selfish old bag.' Eleanor paused, then said

306

with a rush of fury, 'There was nothing to her!'

'Nothing but loyalty and a certain gruff warmth; dependability, integrity—and interest in others.' he suggested.

'So I'm self-centred?' She was swiftly on the defensive.

'Yes.'

'I need not have been. I wanted to give. You have all made me what I have become.'

'Perhaps your Holy Grail was a vision of *yourself*—and not of the Beatific Vision.'

Pain, sharp as her intake of breath, lay savage and raw between them. Once again the abbot knew that he must not intervene: we must each confront our wretchedness. It was as though he watched a cold grey sea gathering force until an engulfing wave crashed over her and swept her along in a current of self-realization. She struggled as drowning men do, then seemed to accept the full horror of truth and relax. When he felt she had been washed ashore, as on to cold grey stones, he said gently,

'You read Teilhard de Chardin?'

'Yes.'

'He says it's impossible to love Christ unless you love other people; and conversely, that it's impossible to love others without moving nearer to Christ. Murder is the negation of love.'

In the silence that followed he sensed her move away from reality: the psychologically sick can take just so much—and then they retreat to a more comfortable world. He was not therefore surprised when she said brightly, with all the cool composure of her normal professional manner,

'One must keep a sense of proportion, Father Abbot! They are both better gone and I considered most carefully before obeying the dictates of my conscience. You must allow me to judge what is best.'

The abbot found himself, for the first time in years, quietly dismissed. She stood up, adjusted the silver buckle on her nurse's belt and, walking towards a framed photograph on the wall, she straightened the picture of her old home. Into his mind flashed the pay-off line of a Compton Burnett novel. 'I have thought you hard and self-righteous; I now feel you were both and should have been neither.' But he suppressed the notion. This woman was sick.

The angelus had rung as they talked and the time for Matins had come and gone. He must make his morning prayer—and he needed breakfast. He got up and laid a hand on Eleanor's arm.

'Shall we go down to the parlour—to meet

Inspector Morgan?'

She walked over to the window and stood looking out upon the walled garden. The abbot did not hurry her and he was grateful for an understanding police officer who, having belief in God and compassion for a poor, unbalanced creature, was prepared to trust him and to wait. Such patience was rare. Too many, he thought, want to hustle along the process of discovery and, by not allowing the sick and bereaved to work their way through a period of grief and acceptance, delay recovery and deep healing. Inspector Morgan doubtless understood the need that we all have to come to terms with ourselves, to recognize sin, to acknowledge it, renounce it—and thereby grow.

Eleanor took a last look at the garden over which a ground mist hovered like a thin shroud. The sun probed delicately and met shoots of peonies and delphiniums piercing the gauze. Lilac and lily of the valley scents floated up through the open window; a blackbird sang and, far away, a cuckoo called.

'I shall miss this place,' she said. 'Such a lovely garden. But it was too good to last. And it never became what it might have been: a haven. It was a mirage, a castle in the air: and now—the mists slowly wash again.' She drew a long, deep sigh—then stiffened and turned suddenly towards him, her eyes wide with terror. 'Don't let me drown!' she pleaded.

'I won't. And we shall learn from what you have said and amend our ways. We will become your fathers and brothers in Christ. I promise. Let's go down and get it over.'

'What will happen?' she asked.

'You will be asked to make a statement, be charged, arrested and taken into custody. Probably to a hospital. You can ask for your own solicitor or legal aid. There will be physical and mental examinations—and interrogations. Presumably you will repeat what you have told me?'

'It's the truth.'

'That you murdered two people?'

'Yes. Perhaps I was wrong. I don't know—perhaps I was mad?'

'Temporarily.'

'Shall I go mad again? I could be schizophrenic.'

'You could. Or—have been maddened by frustration. The lawyers will plead mitigating circumstances. But you are in touch with reality again.'

'I know.' She shivered.

'Keep it that way. It's hard—but more honest. It is not possible to be truly healed if one hides from the truth.'

'A sad ending. Not the one I had hoped

for.' She attempted a wry smile.

'But the one that will give joy to the angels of God and make it possible for the Son of God to come very close indeed. Closer than you can possibly imagine.'

'Why did they all dislike me?'

'Not *all*. The headmaster and I like and admire you. So does Claude le Mesurier and there are many others also.'

'But some—many, even—dislike me.'

'You have told me why. Have you forgotten?' She did not reply so he continued: 'Perhaps you seemed too perfect? Throughout history people have hunted for flaws and justified themselves as they persecuted the saints! You may find, as an acknowledged sinner, that you have more friends than ever before. It's not a good reason for committing sin, obviously, but it may make people gentler towards you when you seem less of a paragon.'

'And if I *had* been a saint? Unmerited persecution seems peculiarly horrible.'

'Well, generally speaking, good people suffering under undeserved attack tend to react in one of two ways: either they accept the judgement of others and believe it must be justified—for some reason they don't understand, but accept—in which case they are purified through humiliation; or the would-be saint is destroyed by resentment.'

'That second alternative is me.'

'Is that the way you see it? It doesn't have to be like that. You could bury yourself in regret and self-preoccupation. Or you can see whatever happens to you as a new beginning, another chance. It will be difficult; but then becoming a saint is. No one is safe until dead to this life and born into eternity. A very good person could be tempted to arrogance, self-satisfied vanity or even the wish to withdraw from others when they ask for help that the would-be contemplative is unwilling to give. Despite the constant generosity of God and His outpouring of grace, we can spoil His work in us. We all have free will: we are all tempted to be blind to our own faults and clear-sighted in regard to those of others.'

'Suppose someone is persecuted for being perfect?'

'Is anyone perfect—except God? It's possible to believe oneself innocent and to be consumed by anger at the unfairness of life and the injustice of others. But if one hits back hard one becomes aware that one is far from sanctity.'

'No one noticed,' she said sadly.

'God did. But I understand your very human longing—which, as you've said, Christ shared. He remarked that only one of the cured lepers returned to thank Him. You

312

would have welcomed even one word of praise. Nothing happened. You were deafened by the silence and perhaps this became destructive of your original impulse to give? Don't ever let this happen to you in the future.'

'What future?'

'Now you are bitter—and bitterness is highly destructive. Eleanor, whatever happens—and however much you are tempted to throw everything away in the years to come—make a gift of yourself, your imperfect self which is very lovable to God, now. Accept in advance whatever punishment or corrective treatment lies ahead. Make it your unavoidable present to God. See its value and open yourself to the pain. Let all your pent-up bitterness flow out in love. We shall hold you most dear at Ambelhurst—'

'You must be joking!' she burst out. 'After I have killed your beloved matron and one of the headmaster's favourite Old Boys? How can you possibly hold me "most dear"?' Mockery and anger had flared once more but he did not withdraw a word.

'You may not be able to see it now—but I do assure you that we shall indeed look upon you with love and keep you in our prayers. Shall we go down and meet Inspector Morgan?' He did not want her to start crying

313

again and felt it advisable to use the energy generated by her anger. 'It will mean telling him what you have told me. That will be the beginning of your restitution.'

There was a moment's silence; then she turned away from the window, held out her hand and said, 'Thank you, Father Abbot,' and, with head held high, preceded him out of the room and down the stairs.

CHAPTER TWENTY-NINE

THE FAMILY

The headmaster felt that he had spent half a lifetime trekking to and from the infirmary and asking Sister Barnes for help. She was making scrambled egg for Hayden and Butcher but left a maid to carry on and took him to the office.

'Sister, I owe you an explanation—especially as you produced the confirmatory clue. Sister Wilbraham has confessed to both murders—of Matron and of Charles Bolton—and signed a statement for the police.'

'Sister Wilbraham?' She was astounded.

'She's to be committed to a mental hospital; at least temporarily. A policewoman is helping her to pack a bag.'

'Good heavens!'

He smiled wryly and said, 'You fitted the last piece to the jigsaw when I asked you whether she went out for a walk last night and what she was wearing. You told me that she wore her hair loose—"in a page boy".'

'So I did. I'd no idea why you were asking about her clothing.'

'I'm sorry I couldn't be more frank. At that stage it was guesswork. Inspector Morgan was on the same track.'

'What a tragedy!'

'It is. I have to contact her brother, Colonel Wilbraham. She's not sure of his present address—but the Army will reach him. I must go and telephone ... May I ask you another favour? I don't want the domestic staff to know anything until she's left: would it be possible for you to take a tray of coffee to Sister and the policewoman?'

'Of course, Father.'

'And I suggest you try to get from her the keys of the surgery, stores, back door and her own flat—before she's taken away. An ambulance is coming and they may give her an injection if she gets worked up. She's behaving more or less rationally at the moment.' He grinned suddenly and his tired face appeared to shed years. 'One would think she's proceeding on a period of convalescence. When I left them she was ordering the policewoman about as though she were a student nurse—or a lady's maid!' His face clouded over. 'I'm afraid there will be a terrible reaction when she appreciates what she's done and the inevitable consequences. The abbot did a great job in getting her to admit to the murders and in preparing her for the dénouement; I gather she swung between reality and fantasy. He's now gone off to say his prayers and get some breakfast. It's been a rotten homecoming: but then he likes to be needed.'

'Don't we all?'

'You certainly arrived opportunely! I haven't felt it necessary to apologize to you for all these goings-on; nor to explain that we aren't normally like this. I feel you already know Ambelhurst. In spite of everything—I hope you are willing to stay on and see us through—at least for the rest of the term?'

'I'd love to!'

Greatly relieved, Dom Erkenwald left the infirmary office for his own, and as he walked towards the Kestrel gate he planned his next moves. He would contact Colonel Wilbraham, then have a quick shower and shave before making announcements to staff and school ... before the pressure of parents and Press interviews began to build up. Yet another day would be severely disrupted. Was it really only seventy-two hours since Mary O'Connell's body had been discovered? He recalled the abbot's complimentary remarks about the apparent stability and normality he had found on his return to Ambelhurst. Would the school and monastery take yet another murder in their stride? They would have to, decided the headmaster grimly!

★   ★   ★

Over coffee in the sisters' sitting-room the abbot, Inspector Morgan and the school doctor listened, with Mary Barnes, to Sister Vera Hanlon's disclosure of her uneasy relationship with Eleanor.

'She was so horribly efficient; so icily cool! I never knew what she was really thinking. It was like working alongside a frozen question-mark! She was so *good* at everything—but,' she concluded, 'I don't really think she likes *people*.'

'Enigmatic—and alas, schizophrenic!' commented James Patterson.

'Oh yes!' Vera gushed. 'That's exactly right! How clever of you, Doctor!'

The school's electric bell system shrilled suddenly and she stopped short, clapping her hand to her mouth in an habitual gesture that Eleanor Wilbraham had found distressingly vulgar. Many things about the junior sister had disturbed her but, ironically, Vera Hanlon admired Eleanor's air of aristocratic disdain and she was rapidly compounding this with respect for a colleague who could despatch two members of the Ambelhurst staff within seventy-two hours.

'Are you coming down to the surgery, Doctor?'

'I am—and I shall return when I've polished off the malingerers.'

The abbot turned to Mary Barnes and inquired, 'Have you enjoyed your first night on duty at Ambelhurst? Or shouldn't one ask? It was a little unusual even by our standards.'

'I imagine so, though I was glad to be needed. I'm sorry about Sister Wilbraham. It seems incredible. What went wrong with her? With her life, I mean?' She hesitated, then added apologetically, 'Oh, I'm sorry! I shouldn't ask a priest such a question.'

'It's all right. I understand your professional interest and it's natural for all of us to wonder where things went wrong and how much we share in the blame.' He sat pondering with head bowed and hands hidden in his sleeves. Then he said slowly, 'She felt undervalued by her family and was over-

318

anxious to prove them wrong—and, in so doing, reassure herself. Resentment can fuel fierce flames, can't it? Perhaps the simplest explanation comes in Paul's second letter to Timothy, chapter three, where he talks about people being—'

'"Selfish, greedy, boastful and conceited—"' Inspector Morgan chipped in, and the abbot smiled and responded,

'I was really thinking of the next words—"ungrateful, irreligious—"'

'Irreligious?' Mary Barnes intervened. 'I thought she was considered *ultra*-religious!'

'In one sense, I suppose that's true,' the abbot responded, 'but one can be emotionally involved and have a heightened sense of the numinous, be deeply aware of the unseen God—and yet lack the moral sense and good judgement essential for balance. Prudence and equanimity are virtues: the need for forbearance with oneself and one's slow progress is as important as forbearance with others. It's essential for humility. Intolerance and self-absorption are danger signals. We need to like ourselves and to be happy with whatever talents we have been given; then we can work with God to overcome our weaknesses.'

There was a long silence, broken at length by the inspector.

'Poor woman!' he said gently. 'Which of us is not a failure? We never quite achieve what God has made it possible for us to be. It's part of the human condition. Most of us are less dramatically obvious failures than people who commit murder—in the sense of taking *life*: but how often we murder reputations or deny people credit for what they do well.'

'Yes, indeed,' the abbot confirmed. 'And yet the wonderful truth is that our broken relationships *can* be taken up and restored in Christ. There is nothing—and *no one*,' he said firmly, 'who is incapable of redemption. That's why Christ died. Not just for the good people, almost transparent to grace; but for the broken, twisted people, overwhelmed by passions or circumstances—or indeed by temperament. Perhaps there's less virtue to be found in the naturally good person, untroubled by violent temptation, than in the tempestuous person who fights against the all too obvious evil that torments him—or her—and breaks out of control at intervals. Fortunately, we're not called upon to judge. Nor do we know which ones Christ prefers. In His lifetime He seemed to yearn for the lost, the sinners, the ones despised by others. And yet again, there were all the good people whom He deeply loved—His mother, John the beloved, Nathanael, "the Israelite in whom there was no guile".'

'He had very catholic tastes,' said Inspector Morgan demurely. All three laughed happily, grateful for this winding-down of tension.

'Do you think,' asked Mary Barnes, 'that Eleanor will recover? Will she be able to appreciate what she has done? Can she regain touch with reality?'

'Mentally, yes,' said Morgan. 'Whether she can face spiritual reality is another matter. That's the abbot's field.'

'I had thought,' the abbot responded slyly, 'that we are no longer encouraged to differentiate. We speak of the whole person; holistic medicine and holistic spirituality are, I believe, the "in" phrases—'

'But also of the split personality!'

'True!' He smiled appreciatively. 'There's always a chance that she may put up a block— as we all can. Christ can do anything at all with people who admit their sin and see themselves as lower than the lowest person on earth. Maybe, for some of us, that's the way to salvation: we have to feel diminished and mean.'

'I noticed something about Miss Wilbraham this morning,' said Morgan. 'She seemed not to have a good word to say about anyone. Her conversation was, not unnaturally, perhaps— in the circumstances—directed entirely towards herself and she mentioned others merely as people who had put obstacles in her path. She expressed no gratitude whatever. It was as though there was nothing in her life for which she seemed willing to thank either God or man. I think that, more than anything, convinced me that she is insane. And yet—I'm like that myself sometimes. As you say: we all need to feel diminished and mean.'

Quick footsteps in the passage announced the return of James Patterson. He came in with a broad grin, delighted to have polished off his surgery with speed. 'Well—?' he looked round in inquiry. 'Have you settled everything? Do you know what made a competent nurse turn to murder?'

'She could be a psychopath,' suggested Mary Barnes.

'If she is, then she had virtually no conscience. A psychopathic state is half delinquency and half mental abnormality and the fact that she sought to further her own position without reference to the ill effects on Matron suggests callous indifference. She may well have *known* that what she did was wrong—but she didn't *feel* it to be wrong. This is the critical fact of an abnormal condition.'

'Umm,' said the abbot. 'A normal sense of responsibility would be associated with feelings of guilt. One ought to feel guilty about committing murder.'

'By contrast,' the doctor resumed, 'victims of neurotic guilt feel guilty without, in fact, being so. On the whole, I think Eleanor suffers from a split personality—and nowadays, schizophrenia is thought to be caused by a disturbance of dopamine metabolism. But the psychiatrists will do extensive tests and decide one way or the other. They may even agree to disagree. I haven't much experience in their field. Whatever the diagnosis, the realization of what she has done will be immensely painful.' He paused. 'She may take refuge in fantasy: refuse to face it. If, however, she accepts the responsibility and sees herself as driven by evil temptation which, at one stage, she could have controlled, she will be your penitent, Father Abbot—or some other priest's—as well as *our* patient, and the lawyers' client. I wonder if there is any real hope of permanent sanity?'

'If she recognizes guilt and failure,' said the inspector slowly, 'then there *is* hope. If, in the words of *Second Corinthians*, chapter twelve, verse ten, she accepts the truth of "When I am weak—then I am strong", all may yet be well. I've seen it happen. From my side of the game you'd think there wouldn't be much opportunity to witness rehabilitation—but

I've seen it: and often when you'd have thought there wasn't a ghost of a chance. But there it is!'

'From the bottom of the well,' murmured the abbot, 'there's one way out—and that is upwards.'

'Well,' said James Patterson, 'I'll say this for you. You certainly have faith and hope!'

'We'd better add love,' said Mary Barnes. 'She'll need it.'

'She will,' agreed Morgan, 'and I believe that her friends at Ambelhurst will supply it.'

'It's an odd thing,' James Patterson reflected, 'I could tell that the headmaster used not to like Eleanor. He admired her professional ability, but she was too inhuman for his taste; he likes real people, warm-hearted, loving people—no matter how damned difficult they are. Now, suddenly, all her cool, competent efficiency, all her cold perfection, has been exposed as a mere façade; she's got a flaw. She may be incapable of really loving anyone but herself—but that's not entirely her fault, she's mentally sick, she's in need of help, she's human—and he will *therefore*, somehow, find time to take her into his heart and prayers. Just you wait and you'll see that I'm right—he'll visit her or write whenever he can. Nothing will be too much trouble. She is part of Ambelhurst and if there's anything he can do, at whatever cost, he'll do it. The man has enough compassion to take on the problem of the whole world. Sympathy, empathy, an infinite capacity for love. I don't know what you call it—but I do know that it's Christ-like. I believe it's the secret of his whole life here and why he's made such a success of his job. For him, as for you, Father Abbot, the reason for living is— loving.'

'Agreed,' said Morgan. 'I've felt this strongly ever since I arrived on Thursday. One doesn't expect hatred and murder in a monastic setting. Here, we've had two murders—and yet—I'll be leaving Ambelhurst with an overwhelming impression of warmth and goodness. And I shall want to return.'

The abbot smiled. 'You're welcome, Evan Morgan. We hope you accept us as your friends.'

Mary Barnes moved around refilling coffee cups and said slowly, 'There's something I once heard—in Cambridge—it was a talk on the priesthood by the Jesuit Master of St Edmund's Hall. He said: "It's a priest's high privilege to be—in a unique way—the face that Christ presents, here and now, to men and women for whom He is seeking and who—perhaps unknown to themselves—are searching for Him." A headmaster has more chances than most of drawing people into—'

'The web?' suggested Morgan.

'Yes. You could call it that—but it's something more. It's a family. And, incidentally, Inspector—you *will* come back—because you, now, are part of the Ambelhurst family.'

★   ★   ★

The trio was reunited. Hodges and Peel-Llewellyn were perched on the end of Brancaster's narrow infirmary bed and all three were wrapped in an aura of self-congratulation. Inspector Morgan had been up to say goodbye, to thank them for their help, and to extend an invitation to visit his Divisional Headquarters at any time convenient to themselves and to the Ambelhurst authorities.

All three had slept until ten o'clock, when Sister Barnes had served them with an excellent late breakfast; and by the time that Dom Erkenwald came up to tell them, as he had already told the school at Assembly, that the murder mystery was solved, that Sister Wilbraham had been removed to a mental hospital and that it was everyone's duty to pray for her and for her victims, the night watchers had completely recovered. It was, they thought, a pity that the sustained excitement of the past three days could not be further extended, but the headmaster had made it clear that the sooner everything and everyone returned to normal, the better. He was, he said, prepared to overlook last night's breach of regulations but no further escapades would be tolerated. In fact, if the trio did not conform a little more, it might be advisable to transfer them to separate Houses. This awful threat struck home but the irrepressible Hodges could not resist asking,

'Sir, we *did* save Cissie from being murdered as well—didn't we?'

'Very likely. And I am sure that she will be quite willing to accord you a measure of hero-worship in due course. But however grateful we are, or should be, it must be clearly understood that no clemency for future misdeeds will be extended towards you on that account. Furthermore, I would advise you not to expect your schoolfellows' congratulations. Some may even be envious and rather bored by your part in the affair, so don't expect adulation from anyone. You've had your fun and I recommend you to get back to normal as quickly as possible. You look fit enough, after your long night's sleep, and I suggest that you two get dressed and come down to school for

327

lunch when the bell rings. I'll have your clothes sent over.'

'A bit damping,' grumbled Hodges when Dom Erkenwald had gone, 'and it puts paid to our plans for a long weekend.' But by the time the dinner bell sounded, his natural optimism was fully restored.

'Ah well!' he exclaimed, rising from Brancaster's bed and stretching luxuriously, 'I *suppose* it's time we went and told the school what's been happening.'

'They won't be interested,' complained Peel-Llewellyn, 'the Erk's already told them.'

'They will!' said Hodges confidently, 'they will—when they've heard *my* version!'

Photoset, printed and bound in Great Britain by REDWOOD BURN LIMITED, Trowbridge, Wiltshire